A YEAR

OF

RHYMES

A YEAR

OF

RHYMES

BERNARD
COOPER

VIKING

VIKING
Published by the Penguin Group
Penguin Books USA Inc., 375 Hudson Street,
New York, New York 10014, U.S.A.
Penguin Books Ltd, 27 Wrights Lane,
London W8 5TZ, England
Penguin Books Australia Ltd, Ringwood,
Victoria, Australia
Penguin Books Canada Ltd, 10 Alcorn Avenue,
Toronto, Ontario, Canada M4V 3B2
Penguin Books (N.Z.) Ltd, 182–190 Wairau Road,
Auckland 10, New Zealand

Penguin Books Ltd, Registered Offices:
Harmondsworth, Middlesex, England

First published in 1993 by Viking Penguin,
a division of Penguin Books USA Inc.

10 9 8 7 6 5 4 3 2 1

PUBLISHER'S NOTE
This is a work of fiction. Names, characters, places, and incidents either
are the product of the author's imagination or are used fictitiously, and
any resemblance to actual persons, living or dead, events, or locales is
entirely coincidental.

The epigraph from "February 11, 1977" by Frederick Morgan is reprinted from
Poems: New and Selected (University of Illinois Press, 1987) by permission
of the author and the publisher. Copyright © 1987 by Frederick Morgan.

LIBRARY OF CONGRESS CATALOGING-IN-PUBLICATION DATA
Cooper, Bernard, 1951–
    A year of rhymes / by Bernard Cooper.
        p.   cm.
    ISBN 0–670–84732–1
    1. City and town life—Fiction.   2. Gay youth—Fiction.
I. Title.
PS3553.O5798Y4   1993
813'54—dc20   92–50771

Printed in the United States of America
Set in Sabon
Designed by Jessica Shatan

FOR BRIAN MILLER

AND IN MEMORY OF MY BROTHERS

Your youngest brother's passed you by
at last: he's older now than you—
and all our lives have ramified
in meanings which you never knew.

—FREDERICK MORGAN,
"February 11, 1977"

The author wishes to thank the following people for an abundance of brass tacks: Bia Lowe, Jill Ciment, Michelle Huneven, the alternate Tuesday nighters, and especially Jeffrey Hammond.

CONTENTS

SUMMER

My brother gave it the gas. Wind poured in through the windows of his Pontiac, rippling our shirts and thrashing at our hair. We sped up the Cahuenga on-ramp, pretending g-force was pressing our torsos deep into the bucket seats. Thirty, forty, fifty—my brother called out the numbers on the speedometer. Once we were on the freeway, I stuck my arm out the window and sifted the night through my fingers. On the hillsides flanking lanes of traffic, lights came on in cantilevered houses. The silhouettes of windblown palms bristled on the crest of the Hollywood hills. A few strong stars burned in the sky. We were on our way to Agoura so my brother could serve a summons.

Though he was only twenty-one, Bob looked like a private detective. His roomy suit was a camouflage that blended into shadows. His big, vigilant brown eyes would dart toward the slightest sound and motion. His square jaw, covered with stubble, worked a stick of spearmint gum. Bob's conversation, peppered with detective jargon, made the city seem riddled with wrongdoing, a place of false identities, rubber checks, and petty scams, where homes were wrecked and livers enlarged, ruin intruding into ordinary lives. Earlier that evening, gazing at the downtown skyline from his small Echo Park apartment, he warned me to be on the lookout for "con artists" who "bilked the public" and "shot at sitting ducks."

Bob worked for my father, Irving Zerkin, an attorney whose clientele that summer included Eve Menassian, a woman suing a Food King market after slipping on a shattered bottle of safflower oil, and Mr. Shoop, inventor of the "manual trash compactor," a cross between a garbage can and a kitchen stool, which flattened refuse when you sat on it. But most often my father went to trial on behalf of people who suspected their spouses of having clandestine affairs or, in one extreme case, of practicing bigamy. Bob was sent to serve the subpoenas, summonses, and writs of habeas corpus that kept the dockets of district divorce courts booked for months. That night he had to make sure that the evasive Mr. Charlie Cantrell would attend a hearing to determine the amount of spousal support for his former wife, a curvaceous, breathy redhead my brother and father secretly referred to as "Mrs. Vixen."

"You should see her," said my brother as we entered the foothills of Agoura, a rural suburb with ranch homes and stables. "What a figure! No wonder she dumped him." He pulled onto the shoulder of the road and turned down the radio; Harry Belafonte was overwhelmed by crickets. Bob flicked on the overhead light, inspected the crude map my father had drawn for him on a yellow legal tablet, and asked me to look for Palomino Road. This simple request seemed to me a crucial responsibility. As my brother's Pontiac slunk down the street, the motor churning its one low note, I scanned the dark intersections and squinted at the street signs as if the fate of decent people everywhere depended upon me. My eyeballs ached. Amber porch lights glowed through the trees. Leaves were rattled by the Santa Ana. When I finally spotted Palomino Road, my heart was spinning like a wind chime in my chest. "This is it," I whispered. We made a left. Bob cut the headlights and we crept along—our progress barely registered on the speedometer—until we reached the right address. My brother gripped the steering wheel even after the engine was dead. He took a deep breath, mustered concentration for his task. "Stay put," he said. "And try to keep quiet." He stuffed the summons inside his coat and closed the car door soundlessly behind him.

A path of round paving stones led to Mr. Cantrell's house. Bob walked up to the bay window and tried to peek in through the parting of the curtains, but judging from the way he twisted his head and pressed his face against the glass, it was hard to see inside. He knocked on the front door and stood as straight and patient as someone handing out religious pamphlets. He tried the doorbell, shifted his weight from foot to foot, waited for a full minute before he returned to the car. "He's home," said Bob, tapping his nose. "I can smell the guy. He knows what's up." We had reached an impasse. The summons couldn't be left at Mr. Cantrell's door; it would have to be delivered in person. Bob chomped gum and stared into space, accompanied by a blustering wind and the distant banter of dogs.

"Burt," said my brother, "how'd you like to go undercover?"

We drove to a nearby Texaco station, where Bob bought us Cokes and hatched his plan, repeating the simple instructions, making me say them back. Once he was sure I had memorized the details—"I'm eleven," I protested. "I *have* a brain"—we sat in the car and guzzled our sodas. In the harsh light of the service bay, we regaled each other with burps.

When we returned to Palomino Road, Bob parked the car in front of a vacant lot, where a discarded sofa and the rusty husk of a stove lay among scrub brush. Like a house, I thought, without its walls. He handed me the summons. I folded it into a square and stuck it in the back pocket of my jeans. "Pal," he said, "you're on your own." He glanced at his watch and made a note in the small ledger he kept in the glove compartment. He had to dodge his own shadow in order to see the page. "Well?" he said, without looking up. "Make your move."

I don't think I was frightened, exactly, but the walk to Mr. Cantrell's front door seemed to last forever, and I remembered Mrs. Robinson, my fifth-grade teacher, telling us about Zeno's paradox—how you travel half a distance, and half of that, and half of that, and you never reach your destination. The air was electric, racing down the mountains, buffeting the hedges that bordered Mr. Cantrell's property. Trees and phone poles and fences shed trembling webs of shadow.

On Mr. Cantrell's front porch lay a clay pot filled with brown flowers, their dry stems bent by the wind. There were other signs of neglect—buckling paint, holes worn in the screen door—that I hadn't noticed from the car. This decay, I knew, resulted from Mrs. Vixen's absence; I'd heard how lovers "give up the ghost," how someone leaves you and life unravels. I jabbed at the doorbell. It played the same tune as the doorbell at our house, a vaguely triumphant ascent on the scales. The door swung open. A man in a sallow T-shirt and madras shorts stood there and snapped, "What are you supposed to be?"

"Oh," I said, as though I'd just woken from a dream. And then I forgot his name. I tried to retrieve it, but my head seemed hollow. This was the pivotal bit of information that Bob made me chant back to him at the gas station. To serve a summons, my brother had said, you must "ascertain the correct identity." That much, at least, I remembered.

"Let me guess," said the man. "You're selling raffle tickets." His voice was coarse from cigarettes. Tall and thin, he tilted forward, his breath as pungent as gasoline. "Well," he grumbled, "what *do* you want?" He gazed at me; his gaze had weight. Behind him were clothes strewn on the floor and plates caked with half-eaten food, the disarray of a banished man.

I slipped my hand into my back pocket; his name came back with the touch of the summons. "Are you . . . Mr. Charlie Cantrell?"

"So what?" he said.

I tossed the summons. His reflex was to catch it. I spun around and leapt down the steps. As I ran across the lawn I could hear him damn me and stamp his foot. Rounding the row of hedges, I looked down the road to where I thought the Pontiac was parked and . . . nothing. Nothing, that is, but the darkness and heat and agitation that filled the giant night. Blood banged at my temples. I sucked the air but couldn't fill my lungs. Had I forgotten part of the plan? I wanted to cry, certain I would be forced to join Charlie Cantrell and the ranks of those abandoned. I didn't even have a dime for the phone. Then a rectangle lit up far away, the figure of my brother within it, waving me to him, reeling me in. The engine revved, headlights came on, weeds and beer cans bleached by the high beams, tires turning and spitting gravel before I reached the door.

"What's wrong?" said my brother as I fell, panting, in the passenger seat. "There's nothing the guy could do to you." My brother ground the gears. The Pontiac fishtailed into the street. We shot down Palomino Road and passed Mr. Cantrell, still standing in his doorway and clutching the summons, paralyzed by indignity. The sight of him made my stomach tighten. "I guess," said Bob, "you're not cut out for this kind of work. Who is?" he added, seeing I was hurt. Houses and stables flicked past the window. I tried to compose myself, to breathe at even intervals, to work the moisture back into my mouth. The lingering effects of fear only annoyed my brother. He switched on the radio and plowed through surges of static till he found a station playing nonstop love songs. *Cupid, draw back your bow and let your arrow go.* Or: *Your love is like an itchin' in my heart, tearin' me apart.* Duos, trios, quartets—they whistled and hummed and wailed, voices melding together, crooning the last word on love. My brother crooned along.

He was thinking, no doubt, of Marion Hirsch, Marion of the black hair, Marion of the measured words, who moved, if she moved at all, as slowly as seaweed stirring under water. Languid, secretive, ravishing Marion, who donned her sunglasses even at night, who snapped her fingers to the strains of jazz, muttering, *Yeah, yeah,* as if music carried to her alone. By day a clerk at a Hallmark cardshop, by night a muse in net stockings, Marion Hirsch was the still center on which Bob doted, speaking in whispers and offering gifts—a squat bottle of My Sin perfume, a gold-plated slave bracelet. Bob would look at Marion as though he could never quite catch her eyes and apprehend her to his satisfaction. He'd inch his body toward her, find ways to make her proximate, to make her yearn toward him in return. The sight of Marion's hips shifting in a cotton dress made him seem restless, too big for his body, his mouth tensed in the shape of her name. I saw longing happen to Bob, knew from movies it was meant to be that way, but I'd never felt anything like it myself. And so, as we barreled through the night, my brother beat time on the steering wheel, sang a popular ballad off key, and knew emotions I couldn't know. I envied his need to wrest Marion's attention, envied the way he was tempted in her presence. Before I knew what I was doing, I found myself leaning out the window and barking at dogs who barked in our passing. Sorry for my ignorance, I arched toward the moon and let out a howl.

"Yikes," said Bob, tugging me by my shirttail, back inside the car. "Get a grip on yourself." My throat hurt from the howl. "Listen," he said, "it's probably best if you don't mention to anybody what we did tonight." He didn't want Mom and Dad to know. "It's a breach of the litigant's right to confidentiality." I kept quiet, knowing it would make him nervous. "Well," he said. "Say something."

"Something," I said.

"I'm not kidding, OK?"

"All right already." I zipped my finger across my lips. I tried to say more, but my lips were zipped.

Bob sighed a sigh of exasperation. We drove for more than a mile in silence. Perhaps we were lost, but my brother wasn't about to admit it. At a railroad crossing on Stanton Boulevard, the gatepost lowered and red lights blinked in time to a bell. A freight train clattered out of the east. It seemed to stretch beyond the horizon, to diminish into infinity. "This is gonna take forever," said Bob, yanking up the hand brake and idling the engine. He propped his chin on the steering wheel, a look of resignation on his face, his back expanding with every breath. The Pontiac rattled as the train came close, and the tassel hanging from the rearview mirror—an odd and purposeless gift from Marion—began to shudder and turn in circles. I could feel vibrations deep in the seats, thought I could hear every nut and bolt nudged imperceptibly loose.

"Let's see who can remember the most numbers on the train," I suggested, "like that guy on TV."

"That guy on TV was an idiot savant," said Bob. "The only thing he remembers are numbers. Poor schmo could barely tie his shoes. Besides," he added, "bet I remember more."

At the age of eleven, I was fascinated by memory. It was, I felt, an ability perfected by adults; they'd left behind a past to remember, a glittering trail of circumstance, like the path a snail leaves on pavement. My mother and father often haggled over the names of people and places from their youth in Chicago. "It was Stella Schwartz." "No, Della Schwartz." My parents could conjure vanished years merely by closing their eyes. Aunt Ida, my mother's older sister, was witness to my mother's former life as a pretty, impulsive ingenue.

"She danced like a dervish," Ida would say, "wore her skirts above the knee and stopped the gentlemen dead in their tracks." Giddy with memories, my mother would hold her sister by the shoulders and tell me that *Ida* had been the beauty, full of verve and brazen jokes, her auburn curls drawing dozens of suitors. And then the gale of protest would begin, each touting the other's loveliness, insisting it was supreme. "Batten the hatches," my father teased. "It's the Battle of the Beauties."

When he still lived at home, Bob had to improve his memory for a class in criminology at City College. There was a lot to remember: the percentage of repeat offenders who were finally reformed, the number of common-law marriages in California. His professor suggested he buy the book *Ways to a Better Memory*. On the cover was a drawing of someone's head crammed with equations and blocks of text. My brother spent his spare time poring over those pages. The book contained lists to practice with: Hammer, Shoe, Island, Tiger, Apple, Clock. I'd walk by Bob's bedroom late at night and see him bent over his desk, incanting words that had no connection; sitting in a dusty shaft of lamplight, he tried, it seemed, to form a coherent story from a random sequence of things. One chapter was entitled "Remember with Rhyme." Bob had tried to explain this method one night while I bounced on his bed. "The mind picks up patterns, see, and stuff stays with you longer when it rhymes. Say you want to remember an address—2391. You just think up a sentence that rhymes, like . . . *You see I'm gone.*"

You see I'm gone. That's exactly what my brother said. Neither of us would have guessed it was prophetic, the numbers rhyming with the phrase, the phrase with eventual facts. For now we sat in Bob's Pontiac and watched a freight train rumble by—Bandy Bros. Cattle, Pacific Produce, Brite Idea —mesmerized by the raucous livestock, crates of lettuce, mounds of ore. Even after the train had passed and the warning lights dimmed and the gatepost lifted, we sat in silence and leaned against the dash, idled on that rise above the San Fernando Valley, both of us eager to fix in memory all that we saw: late commuters on the thoroughfares below us, tract homes spread in all directions, trails of smoke from factory stacks threading through the sky.

The wind persisted into July, would rise without warning late in the day. On hot afternoons, I'd go outside to draw pictures on the sidewalk with a feather dunked in water—portraits of my parents, Bob, and Ida—and watch the shapes evaporate, soaked up by the sun. Hunched over the pavement, sketching the wet features of a face, I'd feel the sky start to change behind me; if I turned around quickly, I could catch a yellow cast to the light and sense the wind like a premonition.

Our Spanish house sat on a cul-de-sac, the end of Ambrose Avenue. We lived at the foot of the Hollywood hills. High above us loomed the Griffith Observatory, its three copper domes blazing in the sun. Late one afternoon, bored with the almost instant disappearance of my liquid artworks, I retreated into the cool kitchen, where my mother, as usual, ironed while watching "Queen for a Day." She was entranced as the host, Jack Bailey, interviewed four female contestants, who each told a story of personal adversity. Mother clicked her tongue at the particularly tragic events—widowhood, bankruptcy, amputation—in lives that seemed composed of endless degradation. "Imagine that," my mother said, eyes fixed on a housewife from Savannah. "Eight months pregnant, no husband in sight, and her mother caught stealing a bassinet." I couldn't imagine how people endured such betrayals and tribulations. Those women, I figured, were rare exceptions to humankind, cursed like the characters in fairy tales, victims of supernatural wrath. At the close of the show's harrowing half hour, we felt, my mother and I, a pang of secret relief. Not so much for the woman who had moved the audience to elect her queen via an applause meter, but for ourselves—two people somehow spared from a sad lot in life. As wrinkles were pressed from my father's shirts, Niagara spray starch fragrant in the air, we watched with selfish pleasure as one lucky woman was led toward a throne by ladies-in-waiting, her shoulders draped in a velvet cloak, a rhinestone tiara pinned to her hairdo. The winner wept and smiled and waved, even though her reign was brief. She clung to Jack Bailey's sleeve, thanked him for her two prizes—a bed to sleep in, a coat to wear in winter—and nuzzled a dozen roses, her crown askew by the end of the credits.

But the coronation wasn't over until my mother muttered one of her three favorite maxims: *Count your blessings. Thank your lucky stars. There but for the grace of God.* Sprawled on an oval rug, I awaited her pronouncement, guessing which of the three it would be, gazing up at her past the plywood underside of the ironing board. The steam iron hissed and glinted as she worked. It was at these moments —dusk descending, the room humid—that she seemed a woman about to fold open: strands of her hair slipped from pins; a button on her blouse would come undone; white socks sagged above her slippers. It's possible that she may, in fact, have looked haggard, but to me she looked relaxed and happy, liable to laugh at anything I did.

That day I amused her by singing along with the TV commercial that followed "Queen for a Day." *Feed him Doctor*

Ross dog food and do him a favor. It's got more meat and it's got more flavor. It's got more things to make him feel the way he should. Doctor Ross dog food is doggone good. Woof! "I know it by heart," I bragged, pleased to exert my memory.

"Amazing," she said from a cloud of steam.

I'd developed an appreciation for rhyme thanks to my aunt Ida. On my eleventh birthday, she'd given me *A Year of Rhymes for Young Adults,* a book containing three hundred and sixty-five poems about the passage of time and the nature of love. There were works by Blake and Yeats and Millay, verses and lines I still remember: "O lonely trees as white as wool / That moonlight makes so beautiful." And "She walks in beauty like the night / Of cloudless climes and starry skies, / And all that's best of dark and bright / Meet in her aspect and her eyes." When Ida visited, we would huddle together on the couch and she would read me that day's poem, licking her index finger before she turned the page, cat-eye glasses sliding down her nose. Her voice blustered like a gust of wind, sending chills down the nape of my neck. I'd stay close to her long after the poem was over, absorbing her warmth, wondering what about the poem had made her sound so grave. Ida looked the way I imagined fortune-tellers to look, her rouge a dusky shade of red, head wrapped in a satin turban, two tendrils of hennaed hair twisting over either temple. Ida possessed a brittle glamour. She was nearly fifty, and her efforts to conceal her age made her look older and all the more resigned. Those interludes with sibylline Ida made me think that poems were some kind of chant, a spell that was cast to alter the future. No matter the subject— falling leaves, first love—the tone of Ida's voice seemed to say, Protect us from our destiny.

Both my mother and Ida were superstitious about the future. They were avid readers of horoscopes, believed that certain colors and numbers had the power to bring good luck.

Ida, however, felt sure that the natural outcome of life was disillusionment, while my mother, when considering the long view, thought the best was yet to come. Their contradictory points of view cropped up in activities as routine as the preparation of dinner, especially if the dinner was meant to celebrate an important occasion—in tonight's case, my brother's bringing Marion home to eat with us for the first time.

"Do you want to use the tan tablecloth or the beige tablecloth?" Ida called from the dining room.

"One is tan and one is brown," Mother called back from the kitchen. "Let's use the brown."

"It's beige," said Ida. "Unless I'm blind, this is beige."

"We know brown when we see it, don't we," my mother whispered to me. I was perched atop the Formica counter, her ally when Ida was out of the room.

"You don't think it's too drab?" yelled Ida. "She'll think we're a bunch of *alter kockers*."

"She'll think nothing of the sort," said Mother, stuffing bread crumbs into a chicken.

"All right," said Ida, appearing in the portal. "It's your life."

Outside our kitchen window, above tile roofs and TV antennae, clouds dimmed in the summer sky. Ida and my mother became so engrossed in cooking—noodle kugel, boiled cabbage—they didn't notice night descending. They sliced and chopped until it was dark, reflections bursting from the blades of their knives.

"What is this?" my father asked when he came in through the back door. "The Carlsbad Caverns?" He switched on the light, put his arms around my mother and her sister. They each gave a hasty kiss to the air and told him to go away. "Jeez," he said, winking at me and dancing backward. "I didn't mean to be a bother." Father's practice was burgeoning, and his easy manner meant we had money, or would have some soon. Mrs. Menassian's case against Food King had gone to trial, and according to my father, her visible cuts and bruises, her plaintive Armenian eyes, made the outcome a foregone conclusion. And thanks to his sound advice, Mr. Shoop's manual trash compactor was patented and under production.

We were watching Ida loosen lime jello from a copper mold when Bob walked in through the back door with Marion on his arm. "Robert," groaned Mother. "The *front* door is for guests. But come in, kids." She dragged Marion into the center of the room and turned her in a circle so that one by one we could say hello. After the round of greetings, Mother asked Marion if she wouldn't be able to see a little better without her sunglasses.

"Oh, that's OK," said Marion.

My mother searched the black lenses for some trace of an expression and, finding none—or finding an expression too cryptic to decipher—laughed a little and returned to the food. Bob escorted Marion into the dining room. My father and I followed. Marion wore a knit dress—painted on, my father said later—the yarn so red it hurt my eyes. The instant we sat down, Bob became transfixed by Marion's profile; it looked as if he was trying to see inside her ear.

"So," said my father.

"Nice walnuts," said Marion, pointing to the centerpiece.

"Thanks," said my father. "Actually, they're plastic."

"I know," said Marion. "I'm big on plastic food. It's the taxidermy of tomorrow."

"Ta da," sang Ida, holding before her a roast chicken. She set the oval platter on the table and clasped her hands together. "Just look at that."

"Is your turban from India?" asked Marion.

Ida wrenched her attention away from the chicken. "It's from Sears," she said, dismay in her voice. She looked at my mother and cocked an eyebrow, thin and dark as a line drawn with water.

Mother ignored Ida, set down the carving knife and miscellaneous dishes of food. She took Marion's plate with one hand and with the other dug out a scoop of cabbage. "Say when," she said.

"When," said Marion.

"But, dear," said Mother, "there's nothing on your plate." My mother was frozen mid-gesture. Cabbage juice dripped from the slotted spoon.

Ida shook her head and sighed, "*Laymene goilem.*"

"I mean," said Marion, "one spoonful is plenty."

"No wonder you stay so svelte," said Mother.

It was then that I noticed Marion's arms, thin and white as sticks of chalk. When she ate—the portions like tiny islands on a sea of blue ceramic—she nibbled her food intently but without the slightest pleasure. Marion's joyless mastication stood out in contrast to my family's noisy feast. Father ripped into the chicken, his forehead sweating. Bob slurped purple strands of cabbage. Ida worked her way through several squares of noodle kugel, protesting that she'd blow up big as a blimp, then helping herself to more. Mother nursed jewel-like bites of Jell-O, transported by the melting of each sweet mouthful.

The dinner conversation was halting, limited for the most part to my father and Bob discussing work. "Bamburger wants me to add a codicil to include his new girlfriend," said my father.

"You're pulling my leg," said Bob.

"What's a codicil?" I asked.

"He's practically broke to begin with," my father continued. "There's a floating lien on his shoe store."

"What's a lien?" I asked.

"How's he supposed to cough up your fee?" asked Bob, his brown eyes narrowing.

I turned to my mother. "What's a lien?"

She waved her hand. "Lien schmien," she said. She was

angry at my father and brother for discussing business and excluding our guest from the conversation. "Marion," she blurted, several decibels louder than was necessary. Everyone stopped eating. "What do you see yourself involved with in the future?"

Marion paused, giving the question due consideration. None of her muscles moved as she thought. "Abstract expressionism," she said at last, then continued to pick at her food.

"How fascinating," said Mother.

"What's abstract expressionism?" I asked my mother.

Everyone looked in her direction.

"We're waiting," said Ida.

"Why, it's exactly what it sounds like," said Mother. She smiled and put down her napkin. "Well," she sighed, "who wants to fight me for the wishbone?"

"I do," said Ida.

"Perhaps Marion would like to be the one to make a wish," suggested Mother.

Marion shrugged her shoulders. "No," she said. "I'm wishless."

"Are you sure?" asked Mother.

"Sylvia," said my father, "the girl doesn't want to."

"I do," repeated Ida, tucking a strand of stray hair back into her turban.

Mother pried the wishbone loose from the chicken carcass and, after sucking away the remaining meat, held one end of it out for Ida. My aunt eyed the wishbone—it was moist and gray—as though she were studying its structure, trying to judge its tensile strength and calculate the exact angle made by the intersection of its two curves. Finally blinking her eyes and emerging from her meditation, Ida rolled up the sleeve of her blouse and placed her elbow on the table. She cleared her throat, flexed her wrinkled fingers, and grasped one end of the wishbone. Her fingernails, opal enamel, were fairly long, and she had to revise her grip.

Mother squared her shoulders, planted both feet firmly on the floor, and with her free hand grabbed the arm of her chair. Despite the fact that the opponent was her sister, my mother steeled herself for battle, had every intention of winning her wish. Her nostrils flared. Her eyebrows furrowed. Her stare could have drilled a hole through a diamond. For several seconds no one spoke. My father's jaw dropped. Bob and I sat absolutely still. Wind blew in through the dining room window, troubled the drapes, strummed the prisms of the crystal chandelier. Even Marion, an expert at disinterest, removed her sunglasses—eyes so heavily lined with mascara, the sight of her made me think of raccoons—and held her breath in expectation.

On the count of three, Mother and Ida began to grunt and struggle. Mother started off with a defensive strategy: she let out a high, triumphant laugh. Ida refused to let this brash assurance distract her. "Oh, no you don't," she said, screwing her elbow even harder into the brown tablecloth, which twisted and gathered and began to drag with it the silverware and dinner dishes. The chicken carcass drifted like a ship-wreck.

As they second-guessed each other's moves, their hands were like one hand reflected in a mirror, thumbs going white at the knuckles. Those women shared a symmetrical will, the same degree of strength. I was certain they'd both made a wish about Marion, though the tenor of their wishes must have been different. Mother, no doubt, wished that Marion might one day change, might shuck away her dark glasses and become—who knows?—a model wife. Ida, on the other hand, must have thought Marion a lost cause, must have disapproved of her odd remarks and, seeing her as the source of future problems, wished that she'd vanish from my brother's life.

Perhaps it is a trick of recall—knowledge suffusing a memory like light—but I think that Marion and Bob were as certain of those wishes as I was. Marion leaned against my brother. She looked like the women on "Queen for a Day" who watch a needle rise on a meter and wait for their fate to be decided. And just as Ida fell back in her chair, startled by her own victory and holding up the wishbone for proof, a shadow passed over my brother's face. He closed his eyes. He laid his head on that red shoulder. He inhaled Marion's fragrance and burrowed into her skin.

Father prospered. Mrs. Menassian received a hefty settlement for injuries incurred at the Food King market. She and her husband, Arnold, who had become friends with my parents, used the money to make mortgage payments on the Cap 'n' Cork, their liquor store on Hollywood Boulevard. Mr. Shoop's kitchen stool was advertised on channel 11 late at night. The commercial featured a pretty housewife who arranged herself on the plastic seat, sank a few inches, and winked at the camera. "So simple," she said, over the crunch of compacting trash.

With their extra capital, my parents went to work turning the den into a rumpus room. Rumpus room, den—the words themselves were worlds apart. A den was a place sequestered from the rest of the house, and ours was furnished with a metal desk that clanged when you closed its drawers, a filing cabinet from my father's office, and a swivel chair on four wheels, my secret entertainment. This was a room sacrificed to practicality, a place for my father to work at home, its musty rug and easterly exposure creating the somber atmosphere we largely avoided (except for my occasional spins into oblivion). A rumpus room, on the other hand, promised a life of loud diversion, of reckless camaraderie, of perpetual play. What better way to suggest the leisure we'd achieved than to furnish the room in a tropical motif. The rug was wrenched up and a parquet floor laid in its place. Rolls of grass cloth were pasted to the walls, the windows shaded with bamboo blinds. Into the room went a new, wide-screen Zenith and a sofa covered in a print of huge hibiscus. But the highlight of our refurbished room, symbol of all the rumpus to come, was a crescent-shaped bar with five tall barstools. Built into the side of the bar was a knob that wound up and played "How Dry I Am" in the tinny notes of a music box. The difference was that these notes, for all their initial harmony, would begin to warp and sour at the end, as though hammered by someone numb from booze.

Much of what I understood about the adult world (especially when it came to matters of passion) I'd intuited from the objects on that bar. There was the hula dancer who wore a grass skirt, thin strands of cellophane that rustled from the breeze as someone walked by. She was frozen mid-swivel, arms akimbo. Her head of black hair, stiff hemp, hung above the shoulders. Her naked torso was carved from teak, the bosom projecting straight from her chest. On the tip of each breast was a pink bulb. The bulbs lit up with a flick of a switch. My father thought she was really something. "It's a lamp," he'd said to my mother at the swap meet where he'd bought it. "We gotta have a lamp, don't we?" Our rumpus room glowed the rose of those nipples.

Then there were the cocktail napkins printed with cartoons. These portrayed a bumbling husband and his bossy wife. Their outfits always stayed the same (she wore a voluminous muumuu, his pant cuffs ended above his ankles), but their quarrels changed from napkin to napkin. She'd chase him with a rolling pin as he panted after a buxom coed. He'd try to sneak out for a poker game while she gabbed on the phone.

Each napkin showed another dismal facet of their marriage.

Eve and Arnold Menassian thought the cartoons were hilarious; with disarming candor, they told my parents how their own spats and foibles resembled that couple's. My parents kept saying, "Don't tell *us*—we know what you mean." Bob and Marion chuckled a little, gave each other troubled looks, put their napkins back on the stack. Ida was the most amused; she peered at the napkins over her glasses and barked a deep and knowing laugh—they confirmed her disparagement of marriage, made her almost glad to be single. Ever portentous, Ida promised I'd get the jokes when I grew up.

We were gathered in the rumpus room to watch my father's television debut; he was going to play himself on a segment of "Divorce Court." Father mixed drinks with zeal, spritzing soda and squeezing lime. He circled the room with a bucket, dropped fresh ice from silver tongs, offered everyone swizzle sticks. Marion liked to scrutinize her ice, watch it clink and swirl in the glass. Bob took swigs of his whiskey sour and watched Marion watch her ice. When Arnold took a sip of his drink, my father hovered behind him and said, "O most illustrious Prince of Liquor, how does it taste?" And burly, nervous, wisecracking Arnold pretended he was drunk and slurred, "It's schwell, Irving, schwell." Arnold gave Mother a sloppy wink. She snorted and called him a wisenheimer. Eve rolled her eyes and said that Arnold should audition for "The Ed Sullivan Show."

Exactly at eight, my father turned on the set. A courtroom bloomed from a dot of white light. He shushed everyone and turned up the volume. The theme music was somber, but Bob and I couldn't stop smiling at the idea that our father would be on TV. As with every episode of "Divorce Court," this was a reenactment of a case that had been decided months before the broadcast, but the producers used the real attorneys to lend an air of authentic tension. When the announcer spoke her husband's name, my mother made a high, invol-

untary noise. The Menassians applauded as my father walked
onto the screen, his receding hair darker than it was in life.
He took to the camera with gusto, pacing back and forth as
he questioned his client, a wife whose husband had jilted her
for the saleswoman who had sold them the prefabricated
bomb shelter for their San Diego backyard. Indignant on the
wife's behalf, my father wove into his speech a word or two
about hydrogen bombs and mass annihilation, telling how
his client was motivated to install the shelter not only for the
sake of her husband and their two small sons but out of a
selfless concern for mankind's survival. His voice spanned its
broad octave. He struck at the air for emphasis. He shot
disdainful looks toward the husband. Love seemed at stake
right then and there, nothing less than love. The court steno-
grapher was frantic to keep up with him. A ribbon of paper
shot from her machine. Beneath the wingspan of a gilded
eagle, the judge sat perfectly still. A bailiff stood to one side,
his wary eyes aimed everywhere.

"Fantastic," said Bob during a toothpaste commercial.
Teeth were singing in squeaky voices.

"A real pro," added Mrs. Menassian.

"It seems so real," said Marion. Her speech was slow and
thick from drink. "How much of this is real?"

"Honey," said Mother, "it's almost real."

Marion echoed, "Almost real," smiling slightly.

"Oh, no," moaned Ida. "Ghosts."

Bob ran up to the Zenith, fiddled with the rabbit ears, and
cursed our poor reception. Arnold suggested the antenna on
the roof might be to blame, or interference from a shortwave
radio in the neighborhood; he stood up in case he needed to
run somewhere. Ida was shouting instructions to Bob: "Stop.
Left. Yes. You lost it." She gave up by saying, "Wouldn't
you know this would happen tonight." Mother said she was
sure the problem would solve itself if people would just stay
calm and help themselves to another drink, but when the

show resumed, the picture was riddled with bands of static and the ghosts had gotten worse; there were double judges, a pair of bailiffs. And then my father was on the screen, pacing back and forth as before, trailed by his translucent twin.

"Is it me?" Marion said to no one, holding up her tumbler of bourbon.

"Get a load of that," said my father. "Two of yours truly for the price of one." He leaned forward on the sofa and stared at the screen, his cheeks flushed. He breathed deep breaths, the monogram on his shirt pocket—I.Z.—heaving in and out. The television's double image only meant that my father's notoriety was multiplied; the gavels slammed, the courtroom twice as crowded as before, his victory beamed across the state, ghosts or no. The plaintiff, still blotting her tears, was granted half her husband's income and full possession of their two-story Colonial house with its backyard bomb shelter.

"Boy," said Bob, during the credits, "that guy's gonna be out of luck when they drop the big one."

"Actually," said my father, "her bomb shelter stinks. She's hired me to sue the contractor. That thing couldn't protect you from a spring shower. It's got cracks and leaks and—"

"The question is," Eve interrupted, "could anything? Protect you, I mean."

"Exactly," said Mother. "Where's a safe place?"

At school, I'd seen a film of a house in the Nevada desert where a family of mannequins waited in a living room to test the effects of a nuclear blast. Those splintering chairs. That melting hair. Those bodies blown like dust from erasers. I pictured, for one awful instant, our rumpus room consumed by light, every one of us seared away, our sorry, insubstantial ghosts rising like smoke from the rubble. I remembered the drill Mrs. Robinson had us practice when, on the last Friday of every month, air raid sirens blared across the city. Before I knew what I was doing, I blurted out, "Duck and cover."

Arnold, who was searching for the switch on the hula dancer, looked at me and dove behind the bar. Ida gasped and clutched her chest, thinking maybe Arnold was hurt. My father laughed and gagged on his drink. Eve groaned, "I give up."

Arnold stayed hidden behind the bar. When he finally reappeared, he was holding a bottle of liqueur in either hand. "Hey," he said, "you've got the ingredients back here for Rainbow Cordials. How about it?"

"What's a Rainbow Cordial?" asked Mother.

"Magic in a glass," he said. Arnold retrieved more bottles from behind the bar, and a set of tall and narrow glasses. He placed the glasses on a tray decorated with a reproduction of Gauguin women, naked and brown and unabashed. Arnold went to work with great concentration, tilting the first glass at a diagonal and pouring crème de menthe down its side. Without shifting the angle of the glass, he reached for a bottle of triple sec and poured an orange layer over the green. We all moved closer (except for Marion, who was sucking ice cubes and trying to straighten the seam on her hose), amazed to see that the two layers hadn't mixed but floated one atop the other. "You need the nerves of a surgeon," Arnold said, reaching for the cassis, holding his breath while it trickled down, making a third, purple layer.

Mother whispered, "Out of this world," and touched Eve's hand.

Arnold proceeded with thin layers of Cointreau and, next, Drambuie, inspired by our reverent attention. "What matters," he said, keeping his hands steady, "is knowing precisely how much and in what order to pour. Liqueurs are like women: each has a unique personality." He cast a meaningful glance at Bob, who in turn glanced over at Marion and motioned for her to join us. She waved, chewed a sizable ice cube, smiled, but wouldn't budge. "You must learn to master," Arnold continued, "their delicate and volatile nature." Eve and Ida looked at each other and stifled their laughter. Finally Arnold tipped the glass upright, as everyone murmured, *Careful, careful.* The five strata stayed distinct. "For Sylvie," he said, handing the glass to my mother. She thanked Arnold and took it gingerly, afraid to move and ruin the effect. And so my mother didn't move. She barely batted an eye. She held the glass at arm's length and stayed that way until Arnold—more adroit with every drink—filled the rest of the glasses. Everyone came away from the bar, Rainbow Cordial in hand.

"Pal," said my father, practically tiptoeing over the parquet floor, "this is bee-yoo-tiful. I can hardly bring myself to drink it."

"Me neither," said Mother. She rose from the barstool, inched toward the sofa as cautiously as a tightrope walker, eyes on the liquid prism in her hand.

Eve and Ida sat down on adjacent chairs. They began to raise their glasses in a toast, but they were so worried about spoiling Arnold's handiwork, they retracted the toast halfway through.

Bob brought a cordial to Marion, walking toward her in slow motion. "I'll be there in a year," he joked, teetering to keep both their glasses level with the earth.

From my vantage point—cross-legged on a barstool—I watched as my family, the Menassians, and Marion sat together in the rumpus room and endured the burden of beautiful drinks, bright bands of fragrance and flavor that everyone seemed afraid to taste. No one could bring himself to be the first to tip his glass, to disrupt the balance, to churn the miraculous into mud. Someone would say, *Here's to you,* or *Down the hatch,* and tentatively raise the cordial to his lips, only to pull it back undisturbed. During a long, awkward silence, they each held a sweet, improbable concoction, determined to keep it intact.

"Well, folks," said Arnold, just to say something, "what's

the word?" He fingered the rim of his glass, looked around the room, waited for someone to speak.

"The word is *legs*," slurred Marion. "Spread the word." Marion became racked with laughter; the layers in her cordial quivered, bled, and collapsed, liquid sloshing out of her glass. She bent over, braying and coughing. Her blouse slid over one shoulder, revealing a bra strap, white against her tan skin. Bob tamped at the spills on her skirt with a wadded cocktail napkin. "Baby," he said. "Baby." She sat up, took a deep breath, and regained her composure. Then she glanced at the murky contents of her glass and began to laugh again.

Arnold and Eve chuckled politely. My mother took my father's hand; both of them tried to sustain a smile. Ida glowered and set down her cordial.

Bob excused himself and led Marion out to the patio. We could see their backs through the double doors, hear every word that passed between them. "My shoes are awful tight," said Marion. She put her arm around Bob's waist to steady herself, examined the redwood fence and aluminum lawn chairs. The yard was frosted with moonlight. "Some enchanted evening," she said.

"Breathe," said my brother.

"Huh?" said Marion. "What's the problem?"

"Breathe," he repeated.

"I'm breathing, for chrissakes," grumbled Marion. "I don't need some man to tie a string around my pinkie to remind me to breathe." She wavered on her high heels. "Dis that make sense?"

"Keep it down," Bob pleaded. "You're embarrassing me."

"Oh, goodness," she said, feigning mortification. And then in mock Chinese, "So velly solly." She waited for Bob to laugh, seemed genuinely surprised that he didn't find her accent amusing. She pried open my brother's mouth and looked inside. "Say Ahhh. You feel all right, Bobby Bear?"

"Uch," said Ida. It was the same sound she used when she

ate a bad pistachio nut. "Don't say I didn't warn you," she whispered to my mother. Ida lurched from the sofa, barreled over, and nearly scooped me off the barstool. "Say good night," she commanded.

"Why?"

"Because," said Ida, "the sun has sunk." She prodded me past the Menassians, whose eyes were larger than usual. "Night," they said in unison. My mother and father grazed me with kisses but looked out toward the patio.

Ida stomped through the dining room, dragging me behind her. Plates and silverware rattled as we passed. All the way down the hall, Ida spat Yiddish invective. She shut the door to my bedroom behind us, leaned against it, and glared toward God. *"Zee helft ihm vee a toyten bahnkess."*

Once I was in bed, Ida plucked *A Year of Rhymes* off my nightstand and thumbed through it till she found the August 28 poem, "Summer's End." "Aloud," she said, and thrust the book into my hands. She crossed the room, sighed, and folded her arms. The window of my bedroom faced our flagstone patio; Ida stood to one side, spying on Bob and Marion. The sound of their argument wavered in the air, shrill and wrong, like the notes of "How Dry I Am." I strained to make out what they were saying, surprised to share with my aunt a role I thought exclusive to children—that of baffled eavesdropper. *Please, never, want, must:* every muffled word was like another piece to the vast and exasperating jigsaw puzzle of my brother's love life. "I don't hear you reading," said Ida, tilting her head to get a better view.

" 'The summer is ending,' " I intoned. " 'Fall arrives. / We lose a season out of our lives. / Memory is all that survives. / And even that will vanish.' " I tried to imbue the poem with sad drama, to read with Aunt Ida's inconsolable tone, but waning time was only an abstraction—for me, summer was a season of long, memorable days—and my rendition sounded insincere. I closed the book (even though the poem had three more stanzas) and slid beneath the blanket. "It's a short one," I said. "It's over."

Ida turned. Her face was drawn. "That girl," she said, "should know to behave better. 'The word is *legs.*' *Vey iss meer.* Don't say things you can't take back." Ida hesitated, tugged at her turban. "Your brother should know better too." Her mouth quivered slightly, as if she were testing words before she said them. "Do you know what it means to *squander* something?"

"Sort of," I said.

"You can waste money. Waste time. You can waste love too. And even if you tell yourself you won't, you will. When it comes to love, things can go rotten before you know it. On the patio is a perfect example." As Ida spoke, I heard for the first time a plaintive tone in her voice, as though she were secretly wishing that someone, anyone, would interrupt, would convert her to a different point of view, would argue against her grim predictions. She fell silent, stood alone in the cold glow of moonlight, and looked at me expectantly. A mild breeze stirred the curtains, bore the odor of honeysuckle, overripe, almost rancid.

"When I get married," I said to my aunt. But I didn't know how to finish the sentence.

The last days of summer were the longest, days of harsh and persistent light. Shafts of it pierced the cover of trees, mottled lawns, and baked the pavement. No wind blew to temper the air. Refuge beneath an awning or umbrella offered little relief; shade was another kind of heat, fierce and dark and indirect. Ripples of heat rose like smoke from the cars parked along Ambrose Avenue. If I dared to look at the sun, my vision was branded with its afterimage, a smudge of molten gold.

I was convinced that one household on our cul-de-sac had hoarded all the shadows that were absent from the street. The King family had taped aluminum foil to their windows, shiny side out; daylight was deflected away from the walls, leaving the interior of their two-story Tudor house (the largest in the neighborhood) comparatively cool, and so dark that, when invited inside, I was forced to thrust out my arms and feel my way like a blind man. And when my eyes adjusted, what came into view was a broad central hall ending in a staircase. Off the hall were two large rooms, their floors a patchwork of shag rugs. Each room contained an odd assortment of furniture—fat chairs on casters, TV-dinner trays, wrought-iron magazine caddies—which the King children rearranged at will. Stephanie, Stephen, Barbara, and Brad: it was, without question, the children's domain. Mr. and Mrs. King were rarely home. He sold used cars on commission in Glendale. She was the vice president of a dating service in Beverly Hills called Miracle Match. Mr. and Mrs. King allowed their children to do or eat anything in their absence, as long as it wasn't life-threatening. And so their refrigerator was stocked with bologna and Mars bars and root beer, their rooms were strewn with the pieces of board games, play money, plastic dice. The Kings' house was a haven where whim and impulse were the only rules. Ida, who had been there once to retrieve me for dinner, referred to it as "that rabbit hutch."

Brad King was my best friend, a plump, quick-witted boy whom I admired for his defiance of adults. For me, being the baby of the family meant a certain shy obedience. I stayed out of the way, spun in the swivel chair (now in my room), vanished into *A Year of Rhymes,* waited to have my hair ruffled, to hear my name volleyed in the Yiddish conversations I'd learned it was futile to ask about. I quietly observed my father, mother, brother, and aunt. Brad, on the other hand, thought of adults as fodder for mockery. He imitated his parents' arguments, making his eyes bulge, waving his fist, and spewing, "Why you . . . just wait'll I . . . I've never been so. . . ." He tormented Mrs. Robinson by making fart noises when her back was turned and, after she spun around, would stare in disgust at an innocent classmate. He once lay on his front steps pretending he was dead, irate when the postman stepped over him. To resist being good was Brad's mission. All restlessness and invention, he led me through his house in search of diversion, his pranks and practical jokes the antidote to those final, indolent days of summer.

It was Brad who taught me how to make crank telephone

calls. He could fashion his voice into that of an old woman, a sniveling child, a census taker. But his favorite trick was this: he'd have me phone the same number over and over, one we picked at random from the telephone book. I'd ask each time for George, and after the person on the other end finally got angry and said, "Look, for the last time, there's no one here by that name," Brad would call back and say, "Hi. This is George. Were there any messages for me?" I listened in, my heart pounding as our victim cursed and slammed down the receiver. From a vestibule in that cool Tudor house, we dialed the gullible, glaring world outside.

When the novelty of fooling strangers had worn off, we turned to experiments that were meant to settle nagging questions. Can a person glue his hands together? Does g-force have the same effect on hamsters as it does on humans? Could the aerosol stream from Mrs. King's hair spray be lit with a match and fired like a blowtorch? Brad's brother or sisters often caught us involved in mischief, and he would be forced to bribe them with Tootsie Rolls or loose change to keep them from reporting us to his parents. Barbara—short and lanky and younger than Brad—was the worst; even after Brad had given her a handful of candy, she would follow us everywhere, repeating, "Loose lips sink ships," and because she was so pale—blond hair, silvery eyes—she seemed like a specter wafting through those rooms, chanting her relentless threat.

By locking the door to his parents' bedroom from the inside, there was one activity Brad made sure no one discovered—our foray into his father's cedar closet. Sound was muffled by rows of Mr. King's clothes. Air was scarce. The scent of cedar made me sleepy. On the top shelf were a dozen black-and-white photographs that Brad had to climb on a suitcase to reach. The photographs showed a voluptuous woman posing in someone's living room. Clad only in high heels or a lace apron or a strand of pearls—each photograph was different—she seemed more naked with these embellishments than she would have been without them. The Tahitian women on the tray in our rumpus room appeared not to think about their nudity; this woman, on the other hand, beamed a sly smile and flaunted her body. She leaned against a stone mantel, lithe and impatient, as though her lover were late again. She draped herself over the arm of a chair, clutching a polka-dot scarf, Kewpie mouth pouting. She contorted atop a coffee table, licking the air, a preposterous knot of seduction, her moist eyes aware of the camera, of the photographer, of curious boys like Brad and me. In image after image, she arched her back, cupped a breast, stroked the black patch of her pubic hair as if to say, *I know who you are and I know what you want.*

"Who is she?" I whispered.

"Who knows," said Brad. "But she's something, huh?" He thumbed through the photographs, greeting each one with an exhalation, touching his fingertip to her nipple or tickling her armpit and saying, "Goochie goochie."

"Come on," I said when I thought he had spent too long on one of the pictures.

"Don't you like them?" he asked. "Those big juicy knockers?"

"Sure," I said, "but. . . ."

Brad fanned himself with the photographs. "I don't know about you, but I'm getting hot." His cheeks were flushed, his eyes shining. Then alarm swept over his face. "What's that?" he asked.

"What's what?"

"Shhh! Somebody's coming. What if it's my dad?"

We jumped up. The hangers we'd hit were rocking and chiming. Brad tossed the photographs up toward the shelf. Most of them fluttered back to the floor. "He'll kill me," squealed Brad. "And he'll kill you too." We bolted from the closet and slammed the door. "Act like nothing happened," he ordered. He ran to unlock the bedroom door. I ran to the little pink chair at Mrs. King's dressing table and tried to appear nonchalant, one arm thrown over the back of the chair, legs crossed, mouth fixed in a grin. I looked toward the door. I waited for the knob to turn. I prepared myself for Mr. King's anger.

No one. The doorknob gleamed in the distance. Brad began to laugh. He held his stomach with one hand and pointed at me with the other. "Bet you're excited now," he said.

I grabbed a pillow from the bed and threw it at him, hard. He caught it, embraced it, fell on the bed. He rolled around like a man in the throes of passion, stroking the pillow's hair and staring into its eyes. "You're mine," he said, several octaves lower than usual, "all mine." He ground his hips into the mattress, the pillow squashed beneath him. "Oh, honey," he moaned. "Gimme that friction."

When he stood up, the pillow lay crumpled in the center of the bed. The bedspread was a mess. "Watch this," Brad said. He stood several feet away, turned his back to me, and hugged himself so tightly he was able to reach around his torso and run his hands up and down along the edges of his own back. It looked as if someone were standing in front of him, hidden from view, caressing him. He tilted his head as if bending to kiss a pair of upturned lips. The illusion that he was making out was enhanced by the dimness of the bedroom; the only light seeped in through the cracks between sheets of aluminum foil. Brad sucked his lips and mimicked kissing. Kisses resounded within the room. The length and intent of each kiss varied, from bold osculations to short, reticent sips, like someone drinking tea. I was mesmerized, certain I could detect in that spectrum of kisses every shade of desire. I heard my parents' kisses, grown halfhearted as that summer wore on, Father immersed in depositions and dog-eared files, Mother washing piles of laundry, erasing stains, ironing the sheets of their shared life. I heard Bob and

Marion's kisses, more conciliatory the more they fought, kisses meant to bridge the distance widening between them. Ida applying her lips to my forehead—*kish in keppela*—extracting herself with a smack of suction. Arnold pecking Eve's neck. Mrs. Vixen blotting her lipstick on a Kleenex.

My elbow was propped on the mirrored top of Mrs. King's dressing table. It was crowded with crystal vials and atomizers full of perfumes with suggestive names: Ardor, Musk, Paris Night. I saw my face gazing up from the murky depths of the mirror, and it struck me, like a whiff of some forbidden scent, that I wished Brad was kissing me. I pictured this as I'd seen it happen in so many movies: unable to resist me a moment longer, he takes me in his arms, and though I fight his advances at first—my fists pummel his back—there comes a gradual giving in, the buttery sway of my body, and soon I grab the fabric of his shirt, drawing him close.

"You're not paying attention," Brad whined.

"I've got to go," I said.

"Come on. It was just a joke. My dad won't be home till ten."

I went for the door. When I turned to say goodbye, Brad had his arm around the pillow as though it were someone standing next to him. "We'll miss you," he said. "Don't forget to write."

I made my way toward the stairs. I could hear Stephen tossing a ball against the wall of his room, the rasp of Stephanie's nail file, Barbara singing "London Bridge." The occupations of a summer day seemed suddenly remote, part of a life I had left behind. The stairwell was dark as a theater. I fled down the steps, the scene of my yielding replaying itself again and again, my hands against the blank expanse of Brad's shirt.

Light and heat blasted through the Kings' front door, bleaching everything in sight. "Duck and cover," I thought, racing down the brick path toward the street. My eyes stung from the glare. The leaves of hedges lining the path shone like shattered glass. I wondered how anything thrived during summer. I wanted nothing more than the silence and privacy of my room.

My mother was busy by our back door, hanging clothes on the line, a wooden clothespin clasped in her mouth. She saw me and smiled, then turned to face one of my father's empty dress shirts.

I shut the door to my room, dived onto the bed, buried my face in the pillow. I waited for a calm that was slow in coming. I considered pretending, like Brad, that the pillow was flesh—but whose? I remembered a movie starring Jeff Chandler and Jane Russell; they glistened with sweat, collided in a kiss, their mammoth lust barely contained by CinemaScope. I reconstructed all the Technicolor details—crashing surf, a canopy of clouds—placing myself in his role, then hers, gauging changes in my heartbeat and respiration. I repeated my experiment again and again. She was striking enough, with her wild eyes and scarlet lips, but remained little more than a stranger on a screen. In the end it was him I preferred to play opposite to, no matter how hard I tried to interpret my physical reactions to the contrary. His image was vivid without my trying to make it so. The blue shadow cast by his jaw. The V of skin within his open collar. The feel of his breath against my neck.

I fell into a dreamless sleep, as vast and dark as a Tudor house. When I awoke, I awoke slowly, fighting each degree of awareness. My eyes would open, close again. Squares of sunlight burned on the ceiling. My arms and legs refused to move. I wasn't sure what day it was. How long I'd slept. Whose bed I'd slept in.

The hiss of plumbing roused me from bed, drew me through the house and out to the driveway, where Bob, wearing an undershirt and denim cutoffs, was washing his Pontiac. He'd uncoiled the hose from a spigot near the kitchen door, stopping now and then to tug out the knots. A jet of water splashed over the hood and cascaded down the grimy fenders. Puddles expanded on asphalt. Without his having to ask me, I fished the sponge from a bucket and began to suds the body of the car, watching the rivulets of water, the incongruous splotch of sun that burned within the midnight-blue enamel.

"Were you asleep?" he asked. I gaped at him, startled by what I thought was clairvoyance. Maybe he knew what had happened at Brad's. "I can tell because the pillow made a mark." He touched his cheek. I touched mine and felt a scar embossed by sleep. I held my hand there, as if to hide it. Water dripped into my tennis shoes. "Don't worry," he said, puzzled by my embarrassment. "It'll go away in a while." He continued to circle the car, stroking it with the stream of water, holding his thumb over the nozzle when he needed extra pressure. "If Dad would stop sending me out to the boondocks," he shouted over the sound of water, "I wouldn't have to wash this baby so often. Once a divorce is under way, it slips people's minds they were ever married. You have to trail them all over the map just to slap a summons in their hand and smile like a fool so they don't know what hit them. And when a couple shows up for the hearing—*if* they show up—it's 'This plate is mine, that sock is yours.' Like some damn ashtray was the end of the world. Every settlement is a fight to the finish." He drank from the hose and shook his head. "No joke, tooth and nail. But the minute their stuff is divvied up—hasta la vista. Remember Mrs. Vixen? Gone With the Wind."

"That's bad?" I asked.

Bob went to turn off the water. "Well," he said when he came back, "you can't really blame her. Why not make a clean break? Especially when there's no kids in the picture. What's the point of dragging out disaster? My theory is: Love is good as long as it's good. When it's over, that's that." He grabbed the chamois that stuck out of his back pocket but, instead of wiping the car, closed his eyes and craned his face toward the sun. His forehead gleamed. He stopped chewing his spearmint gum. My brother's sunlit expression went lax. He stayed that way for a long time. I thought of Mrs. Robinson's lesson on photosynthesis, how plants yearn toward available light. "I wonder," he said, eyes still closed, "what Marion is doing right this minute." If it unnerved my brother to recount the ways a bond can be severed, the antidote was Marion, the filament of her image bright behind his eyes.

When his reverie ended, Bob began to polish the car, rubbing with rhythmic passes of his hand, scratching off stubborn chunks of grit, buffing metal and chrome. "While I finish this," he said, "go ask Mom if Marion can come for dinner."

"Let's see," said my mother, unwrapping a wax-paper package filled with knockwurst. She pointed at each ruddy piece of meat: "Dad, me, Bob, you, Arnold, Eve, and Ida. That leaves one for Marion. I'm certain one's enough." Mother rummaged through the spice rack. "She eats so little it's a wonder she's alive. But," said my mother, "we'll fix that. Tell your brother I'll set another place." Before I reached the back door, my mother had gathered all the jars of spice in the kitchen, sniffing paprika, shaking loose the lumps in celery salt, touching to her tongue one incendiary dab of cayenne. She contemplated every flavor and its potential effect: Marion might be enticed by a meal steeped in the perfect spices, the seed of her appetite brought to blossom.

"Mother's wrong," said Bob as we pulled out of the driveway. We were going to pick up Marion from work, the Hallmark cardshop on Western Avenue. "Marion is *always* hungry. It's just that she doesn't give in to it. 'Hunger puts the edge on the razor.' That's what she says. She says being hungry makes her alert."

"I don't get the things she says."

"That's exactly what I like about her. She says what she wants. Does what she pleases. Breaks the rules."

"Like a criminal?"

"Like an outlaw," said Bob. "There's a big difference." Our sunstruck neighborhood slid past the windows. "She's bad in a good way. Catch my drift?"

"What about your fights?"

"What about them?"

There was no use probing; my brother would make a display of devotion, every aspect of their ardor defensible, flawless. "I like her," I said. "I didn't mean I didn't." As the Pontiac sped down the street, the tassel Marion had given to Bob shuddered and twirled from the rearview mirror. "She kind of reminds me of Jane Russell."

"Yeah?" Bob was pleased by the comparison. Wherever they went, he told me, Marion was magnetic in her tight red dress, drawing whistles from thin air. He smiled, and I could see why women found him attractive: cleft chin, disheveled hair, the thick eyelashes Ida envied. It frightened me to see him as a woman might, but as he spoke—thoughtful, halting, trying to define the ineffable aspects of his girl—the light and shadow shifting on his features caused me to stare. "Sometimes—this is going to sound really crazy—sometimes I can't remember what Marion smells like, so I have to be around her to remember."

We turned south on Finley. Modern houses with A-frame roofs and spacious carports lined the street, their walls painted coral, sea foam, canary. Front yards were landscaped with cactus and colored gravel. Soon single-family homes gave way to stucco apartment buildings, the name emblazoned on each facade a promise of glamour and ease: Starland Court, Pacific Terrace, Sunset Royale. Balconies loomed like honeycombs. Long and blue in the late afternoon, the shadows of palm trees incised the street, intervals of asphalt baking between them.

A voice on the radio announced a back-to-school sale on three-ring notebooks and lined filler paper. The mere mention of school—I was about to enter the sixth grade—made me feel as though I had swallowed a stone. I changed the station. "Listen to this," yelled Bob. He pushed my hand away from the knob and turned up the volume till the song was distorted, the treble like someone scratching on a blackboard. "It's 'Louie Louie.' You know, the one that's supposed to be dirty." We leaned toward the dashboard and tried to decipher the lyrics. The Kingsmen rasped the first verse: *Louie, Louie, oh, oh, baby, now.* But after that, any sense was speculation.

Bob guessed the second verse aloud: "I'm going to love you with a . . . something . . . in me."

"No," I said. "It's: I'll take my dog for a walk by the sea."

"That's not dirty."

"It's what they said," I insisted.

He squinted at the AM band, periodically glanced at the

road. "I come up to the something something in your something bed."

I decided to improvise. "And dump a bunch of something all over your head."

Bob leaned closer, turned the radio louder, hoping the volume would obliterate my comments. Then he smacked me in the arm. "Did you hear that? They said *screw*. No kidding. Did you hear?" He sat upright, hands firmly on the wheel; Bob was braced by that one illicit word issuing through the speaker.

I tried to picture Marion and my brother alone in his apartment, what they did to each other. She is looking toward the skyline, the silhouette of City Hall, the clapboard bungalows crowding the hills, the paddleboats skimming Echo Park Lake and leaving silver wakes. She says something odd about the view, what the clouds remind her of, or how powerful she feels surveying the world from this height. He comes up behind her, slowly, like a man approaching a deer. Her hair is straight and smooth, the only view that could hold his interest. He parts it—the weight of two black wings—exposes the nape of her neck, the clasp of her necklace, the zipper of her dress. My brother inhales Marion's scent and remembers what he could not recall from across the room.

That's as far as I could go; beyond the imminence of love-making, lovemaking itself was a mystery. There were some scenes I gleaned, how their faces may have flinched when he entered her, how their bodies may have arched before it was over, but only in a vague and momentary way; to try to imagine the feel of sex was like straining to hear a song's obscure verses.

A bell tinkled above the door when we entered the narrow cardshop. Marion stood behind a glass counter at the far end, gift-wrapping a package for a man who drummed his fingers on the countertop. Even from the other end of the store her concentration was apparent; she pressed each fold with such care I was reminded of the time Mrs. Robinson made an origami swan. "Young lady," said the man, glancing at his watch, "it needn't be perfect." Marion didn't respond. She tugged the paper tight, secured the flaps with snippets of tape. She ran a scissors along a length of yellow ribbon, again and again, like a barber stropping a blade. The ribbon curled, became a fat and tangled bow. She taped the bow to one corner of the box, arranged several tendrils of ribbon artfully over the edge. The man grabbed the box and dashed out the door the instant she was finished. "Where's the fire?" Marion said once he was gone. Rotary fans dangled from the ceiling, slapped at the air. High windows behind the counter admitted slanting shafts of light.

Bob asked Marion over for dinner and, after she agreed, watched her tally receipts in a ledger. I took an inventory of my own, sniffing the scented stationery, examining the apothecary jars filled with jelly beans, the Gift Plaques for Home and Office: *World's Best Mother, Husband, Lover, Daughter, Son.* A rack of greeting cards divided the store into two aisles. The cards spanned every occasion from baptism to bar mitzvah, every sentiment from sorrow to thanks. There were more rhymes on those racks than Aunt Ida could keep count of, more than a mere year's worth, rhymes written in lavish calligraphy. On the covers of the cards were clustered balloons, blizzards of confetti, an abundance of bouquets. Cornucopias spilled their plenty: apples, walnuts, stalks of wheat, and, on one glossy card, a cache of gold coins. Tiers of cake—birthday and wedding and anniversary—rose like miniature Towers of Babel. Saint Valentine was commemorated with a palpitation of crimson hearts. Moses hoisted stone commandments, his beard and robes blown by the wind. Cards for women, I noticed, tended to show gingham aprons and wooden spoons, while cards for men featured Model T's and mallards. My parents' embroidered towels came to mind—His, Hers—words that cleaved the world in two. Just as I was about to investigate the section marked

Miscellaneous, the lights in the store flickered and dimmed. "Time to split," Bob said. Keys jangled in Marion's hand.

On the way back home, Bob tried to find a station playing "Louie Louie," but Marion asked him to stop on a meandering jazz piano. She wrenched off her high heels, propped her stockinged feet on the dashboard. "What's for dinner?" she said through a yawn.

"Knockwurst," I called from the back seat.

Marion threw back her head and laughed. "What a miserable word." She rested her head on the back of the seat. Her long hair fell over the edge, swayed back and forth with the motion of the car. My fingers became the tines of a comb I drew through Marion's hair.

"Mmm," she sighed. "That feels fantastic."

The pleasure in her voice made me feel older, and I wondered if my brother was jealous. I raked her hair, heavy lengths of it slipping through my fingers. She turned her head to gaze at the cavalcade of pastel houses. My hand grazed her forehead, the rim of her ear. Damp heat rose from her shoulders.

"It's a shame," she said.

"What is?" asked Bob.

"Pink and green and yellow, everyone in their proper box. Just look at those yards." We passed a statuette of a man holding up a lantern. "Nothing," she said, "is more despicable than a plaster lawn jockey."

"We'll find the kind of place you want."

"What kind of place is that?" she asked.

"Wherever you are is OK with me."

"You know what I told you," she whispered. "Love is good as long as it's good. I'm bad at plans."

My brother bristled at her reticence. He muttered, *That again,* under his breath.

"What do you want from me?" Marion asked. "What do you want?"

Waves of warm air. The din of passing traffic. How many

theories, I wondered, had Bob borrowed from Marion? How had my brother, who warned me of deception so often, convinced himself that Marion loved him, her devotion beyond reproach? It was then I was certain they would part. I lifted the sheath of Marion's hair. Bent close. Inhaled smoke.

Marion bolted up in her seat. Her black hair vanished from my hand. Her forehead furrowed, nostrils flared.

Bob switched off the radio. "I can smell it too," he said.

The three of us were speechless as ashes billowed toward the Pontiac. A few at first. Then erratic droves of ash. Ashes skidded across the hood, gathered in a fine silt beneath the windshield wipers. Flurries corkscrewed into the car. Marion and I batted at ashes, rubbed them between our fingers. They yielded no sensation apart from their smell, a pungent char, and a weightless paste they left on our skin. She and I held out our hands and showed each other the gray stains.

Traffic slowed. Hands were thrust from car windows, catching ash. Passengers peered into other cars, seemed to require confirmation—yes, yes, the world is burning—their faces pale, unbelieving. A carload of people pointed toward flames that crept up the slopes of the Hollywood hills and inched toward the Griffith Observatory, its copper domes gone dull. I craned out the window, strained to see the commotion on the mountain. High ridges incinerated. Parched tinder smoldered in gullies. Above a row of stucco houses, embers sputtered from trees.

Helicopters thundered above us on Ambrose Avenue. Dazed neighbors drifted from their doors and, heedless as sleepwalkers, milled in the street, heads turning this way and that to find the source of the sirens. Bob had to dodge astonished pedestrians who sniffed the air, then cupped their palms over mouths and noses to filter out the odor. A woman called the names of her children, all the while staring into the sky. One man sat atop his parked car and watched the fire with his hands in his lap, like a boy learning a lesson in school.

By the time we pulled into our driveway, a pall had snuffed the afternoon light. Evening was blurred and premature, the crescent moon aloof. Bob and Marion and I leaned against the trunk of the car, shielding our eyes from sifting ash and looking toward the hills. The tiny, frantic figures of people moved on distant roofs. Threads of water glinted from hoses, darkened shingles, and wooden walls. Far away, the fire brightened. Cinders fell faster, held more heat, a steady, stale precipitation. Though the light had faded, the temperature rose. The car, the pavement, my own clothes—the sum of a season's heat seemed to blaze beneath every surface.

Across the cul-de-sac, the King children filed from their house, pivoted to find the flames. Stephanie and Stephen stood perfectly still, made reverent by the bright destruction. Brad and Barbara squealed with delight—neat; wow. Brad waved in my direction.

My parents, Ida, Arnold, and Eve wandered out of our back door, huddled close together. Ida, who must have become aware of the fire while setting the table, still gripped a folded tablecloth. Her jaw was clenched, muscles taut in her thin neck. She glared at the fire as though she were willing the flames to retreat. "You got fire insurance?" she asked my father. Ashes dusted the top of her turban.

"I'm covered," said Father, "up to here." He lifted his hand above his head. For a moment I thought he meant covered with ash. Father leveled his gaze toward the hills and asked if he should wet the roof.

"I'll help," said Arnold. But neither of them budged.

"Thank your lucky stars," murmured Mother. "I don't think it's too bad yet. Wait awhile and see what happens." She turned around to look at the laundry. White sheets, darkened by soot, drooped from the line. The smell would tinge the linen for weeks. She cast a glance at Bob and me, then took my father's listless arm and draped it over her shoulder. Heavy-lidded, pressing against him, Mother seemed eager to sleep.

"When you invited us for dinner," Arnold said to my parents, "I didn't think you meant a barbecue." No one laughed. He shifted his weight from foot to foot, then slipped his arm around Eve's waist.

"Maybe we should go," Eve said. "Sylvia," she asked my mother, "should me and Arnie go?"

"No," said Mother. "Don't go."

Father said he'd better check the property, then walked in circles around the house. Sometimes he'd stop and touch the walls. I didn't know why.

Helicopters flew in haphazard patterns and doused the hills with chemical clouds. From our vantage point, it seemed miraculous that they didn't collide. A few shot directly overhead, bombarding us with an uncanny racket. All the dogs in the neighborhood howled. "It hurts them to hear this," Ida said.

After almost an hour of standing on the driveway, we all retreated into the house. My parents closed the windows and doors, hoping to keep the smell at bay, the fine, invasive flecks of ash. Instead of eating dinner that night—the knockwurst, potatoes, and cabbage cooled—we crowded into the rumpus room, where we watched a newscaster (trailed by his ghost) give reports on evacuations, acreage consumed, the locations of fire lines breached by flames. The fire seemed tame in black and white, a story unfolding somewhere else.

How long it took to contain the flames, I can't recall. Four hours. Five. What I remember best about that night is not the sight of encroaching fire, sirens blaring into the night, frightened families milling in the street. I remember best one image of my brother (and though he's been gone for thirty years, it is still the image I mourn him with). Before we turned to go inside the house, Bob blinked against an onslaught of ash. Ashes were falling thick and fast. They caught in his lashes, coated his shoulders. Even though I knew that their source was the fire raging in the hills, I pictured the cards I had seen on the racks—the hearts and clovers and horns of plenty, the countless ornately lettered rhymes—ignited at the edges, bursting into flame, their charred remnants carried on the air, ruined sentiment raining on my brother. Bob and Marion stood side by side but could not touch or speak to each other, my brother made sullen by useless affection. Helicopters clattered overhead. Across the street—faintly at first, then louder and louder—Barbara King sang "London Bridge." "Ashes," she chanted, "ashes. All fall down."

AUTUMN

hief Altoon, the fire marshal of Hollywood, walked to the center of the stage, spun on his heel, and faced an auditorium full of fidgeting kids. A spotlight fell on his hirsute forearms, his black uniform with epaulets. The word *fire* rose like smoke, lingered in the air, the chief's deep vibrato resounding within my chest. "Be alert," he warned, "for hidden dangers." That was the cue for Mr. Mullen, the principal of Los Feliz Elementary, to switch on the slide projector. "An octopus," boomed Chief Altoon, his shadow thrown against the image of an overloaded electrical outlet, wires writhing from a single socket. "Notice," he continued, "how some cords are frayed. This is a tragedy waiting to happen. *Spark plus carpet equals flames:* now, that's some math you need to remember." Next there appeared a picture of a housewife gasping in horror at a grease fire erupting from her skillet. "A lady's best friend is baking soda. Pour it on and the fire is gone. Tell Mom to keep a box by the stove." We saw the consumption of a Christmas tree, Halloween costume, shingle roof. A candle ignited the corner of a curtain. A lit cigarette smoldered on a mattress. During his slide presentation, Chief Altoon paced back and forth in front of the screen, the projected flames twining up his arms and face with no effect but to tint his skin, and I got it in my head that his angular, masculine beauty made him somehow impervious, that his broad stride and resonant voice kept pain at bay, his body burning but not consumed, his badge glinting like an armored heart.

I turned to see if Brad was as fascinated by Chief Altoon as I was, but Brad, breathing audibly through his nose, squinting to see in the dark, was busy drawing a tattoo on the back of his hand with a ballpoint pen. His head was bent, and he didn't see Mrs. Beswick, our new teacher, glaring at him from the end of the aisle, her taut mouth like a minus sign.

The final slide showed the layout of an average house—two bedrooms, two baths—with arrows pointing toward windows and doors. Chief Altoon encouraged each of us to sit down with our families and draw the floor plan of our own homes and apartments, marking a way out of every room. "Be wise," he advised. "Prepare for escape."

All the kids blinked and coughed and shifted in their seats when the lights came on. A couple of teachers fanned themselves with their green grade books. Mr. Mullen thanked Chief Altoon, who stood in the center of the stage with his arms folded and his legs spread far apart; he responded to our accolade with one quick nod of acknowledgment. Then Mr. Mullen dismissed the assembly according to grade, starting with first. Wooden seats creaked, and feet pummeled the hardwood floor. As a throng of first graders filed into daylight, Mrs. Beswick rose at the end of the aisle and calmly asked her class if we were aware of the sailor in our midst. Blank looks from two rows. Even Brad didn't see it coming. Yes, she insisted, or at least a boy masquerading as a sailor, tattoos and all. Brad stiffened. He slipped his hand and its inky image beneath his thigh. To pay for his discourtesy, Brad had to stay after school and "swab" the blackboards.

Walking home alone gave me time to think about Chief Altoon. I tried to convince myself that I was drawn to his kindness—he broke the falls of children with his net—and not his good looks. Still, every time I closed my eyes, his tall body flared up from nowhere, persistent and bright, a trick candle that wouldn't blow out. What did my brother see in his reveries—the swaying flame of Marion's hips? Did Bob feel as helpless as this?

On Ambrose Avenue, the sidewalk was humped and broken by the roots of old carob trees, and I had to pay attention to where I was stepping. A pewter sun hung in the sky, too dull to burn the haze away and reveal the expanse of blackened hills. It was the kind of day that caused Aunt Ida to complain of autumn's absence in our city; she'd point to illustrations of orange leaves drifting down the margins of *A Year of Rhymes*, grazing the stanzas of "Maple Feast," "This Country Called Autumn," and "Uncle Pumpkin." She'd tell me about the winds of Chicago, the leaves carpeting public parks, and her opal fingertips wafted through the air, settling at last in her lap. "So brisk," she'd sigh. "You can't imagine."

Few leaves covered our busy streets, but one couldn't deny that the season had changed. Hollywood autumn was strange, opaque. Grainy September afternoons infused even the most ordinary occurrences—passengers jostling on an eastbound bus, the cautious migrations of crossing guards—with a sense of distance, as if local lives were minor, remote, random habits enacted far away, the sound and sight of them filtered through wool. Viewed through thick, unmoving air, my house seemed to hover on our dead-end street, its stucco walls gone dim and soft, the mirage of a place where I slept and ate.

As I neared the kitchen door, I heard the low, incredulous register of Marion's voice. "Big deal. Everyone has to have an operation sooner or later. She'll never win."

"But she's a rare blood type," said my mother.

"*Says* she is. But how do we *know?*"

"Such a cynic for a girl your age."

"Suspicion," said Marion, "keeps Bobby in business."

Marion sat hugging her knees on the rag rug, while my mother absently ironed a blouse. They greeted me without taking their eyes off the gaunt, sniffling woman on the television screen, her tear-streaked cheeks glistening in close-up. Jack Bailey reached within his coat and flourished a handkerchief. "Darlin'," he crooned, "perhaps you'd like to tell the audience exactly what will happen if you can't have the operation."

"I'll keel over and croak," sputtered Marion through mock sobs.

"Don't you just love the way he says that," sighed my mother. " 'Darlin'.' " Fingers of steam seeped from the iron.

"Sylvia," said Marion. I was shocked to hear her address my mother by her first name. "You don't mean to tell me you find him attractive." Her face puckered with disgust.

"So what's with the face? The man makes me melt."

Marion turned to me and shrugged. "To each his own. Give me Lloyd Bridges any day. Those huge hams stuffed in a wet suit." Marion raised her hands and tried to approximate the circumference of Lloyd Bridges's thighs. She winked at me, as if I shared her predilection. I leaned against the wall, my vinyl binder, my sixth-grade textbooks—*People of the Western World, Success with Spelling,* Today's Mathematics—heavy as bricks.

"Just ignore us gals," said my mother. There was a buoyancy in her voice, an abandon that, more and more often, Marion's presence teased into being. Despite Aunt Ida's admonitions, or perhaps because of them, Marion and my mother had grown fond of each other.

"Yeah," said Marion. "Us gals got carried away."

Applause reported from the television set. Jack Bailey lowered a tiara onto the head of a woman with a neck brace and a beehive hairdo. The tiara jittered with highlights.

"Which one was that?" asked Marion.

"The elevator operator. Poor thing."

"It's her own fault," insisted Marion. "Don't they have to go through some kind of training, like airplane pilots?"

On my way down the hall, I heard Mother playfully scolding Marion for her lack of compassion. There were blessings to count. Stars to thank. And then there came the chorus of the Doctor Ross dog food commercial.

Pale light suffused my room. I collapsed into the swivel chair at my desk. Above me, the model of a B-52 bomber twirled on a length of fishing line and cast a mammoth shadow that slid across the walls. "Knock, knock." Marion stood in the portal, rapping her knuckles on empty air. She had on a white crop-top and white capris. Standing against the white wall of the hallway, her bare midriff was perfectly smooth, the vivid emblem of all her flesh. "Are these premises quarantined?" she asked, sweeping into the room. She left a wake of My Sin perfume. Sensing that I was upset, she offered consolation in the most effective way she knew. "You're going to be a real knockout someday." Her pronouncement contained the same prescience I associated with Aunt Ida, a sure and womanly knowledge of the future. Marion bellyflopped onto my bed, propped her chin on her palm—plastic bracelets clattered together—and scrutinized me so frankly I found myself unable to breathe. "Better even than Lloyd Bridges."

Marion could never—never in a million years, I assured myself—have guessed that what was bothering me was my attraction to our district fire marshal; she must have assumed I was troubled by my mother's erotic admission, or her own—adult comments a boy might find confounding. And I realized—in a wordless, unnerving way—that it was precisely the exceptional nature of my desires that promised safety; if my longing was an unthinkable thing, it might easily be hidden from the judgment of others. For now I was protected from consequences, from the fates that made people weep on TV. On that temperate and still September afternoon—suburban from every placid angle—years of subterfuge began, the determination to guard my secret like a monstrous jewel.

"What have we here?" asked Marion. She stretched toward my nightstand and picked up *A Year of Rhymes*. "You can tell a lot about a man by the books he reads." As soon as she saw the illustrations and the big print, she seemed to regret having said it. She quickly thumbed through the book, the pages a blur of seasonal color, dates catapulting into the past. It could have been the otherworldly light—the day's luminous residue—or the shadow wheeling around the room, or the heady scent of Marion's perfume, but I found myself pretending that my wife, happy I'm home from a hard day at work, reads me aloud a poem by Yeats, her bare stomach undulating. " 'And pluck till time and times are done, / The silver apples of the moon / The golden apples of the sun.' " Read in Marion's dulcet voice, all the sweet, impossible longing in those lines shook me like a chill. She stopped her recitation and looked up from the book. Her face, framed in parentheses of black hair, was brimming with such ardor and surprise, I thought I had willed our marriage into being. "You made me wait and wait just to drive me crazy," she whispered. I could see her eyes; she wasn't joking.

"I told you I'd be late." Bob was standing in the doorway. He came up behind the swivel chair and rested his palms on my shoulders. "Remember? The subpoena for the Ludlow trial?" His tie grazed the nape of my neck. I welcomed the weight and heat of his hands.

At the mere mention of the Ludlow trial, Marion bristled; the premise of the case put her on edge. My father's client, Eugene Ludlow, insisted that Vivien Ludlow had intended to become his wife "in name only," and he was suing for the annulment of their sixteen-day marriage. Mrs. Ludlow, on the other hand, denied that she intentionally withheld affection from her husband and claimed she was so busy preparing "unheard-of meals" to satisfy his insatiable appetite that she didn't have time for anything else. The case provided my father with considerable publicity in the local newspapers. A reporter from the *Herald-Examiner* dubbed it "The Case of the Baking Newlywed," and the epithet stuck. An excerpt of Mrs. Ludlow's deposition was included in one of the articles; it read like a menu, itemizing an array of dishes that allegedly kept her confined to the kitchen. One breakfast alone consisted of a rasher of bacon, a nine-egg omelet, pancakes, toast, cereal, freshly squeezed orange juice, and rice pudding.

"What kind of man eats an entire rasher of bacon for breakfast?" asked Marion. She tossed aside *A Year of Rhymes.*

"What kind of woman," asked Bob, "calls bacon and eggs an 'unheard-of meal'?" He sat down next to Marion. It was odd to see them together on my bed. They made eye contact only intermittently, staring instead at the olive-green carpet.

"A man who needs a trough," mumbled Marion.

"Whose side are you on, anyway?"

"Hers."

"I mean," said Bob, "mine or theirs."

"Don't you understand? Vivien Ludlow isn't some kind of criminal just because she won't"—Marion shot a glance at me, then looked back at Bob—"do the deed with her precious husband."

"For chrissakes, Marion. I've never even met the woman. I have nothing against her personally."

"Exactly," said Marion. "You're a man. You have something against her impersonally."

It astonished me that Marion, who scoffed at the women on "Queen for a Day," displayed such obstinate empathy where Mrs. Ludlow was concerned. And it astonished me that Bob, who could fire back retorts in any altercation, did nothing now but shudder; light moved through his iridescent suit, and I felt a swift, vicarious contraction. Silence ensued, a silence that threatened to last forever. I couldn't think what to say to end it. In my head I tested jokes, comments on the weather, news of school, but no remark could have dislodged the wedge of indignation between them. They didn't budge from my sagging bed. A clock ticked on the nightstand. A shadow circled the room.

"What's up?" It was Brad. I wasn't sure how long he'd been standing there. Chalk dust covered his shirt. "Beswick is cracked," he said, tapping his temple. "A basket case." Oblivious to the discord in the room, Brad turned his attention toward Marion and Bob. "The whole time I cleaned the blackboards, she looked out the window and talked to herself." Cocking his head, he made his eyes inanely wide and mimicked the babbling Mrs. Beswick. Bob and Marion stared at Brad without quite comprehending his presence. "And you wanna know why I had to stay after?"

Seconds of silence.

"Because of this." They practically flinched when Brad thrust his fist toward their faces. Innersprings creaked as they leaned closer to examine his tattoo. Brad's nostrils flared at the scent of My Sin. While Marion's head was bent, he tried to peer down her blouse.

My brother squinted at Brad's hand. "Gee," he said, without conviction.

"Hmm," Marion barely added.

Brad barreled over and showed it to me. Most of the ink had smudged when he tried to hide it from Mrs. Beswick. The figure was either a woman's or a man's—it was too smeared to tell. Arms and legs of differing lengths jutted out from a rotund torso. Its hair was a nondescript clot of ink. The face wore a blue, inscrutable expression. Brad stood before me and held out his hand, a slapdash impression embellishing the back, little more than a stain on his skin.

After Brad had gone home, after Bob took Marion back

to his apartment, I swiveled in circles, as if by centrifugal force the day's events could be flung from my head: Chief Altoon's persistent image, Bob and Marion's harsh exchange, Brad's awkward interruption. My room grew dark by rapid gradations. The bed and desk surrendered their edges. The shadow of the bomber blended with the walls. These autumn evenings, I suddenly understood, would continue to arrive earlier and earlier, a drop of ink added each night. I kept telling myself to stop revolving, to sit at my desk, to tear a piece of paper from my binder and try to render the layout of our house, a maze of rooms whose doors and windows a person could grope toward to save his life. But I stayed in the chair and continued to spin, aware of my blood's velocity, of all the foreshortened days ahead. I must have looked like Brad's tattoo, a small, blurred, uncertain body.

My brother adjusted the visor, his senses alert to the world beyond the windshield. I stuck my arm out the window and cupped the rushing air in my palm. We were trailing a lunch truck through afternoon traffic. At a stoplight on Third we almost lost it; our view was blocked by pedestrians surging through the crosswalk. Groups of men in drab suits and narrow neckties clutched their briefcases, greeted one another, inserted words edgewise in conversations. Every woman who passed before our car seemed to levitate atop her high heels and smile beneath a stiff bouffant. Bob smacked the dash, and the traffic light changed. People parted like the Red Sea. The Pontiac shot through the intersection. Along the congested avenue, shopkeepers stood in the doorways of their stores, eyeing passersby. Overhead, flat clouds covered the stratosphere, the office buildings and parking lots below bathed in lusterless sunlight.

Within seconds I spotted the lunch truck, making a left on Alvarado, and I shouted, "Thar she blows." My brother jumped. He made the turn just in time. Deftly changing lanes, he pulled up right behind it. "Good work," Bob said, and poked me in the ribs. "I'm going to stay on his tail if it kills me." CHOW NOW was emblazoned in big block letters above the lunch truck's taillights. The body of the truck—quilted aluminum, white enamel—rocked on its springs as it traveled down the street. We followed it past the county courthouse, the hall of records. Diamond rings sparkled behind the rusted iron grate of a pawnshop. A bus bench advertised the twenty-four–hour telephone number of a bail bondsman. Bob sat erect and drove with both arms; as if impelled by magnetic force, he stayed three feet from the lunch truck's bumper, smooth with the power steering and easy on the brakes. Attuned to our task, all silence and nerve and stealthy maneuvers, Bob and I became more than ourselves, greater than a sum of brothers. We negotiated busy roads, refused to lose our prey to a stoplight.

Soon we were trailing the lunch truck through a part of town where mannequins were married on every block. The grooms appeared to be interchangeable—tuxedo, cummerbund, black bow tie—while the brides grew more and more ostentatious, their gowns blooming with crinoline roses, their satin trains like wakes of white foam. Some gowns rivaled the dusty plaster wedding cakes—tier after tier encrusted with icing—on display beside them in the bridal shop windows. I tried to imagine Marion and Bob standing side by side on the threshold of wedlock, quiet and pious and beautifully dressed. But my brother's tuxedo was rumpled, and Marion gazed down at her dress through pitch-black glasses and was racked with laughter; their ceremony had all the aplomb of a cartoon on a cocktail napkin.

I was wrenched from my fantasy when Bob swerved the car into a parking spot in front of a construction site. The lunch truck pulled onto the dirt a few feet away. The driver, a squat balding man in a crewneck sweater, sounded his horn and leapt from the cab, a metal change belt strapped to his waist. He swung open the side of the truck, revealing candy bars, doughnuts, bags of potato chips, and triangular sand-wiches. Small bottles of tropical punch were nestled on a bed of crushed ice. Water from the melting ice drizzled out of a drain near the bumper.

"That's our man," said Bob. He glanced at his watch, made a couple of notes in his ledger.

Hard hats laughed and whistled and called to one another within the shadowy recesses of the unfinished high-rise. Then they descended in wire elevators and converged on the truck by the dozens, jockeying for a look at the food, blowing on cups of hot coffee while they waited for the driver to dole out change.

"We'd better wait," said Bob, "till the crowd clears out." He offered me a stick of spearmint gum and settled back in the bucket seat. Calypso music wafted from a record store down the block—The Platter Party—and a group of women huddled nearby and spoke in a rapid foreign language, their exclamations rising in waves. The interior of the car grew warm, redolent of new vinyl, spearmint gum, and Old Spice. My brother struggled to keep his eyes open. The muscles in his face went lax. His shoulders succumbed to gravity. I no-ticed his roomy collar, an arm protruding from his short-sleeved shirt; he was thinner than usual, as though he'd sacrificed some of his substance to look as lean as the girl he loved. Bob's closed eyes and upturned face no longer sug-gested the reverie with Marion at its center. My brother seemed tired, simply tired, purged of longing at last.

A subpoena for Mr. Pomeroy, the lunch truck driver, was sticking out of Bob's shirt pocket. I reached over and gently tugged at the paper. My brother stirred, and I froze for a moment. His eyes darted behind closed lids, in pursuit of a fleeting dream. I could see every strand of his long lashes, the whiskers that darkened his slack jaw. A small blossom of chewing gum rested between his tongue and his teeth.

The construction workers eventually wandered away from

Mr. Pomeroy's truck, sat on stacks of cinder block or leaned against rolls of insulation. They were too involved in their lunches to notice me milling among them, kicking up dust with my sneakers. Mr. Pomeroy, busy burrowing new bottles of punch into the crushed ice, had his back to me. I decided that a surprise ambush was the best tactic, and I hurtled toward him, clutching the subpoena behind my back. Blood banged through my heart, but it wasn't as bad as that night with Mr. Vixen; after all, I'd successfully served a summons before, and this time the car would be where I left it, my getaway driver sawing wood. "Excuse me," I blurted.

"I'm listening," said Mr. Pomeroy. But he didn't turn around.

"I need to give you something."

"Is this something made of paper?" he asked. The ice made a muffled crunching sound.

"Yes," I said, a little stunned.

"Does this something have a picture of one of our illustrious presidents on it?"

I unfolded the subpoena, but there weren't any pictures on it. "Just words," I said. It became clear that Mr. Pomeroy was not about to interrupt his work for mere words. "It's important," I insisted.

"It's important if you're telling me you want to make a purchase."

"That's it," I said, thinking he'd set his own trap. "I want to make a purchase."

The instant Mr. Pomeroy turned to face me, I tossed the subpoena toward him. It arced through the air, grazed his shoulder, then fluttered toward the ground like a pigeon come to scavenge crumbs, landing at last in the dust between us. The lunch truck driver stood there, his ruddy features unperturbed.

"Mr. Pomeroy?"

"That's right," he said, wiping his hands on a towel stained with fruit juice. "How'd you know?"

"Please pick up the piece of paper, Mr. Pomeroy." Desperation invaded my voice.

Mr. Pomeroy looked around, hoping to catch the eye of one of the construction workers, who'd surely find this exchange as absurd as he did. Finally his gaze returned to me. "Son," he said, "I got people to feed. You wanna buy something, fine. You wanna play catch, find someone else."

"OK," I said. "OK. If you just pick up the piece of paper, I'll buy . . ." I dredged my jeans for change and brought up a lonely dime.

Mr. Pomeroy reached into the truck and tossed me a pack of Life Savers. "Good catch," he said. "They're free. Now scram." He turned his attention back to the food and began to stack coconut-covered donuts into a pyramid.

I pocketed the Life Savers and picked up the subpoena from the ground. One corner had gotten dirty, and walking back to the car, I tried to blow the dirt away, worried that the slightest trace of grime might alert Bob to my failed scheme. I blew harder and harder, growing dizzy, and when I looked up, the city seemed different. Girders and glass and passing traffic—every surface repelled the sun. The very air was restless, glaring. Sound ricocheted in all directions: welding torches whispered high in the skeleton of the skyscraper; Calypso percussion stuttered through the street; waves of foreign gossip inundated the afternoon. This was a world of noise and fervor whose rules I might never master, whose discord might last forever, and just as I began to swoon, I saw framed by the window of his car the familiar face of my sleeping brother—the family profile, olive skin, unruly profusion of black hair. Bob's head was tilted back, a fixed point in the midst of commotion.

I dashed toward the Pontiac, climbed quietly inside, and held my breath as I slipped the subpoena back in Bob's pocket, relieved to be sitting beside him, insulated from the rush around us, a boy basking in the heat and fragrance of his big brother's car. The tassel turned from the rearview mirror. The windshield tinted the city blue. I let go of the subpoena and was about to settle back into my seat when Bob's eyes snapped open. He caught my wrist and gripped it hard.

"I was only—"

"No tricks," he hissed.

"I was only—"

"—getting into hot water." My brother wouldn't let go of my wrist or lighten his grip. "Never sleep," he said, "with both eyes closed." I struggled to pry his fingers off me. I couldn't cry out or breathe or speak. I tried to strike him with my free hand. "Say it," he demanded. He had me by both arms now. "Never sleep with both eyes closed." Time was protracted, each of us fixed on the face of the other. Tension would not relinquish his features. He had to hear this phrase repeated. I couldn't respond, couldn't grasp what was asked of me—wakefulness that lasts a lifetime, wariness without relief. I freed myself from my brother's hold, clamped my aching wrists between my knees. Bob turned away and looked out the window. A sign showed an architect's rendering of the finished high-rise; it gleamed like a prism from my parents' chandelier, fifteen floors of steel and glass rising into a cloudless sky. Bob stared at it, his expression so despondent I forgot that I was angry. I'd scared him, I thought. That's all there was to it. Maybe he thought I was someone else, someone trying to rob or harm him.

"Never sleep—" I began.

"Don't," said Bob. Then, softer, "Don't." He yawned and rubbed his eyes. As he was leaving the car, he mumbled, "Too damn tired . . . nodding off on the job . . . It doesn't figure."

It took Bob only a few minutes to serve the subpoena to Mr. Pomeroy. I watched them talk, then my brother handed over the paper. His job accomplished without a hitch, Bob had lightened somewhat by the time he returned to the car.

He reported that Mr. Pomeroy had, of all things, smacked his forehead and said, "Now I get it," taking the subpoena almost gratefully, willing to testify that after months of catering at the office where Eugene Ludlow worked, he could safely say the man's appetite was meager, if not downright picky, despite Vivien Ludlow's claims to the contrary. What my brother hadn't found out—and what I wouldn't dare tell him—was that Mr. Pomeroy was glad to have the mystery of the persistent eleven-year-old solved; I'd paved the way for my brother's work, the lunch truck driver primed by me to accept his day in court.

The trip from the construction site to our father's office required a lot less skill than trailing the lunch truck. The Pontiac rode the flow of traffic, meandered long city blocks. Typical of September weather, clouds thickened as the day wore on, and only the thinnest light strained through. Sometimes my brother would slow the car, absorbed by a billboard or a poster in a travel agency without regard for the honking behind us. One theater displayed the titles of a double feature on its marquee—both filmed in Blush Color—and my brother laughed to hear me reading: "*It Happened in a Nature Camp* and *Torrid Teasers.*" I asked him what *torrid* meant. "It's when your blood boils for a girl. When she makes you pant like an animal." Bob's definition reminded me of a wolf I'd seen on a Saturday-morning cartoon; at the sight of a woman in a side-slit dress, the wolf's eyes popped out of their sockets, the ribbon of his tongue unfurled, jets of steam shrieked from his ears, and his polka-dot bow tie spun like a propeller. "What're you smiling at?" asked my brother. "You're not keeping something from me, are you? Don't tell me you've flipped over some doll in the sixth grade." Silence seemed like the perfect reply to a question charged with pride and innuendo; I let Bob believe his younger brother was a ladies' man in the making.

As we pulled into the parking lot of our father's office, I

felt, I admit, a certain satisfaction in having deceived my brother. Though Bob's physical strength was superior—a phantom grip still burned my wrists—he could be made to believe about me what I wanted him to believe. Something as simple as a grin and well-timed silence could placate him, assure him I was a typical boy, freeing me for my private desires. And despite my continued fear of exposure, despite my understanding, however dim, that these desires would set me apart forever, every clandestine urge—to feel Brad's lips as he mimicked kisses, to lay my head on Jeff Chandler's chest, to touch the arms of Chief Altoon—infused me with a lust that was, I knew, as powerful as the lust of adults. In secret, I was equal.

The door to my father's fifth-floor office was a frosted pane of glass that read IRVING ZERKIN, ATTORNEY AT LAW in gold letters. Throughout my boyhood, I visited my father's office only occasionally, but every visit renewed my amazement: this was a place where fates were decided. Above the love seat in the waiting room hung a reproduction of a nineteenth-century etching; it showed a juror's box inhabited by homely caricatures—cross-eyed men and toothless women whose heads were larger than their bodies—and even then I wondered if it might deter prospective clients with its irreverence. In a small, lighted alcove, chiseled from a single piece of marble, sat a sculpture of a gavel on a pedestal; since the gavel couldn't be lifted from the pedestal and banged, I imagined it belonged in a courtroom where order could never be restored and verdicts never handed down. Along the opposite wall stretched a towering bookcase, the books within it bound in blue leather, silver titles shining on their spines: *Contract Law*, *Law of Torts*, *California Jurisprudence*, *Forms of Pleading and Practice*.

Bob and I moved to the doorway of my father's consulting room. He was seated behind a vast desk, head bent, doodling on a legal tablet as he talked on the telephone. The desk was piled with paper: stacks of manila files, unopened mail, memos skewered on a wire spike. My father's caseload was heavier than ever. Bob knocked on the wall to get his attention. My father motioned for us to come in. There was no question that it was men who made and argued the law; like every other office I'd seen in his building, my father's was staunchly masculine—leather upholstered, brass appointed, and walnut paneled. Shafts of failing sunlight streamed through the venetian blinds. Bob walked up to the window, pried open two slats, and gazed at the grid of streets below. As on that night we stopped at a railroad crossing to stare at the lights of the San Fernando Valley, Bob was transfixed by the vista before him; Chow Now, I said to myself, is the rhyme he'll use to remember what he sees. There was a pause in my father's conversation. The room was hushed, the sound of downtown traffic so vague it seemed recollected rather than heard. Somewhere a typewriter clattered, a door slammed. My father's assent broke the silence. "Yes," he said to the party on the other end of the line. "That's right. My client is requesting a voluntary separation. She will not pursue charges of marital misconduct. What we're asking the judge to consider is a statutory presumption of incompatibility." At one point my father held his hand over the mouthpiece and whispered to Bob, "How'd it go?"

"Like a dream," Bob said, turning from the window. "The case is going to be a cinch; Pomeroy's with us all the way."

My father took Bob's hand and shook it. A gust of goodwill passed between them. I was gratified too; whether or not my brother and father knew it, I was also responsible for serving the subpoena, and the fact that my assistance went without acknowledgment or reward made it, as far as I was concerned, all the more noble. Best of all, I'd be able to brag about my accomplishment to Brad, casually tossing out the word *torrid* as I enlightened him to the difficulties of detective work.

As I look back on that day, it seems remarkable that my

father hadn't noticed the physical changes in Bob. Perhaps he was so steeped in work he hadn't the time or attention to notice. Or perhaps he did and attributed them to his son's bachelor life, with its late nights and poor meals and pained romance. In either case, that was one of the last happy afternoons I'd spend among the men of my family, the three of us bearing our shared victory like one of the delicate, short-lived bubbles that Brad's younger sister, Barbara King, blew from a plastic pipe. If I suspected how fragile our contentment was to prove, if I had any inkling of the trouble to come, my doubts were expressed in what I did next. On a console there stood the statuette of a blindfolded woman holding scales from her outstretched arm. Her toga cleaved her figure as though she were walking against the wind. Her scales, loaded with hard candy, teetered up and down when I touched them. No matter how carefully I tried to tip the scales, I couldn't make them level. I reached in my pocket and added the pack of Life Savers to one side and, when that didn't work, added my dime to the other side and, when that didn't work, transferred candies to equalize the weight. The cellophane wrappers were bright and hypnotic, catching the light as I moved them back and forth. My father continued his conversation, idly drawing spirals on a notepad. My brother peered through the venetian blinds, a witness to distance. And I found myself obsessed with symmetry, unable to stop till a balance was struck.

September ended in a stretch of white weather. The monotone of morning would continue into noon. At the height of every day were warm but pallid hours. By three o'clock the light declined; I could sense it wherever I happened to be, watching "Queen for a Day" with my mother or riding my bike with Brad. Failing light alarmed the birds; hundreds called from the carob trees. Shadows gathered beneath the eaves of houses lining our circular street. As layers of gray darkened the sky, women leaned from windows, shouted names, urged their children to hurry inside.

One evening, when the panes in my window had just gone black, losing their view of our narrow backyard and mirroring my room, I began to swagger back and forth, watching my reflection.

"What on earth are you doing?" Aunt Ida asked from the hall.

The sound of her voice made me jump. "I'm exercising," I lied.

Ida walked into the room and told me she got *her* exercise by helping my mother in the kitchen. She sat on my bed and examined her hands. Unlike Marion, who had sprawled on my bed and claimed the air with her scent and presence, Aunt Ida, shoulders sagging, looked ready to wilt. "Your aunt," she announced, "has dishpan hands." I insisted she had nice hands. She held them up and wiggled her fingers. "Nice like lobsters," she said, and laughed. "But thanks," she added. "I wanted to hear that." I sat down beside her. If sensuous Marion Hirsch made me feel embarrassed to be young, weary Ida made me realize, with equal amounts of regret and relief, the pretense of acting older than I was. Ida asked, "What's today's date?" and grabbed *A Year of Rhymes* off my nightstand.

"It's September twenty-first," I said.

My aunt put on the pair of cat-eye glasses that hung around her neck from a gold chain. Peering down, eyes slightly magnified, she gave the impression of alarm or consternation. Ida licked her index finger and thumbed through the Autumn section until she found the right poem. On the days when it was my turn, I'd read the poem cold, without so much as clearing my throat, unconcerned about mistakes. For her rendition to be as memorable and edifying as possible, Ida made sure that there were no odd words or difficult rhymes to trip her up. She scanned the stanzas of Ben Jonson's "The Shadow," then read the poem out loud: " 'Follow a shadow, it still flies you; / Seem to fly it, it will pursue. / So court a mistress, she denies you; / Let her alone, she will court you. / Say, are not women truly, then, / Styled but the shadows of us men?' " The pitch of her voice rose dramatically on "us men." Ida's shadow fell across the carpet, a tall shadow without a trace of the slumped and disgruntled woman who cast it. She turned her magnified gaze on me. "Do you agree with Mr. Jonson, Burt?" I could tell from her tone that she hoped I'd say no.

"No," I said, even though I hadn't been paying enough attention to fully understand the sentiment behind the words. "I don't think the poem is true."

Ida's glasses slid down her nose, and she poked them back in place. "I'm not asking if you think the poem is true. I don't believe you can say a poem is true or false. But you can say whether or not you agree." Pleased at this distinction, Ida grinned and fussed with her sleeve. Her yellow turban almost glowed.

"I think everyone has a shadow."

"*Gevalt*," she groaned. "That goes without saying. The question is: who is more like a shadow, men or women?"

I tried to picture each of the King children—Stephanie, Stephen, Barbara, and Brad—transformed into flat and fleeting shadows. It was easy to imagine with both boys and girls. "They both are."

"Are what?"

"Like shadows. Men and women are both like shadows."

"Now, that," she said, "is the absolute truth. If what Mr. Jonson is talking about is the elusive—do you know what that means?: hard to hold on to—the elusive nature of people, well, he should've asked me, because I've seen it all. Just last week I had to call a cab for some poor girl whose husband deserted her in bungalow two. She wakes up one morning, and poof, the groom is gone. Nothing, but nothing, would make her feel better. Even when I told her I'd tear up the bill, she didn't stop sobbing. *Vey iss meer,* if I had a nickel for every miserable member of the human race I've registered in that motel, I'd be a millionaire. And that's not counting couples without luggage."

"Couples without luggage?"

Ida shot me a sidelong glance. "I'm just saying that I've seen everything, that's all, and the knife cuts both ways."

The Nite Light Motel was a bungalow court on Sunset Boulevard, within walking distance of our house. Ida's shift at the reception desk ended at four o'clock, just in time for her to hurry over and help with dinner. Whenever I saw Ida huffing up the street, her anticipation was palpable; she couldn't wait another minute to leave the lives of strangers behind, huddle around a table with family, and immerse herself in a meal.

"Did you know," asked Ida, "that shadows brought your parents together?"

"I know," I said. "Mom told me that story."

Ida pretended not to hear me. She took off her glasses. The bridge of her nose bore two red impressions. Her face looked naked. "We were at a party given by . . . what was his name?" Ida closed her eyes for a moment. "Aaron Lipsky, that's it. Your mother was just as pretty as a song. All she had to do was look at a man. Anyway, this Lipsky fellow was moving out of a condemned building—it seemed like all Chicago was being rebuilt—and he puts a lamp in the middle of his living room, gives every guest a bucket and a brush, and tells them to paint each other's shadows on the walls. Isn't that a darling idea for a party? Unless you had to live there after. So Sylvia was standing and talking to Aaron—I can picture it fresh as yesterday—and he says to her, he says, 'Don't look now, Sylvie, but Irving Zerkin, the husky one with the navy-blue paint, is filling in your figure.'" Ida bit her lower lip, as if by submitting to some small pain she could stop the unreeling of reminiscence. She slipped *A Year of Rhymes* back on my nightstand. "Well"—Ida sighed—"I'd better check on dinner. Bob and the Menassians should be here any minute." Her knees cracked as she rose to her feet. My room was rich with the smell of brisket.

Ida turned around before she reached the door. "Who knows," she said. "Maybe that's how you'll find one."

I must have looked puzzled; I thought she meant a shadow. Ida laughed and said, "A wife." She inhaled the odors wafting down the hall. "Let's hope she cooks as good as your mother."

"I like TV dinners," I said. "Salisbury steak is my favorite. Anyone can make it. It only takes twenty-five minutes."

Ida echoed, "Twenty-five minutes." Her mouth looked small, as though the words were sour. "That has to be one of the most ridiculous things I've ever heard. Believe me, if your wife loves you, she can show you she loves you by cooking good food." The Baking Newlywed popped into my head, stirring pots, her apron stained, all the gas jets burning at once. "You and your brother," Ida muttered. She thrust her hands into the pockets of her pantsuit, shaking her head as she walked away. "Two of a kind when it comes to women."

The comparison pleased me. In the minutes before dinner, I resumed pacing back and forth—this time with the door locked—scrutinizing my movements in the window and stopping only after I was satisfied that any gingerly step was buried by a broad and confident stride. I worried that, in an unguarded moment, I might cross my legs or hold my cup or run from a bee like a girl, a sure way to invite the condemnation of my classmates or, far worse, their laughter. But greater than this worry was the ponderous task of dividing everything on earth into its appropriate category—His, Hers—so that I knew what I mustn't like or do. Though I glued together model planes, though making crank calls had become second nature, nervous classification was my real hobby, my nagging avocation. Certain assessments were as easy as Jane Russell / Jeff Chandler; pink / blue; cats / dogs; slapping / slugging; dances / drag races. But so much of the world didn't fit neatly into either camp: clocks, weeds, Wonder bread, our two-tone hi-fi, just to name a few. Fitful nights were spent tangled in pajamas, the world's bounty amassed in my head, a bounty I had to divide into piles, two distinct piles, or risk humiliation.

On nights like those I'd stir from sleep, suspended in a netherworld; I couldn't feel the limits of my body, where my flesh left off and the world began. Who I was seemed to hover all around, neither ghost nor angel, boy nor girl, but some essential element released into the air at last, dissipating the instant I awoke.

After a dinner of beef brisket and Eve's rice pilaf, my family and the Menassians scattered in different directions. Men in the rumpus room. Women in the kitchen. Arnold was showing Bob and my father the Dial-a-Drink, explaining how he believed it was "the best little bar aid currently on the market." He said his customers at the Cap 'n' Cork were clamoring for them. By turning a dial, the alphabetized recipe for one of eighty exotic drinks would revolve into view. Arnold stood behind the bar, bathed in the rose light cast by the hula dancer, nudging the dial with his thumb while Bob and my father perched on bamboo barstools, working toothpicks into their teeth; they watched intently and read the names of drinks out loud, from Adonis and Between the Sheets to Pink Lady and Widow's Dream. Whenever my brother or father expressed curiosity about the flavor of a particular drink, Arnold would whip up a sample, deft magician with a swizzle stick. "You'd think it was *his* bar," my father teased. Soon half a dozen drained highball glasses sat atop the bar, and Arnold had slung his tie over one shoulder to keep it out of the way. The blond TV was on; I watched a woman croon a sultry song as her body was squeezed from a huge tube of Brylcreem. To win back my interest, Arnold mixed me a Sputnik, a "children's cocktail" made from 7UP and maraschino cherry juice. He skewered cherries on toothpicks—the vague semblance of a satellite—and put them into the drink. As I left the rumpus room, glass in hand, I heard Arnold say in confidential tones that a Sputnik was really a Shirley Temple, the name changed to appeal to boys.

Mother and Eve and Ida shushed one another the second I stepped into the kitchen. I never seemed to catch their secrets, though secrecy lingered in the air like steam whenever they were together. Eve took one look at my drink and said, "Call the vice squad; my hubby is foisting alcohol on minors."

Mother extracted her hands from the sink. "Hide the lampshades," she said as she grabbed me. Her damp, warm hands seeped into my shirt. I pressed against her and sipped my Sputnik.

Eve licked the tip of a pencil. "Where were we?" she asked. She leaned against the stove, examining a questionnaire from Miracle Match, Mrs. King's dating service. Behind her back, a kettle sat on a ring of flame. "Oh, yes. 'Your Date's Preferred Social Activities.' "

"What were the choices again?" asked Ida. She dried a plate till the blue ceramic squeaked.

"There's 'Listening to Music,' " said Eve.

"Yes," said Mother. "Ida's date should like music."

Eve put a check next to music.

"What difference does it make if he likes music?" asked Ida.

"It shows if a man is cultured," said Eve.

Ida snorted. "Have you listened to the radio lately?"

"How about 'Skiing'?" said Eve. "Sure," she answered herself. "Who wouldn't go for a guy who skis?"

"That's all well and good for you," said Ida. "But I want a Jewish date, and I've never heard of a Jewish man who skis."

"All right," said Eve. "Forget skiing. 'Date's Occupation'?"

"Retail," said Ida.

"Oh, Ida," sighed Mother. "Retail is so . . . run-of-the-mill."

"Excuse me if I'm not more adventurous," said Ida. "Maybe a rocket scientist would be more to your liking."

"Honey," said Mother, "don't take it so seriously. We're just fooling around."

"Speak for yourself. I happen to be unattached, in case you hadn't noticed." Ida went to the sink, rolled up her sleeves, plunged her hands into the water. Mother moved to the dish rack and dried.

"Shall we go on?" asked Eve.

"Go on," I urged her.

" 'Date's Favorite Foods.' "

"Salisbury steak," Ida said with disdain.

"As long as he has a good appetite," said Eve, her dark eyes shining. "I've always thought that men with big appetites were . . . you know . . . insatiable in other departments."

"That's the absolute truth," Ida testified. "Just ask room service."

"And now," said Eve, "for the dream date's build: 'Slim, Average, Stocky, or Heavy.' "

"Average," said Ida.

Eve said, "Right," her pencil poised.

"But," said mother, "if his appetite is big . . ."

"Hmm," breathed Eve. "I guess he'd be heavy."

Everyone was quiet for a time. Mounds of soapsuds crackled in the sink. Eve stroked her neck, deep in thought. My mother turned a bowl in her hands, over and over, as though she were molding it. Ida had her back to us, but I could tell from the angle of her turban that she was gazing into the depths of the dishwater as one would gaze into a crystal ball, waiting for meaningful shapes to appear, waiting for revelations. "Don't tell this to Mrs. King," said Ida, the feistiness gone from her voice, "but I'm not so sure these questionnaires do any good. Who can say what brings people together? You can't force it. You just have to keep your fingers crossed and try to be cautious." Ida fished up a dripping skillet. "If you ask me, it's a mystery. A mystery we're not supposed to know."

"Do you think," asked Eve, "love happens by accident?"

"I hate that," said Mother. "I hate thinking that something as important as love is accidental. What if Aaron Lipsky's building hadn't been condemned? He wouldn't have had that party and Irving wouldn't have painted my shadow on the wall and we never would have met and we never would have married and Bob and Burt wouldn't have been born and none of us would be standing here tonight."

"Don't get worked up over nothing," Ida said to Mother. "Look at it this way: every accident happens for a reason, but the reason is mysterious."

Eve blinked and leaned against the counter. "Gee," she said. "You should write that down."

Ida smiled.

"Well," said Mother, "I've had my chance at love, accident or not. It's Robert I worry about."

"I'll second that," cried Ida.

Eve asked, "What happened to Mary?"

"Marion," corrected Mother. "Oh, she still comes around once in a while, but it's really to see me. We gab about this and that while I iron. Sometimes we even talk about Bob. It's the strangest thing, the way she talks about him, what he should do and who he should see. She says she loves him, and I think she does. But she loves him—I can't explain it exactly—like someone who lives in another town."

"She's concerned," said Eve, "but not involved."

"Uh-huh," said Mother. "I guess it could be worse. But he mopes around. He's losing weight. It breaks my heart to see him lonely."

Eve pointed a finger at my mother as though she were going to scold her. "Sure, he's disappointed. But I'm telling you, Sylvie, that boy is resilient. Everyone has to go through it once. At least," she added.

"Besides," said Ida, "he's better off. Marion was too strange for my taste. Especially her clothes."

Eve and Mother looked at Ida, then at each other.

"Anyway," said Mother, "if I tell him I worry, he says, 'Then don't. I'll be OK. The case is closed.' " The kettle began to hiss and whistle. Mother turned off the burner. "Burt," she said, "go tell the guys their coffee is coming."

I hurried toward the rumpus room, careful not to spill my drink or drop the cherry satellite. I pretended I was flying behind it, hurtling through outer space, light-years away from planet earth. A black vacuum sucked at the windows. "Is it instant or brewed?" my father asked.

I orbited back to the kitchen. "I was going to make instant," Mother said. She reached into the cupboard and found a can of coffee. "But I could make fresh."

"She shouldn't go to any trouble," Arnold told me. He held up a tumbler full of amber liquid. "And this," he said to my father and Bob, "is the last word in booze: a Zacarac."

"It's no trouble," said my mother. "Tell them it's going to take a while."

Bob had moved to the couch by the time I returned. "It's going to take a while," I announced. He was watching the last of "This Is Your Life"; sand dribbled through the waist of an hourglass. The reception was weak. Ghosts filled the screen. Bob didn't bother to make it better. My father took a swig of the Zacarac, pivoted on the barstool, and asked, "Whose life is tonight?"

"Beats me," said Bob. He lay down on the floral couch, propped his head on a pillow, and instantly fell asleep.

"It's my fault," said Arnold. "I let him get carried away with the liquor."

"It's not," said Mother, gazing down at Bob. "He was tired to begin with." She held a tray of cups and saucers and was flanked by Ida and Eve.

My father suggested we wake him.

"He looks comfortable right where he is," said Mother.

Ida went to get a blanket.

Eve whispered, "He's sweet when he sleeps."

Everyone had begun to whisper, to move about the room in silence. My father tiptoed up to the television, turned it off; a life contracted to a dot of white light. Arnold quietly tidied the bar. My mother handed the tray to Eve and stroked Bob's shoulder. Ida shuffled back into the room, a blanket under her arm. She positioned herself before the couch, cast the blanket high into the air. It unfurled and let out a muffled snap, billowing down. Its fall caused a sudden breeze, a pressure that grazed our faces and lifted strands of our hair. The hour was late. The room was hushed. The blanket seemed to float so slowly. We watched its shadow move across the couch and eclipse the dreaming body of my brother.

The Case of the Baking Newlywed came to trial. During the proceedings, my father referred to Eugene Ludlow as his "kissless client," a man denied "routine conjugal satisfaction" by a wife whose obsessive cooking was motivated, my father claimed, by coldness rather than love. Vivien Ludlow, on the other hand, swore that her husband's demands for enormous meals left her "too tuckered out for anything romantic." The two witnesses Bob had subpoenaed to appear in court, however, challenged her contention. Mr. Pomeroy—whose lunch truck had stopped at Eugene Ludlow's office for the past three years—characterized Ludlow's appetite as "kinda sorry for a grown man" and "generally way below par" compared to his other customers. "I've seen every type of eater in my line of work," said Mr. Pomeroy, "and I know who's who when it comes to food." When Vivien Ludlow's attorney countered with the suggestion that Mr. Ludlow was simply too full from one of his wife's huge breakfasts to consume a noteworthy lunch, my father produced Loretta, Eugene Ludlow's first wife. In a hasty testimony that had to be repeated for the court stenographer, the former

Mrs. Ludlow said her ex-husband never touched the tasty breakfasts *she* slaved to make; according to Loretta, Eugene Ludlow was a man whose metabolism was so overwrought he could barely sit still for one meal, let alone demand second and third helpings. Even Vivien Ludlow's collection of long, curling receipts from the Safeway market was insufficient to prove her story of virtual imprisonment in the kitchen. "The receipts are compelling," said the judge, "but there is no way of knowing for certain that these purchases are the direct result of your husband's coercion." In the end, it was probably Eugene Ludlow's starved appearance that clinched the case; my father pointed to him repeatedly during the trial and likened his build to a broom. And so Mr. Ludlow was granted an annulment—with no further financial obligation—of his sixteen-day marriage to a woman whose perpetual cooking, according to an article in the *Herald-Examiner*, had been merely a "ploy to avoid her wifely duty."

Our telephone rang continuously that week. Arnold and Eve said they were tickled to death to know a bona fide celebrity and told my father that they had shown the article to several of their friends. Mrs. King phoned to say that it took her a minute, but she finally recognized the photograph in the newspaper as that of Irving Zerkin, none other than her neighbor, posed beside the triumphant Mr. Ludlow. My father relished the attention, leaping at the phone whenever it rang. He was swamped by calls from prospective clients—spouses despondent in San Bernardino, enraged in Orange County, rankled in Tarzana. No case was unwinnable, no accusation too absurd to warrant legal recourse. On the temperate nights of early October, through the living room of our Spanish house, my famous father paced back and forth, the black receiver pressed to his ear. He asked questions, jotted notes. He listened to tales of soured vows, rekindled suspicions, envelopes held over steaming kettles, withdrawals from joint accounts.

The only person who didn't call was Marion Hirsch. During September, her connection to my family had held by a thread; by early October that thread was severed. My mother, who hadn't heard from her for weeks, confided in Ida that she missed seeing Marion step through the door, a girl exuding pungent perfume, eyes obscured by black glasses. My brother rarely spoke of Marion, but when he did, he blamed her departure on the Case of the Baking Newlywed. "We had tiffs from the start," he told me, "but after Dad took that case, we never agreed on anything. It got so I couldn't tell if she was contradicting me on purpose. Then it got so I couldn't tell if I was contradicting her on purpose. She'd say, 'Let's take Vine Street,' and I'd say, 'Highland,' and before you'd know it, up came the Ludlows." My brother—I believed it then, believe it now—would have preferred those recurring contradictions to Marion's absence. With Marion gone, Bob suffered a phantom affection; he seemed keenly aware of his ungiven kisses, his reserves of yearning, his penchant to turn toward a woman's voice.

How much my brother missed Marion became clear to me one Saturday afternoon at his Echo Park apartment. Bob slid an album out of its jacket, coddled the edges of the record in his palms, and lowered it onto the spindle. I'd seen him play records a dozen times before, but now he was a man immersed in reverie, all his tenderness given over to that task. Marion had left a selection of her favorite jazz at Bob's apartment—Gene Krupa, Dave Brubeck, Keely Smith—and my brother, careful not to scratch the vinyl, played the records again and again, humming under his breath. "You'll like this one," he said as the record dropped onto the turntable. "It's called 'Pick Up Sticks.' I get lost in it." The needle hissed and drifted through the grooves. Then the ascent of saxophone, brisk and hoarse on the highest notes. A brush swept and swept a cymbal, the sound of something coming clean.

Bob sat on the floor, with his back to me. I sat on the sofa behind him. Beyond the picture window, above the lake and the clustered hills, opaque air was breaking up, the sky giving way to an orange emanation whose source was unseen but gathering strength. Second by second the white sky ignited. Light burned through the gauze of autumn and tinted the walls of houses on the hills. Faraway windows, windows blue only moments before, were glaring with reflected flame. The afternoon's new, fiery hue blazed in the depths of Echo Park Lake.

My brother was right about the music; he closed his eyes, got lost in it. "This was Marion's favorite tune," he told me. "She said it had a—how did she put it?—'crazy invisible architecture.'" From the back, his shoulders bore the orange apartment, carried the flaring light of day. He hummed along to "Pick Up Sticks." I studied the slope of his shoulders, the haphazard part that ran through his hair. We sat together in brightening sunlight, sunlight that warmed my face and chest. For an instant I thought that, listening so intently to a missing girl's music, Bob had caused the air to color, had caused the world to flush with his wanting.

I lifted a hand toward my brother's back. What I would do once I touched him, how he would feel beneath my fingers, how my humming brother would react—consequence was held in suspension. The smell of soap rose from his skin, but beneath it lay a scent that belonged to Bob alone—turned earth is the closest odor—and I breathed that base, unnameable fragrance. Somewhere in the park a group of teenagers played volleyball, their urgent shouts like admonitions. My brother tightened when I touched his back. The white shirt went taut across his shoulders. He stopped humming, froze for a moment. Then he yielded to my design.

I drew a square with my index finger. A roof. A door. I used the careful strokes I'd used to paint on the pavement with a feather dipped in water. Some shapes made my brother shudder. Others caused him to tilt his head and wonder where the lines would lead. He leaned forward and arched his back, making his body easy to reach.

"A house," he said, his eyes still closed.

"Not just any house." I added a patio and a TV antenna.

"Our house? I mean, Mom's and Dad's?"

"Right," I said. "Our house."

"It's not my house anymore."

I ran my hand across his back, and our house was erased in a single stroke. My brother waited for another drawing. I scanned the room for inspiration. He'd figure out the chair in a second. The lamp was too easy. So was the sofa. My goal was to keep my brother guessing; I wanted him to concentrate, to anticipate my touch. Taped to the wall above the hi-fi was a picture of a Jackson Pollock painting Marion had cut from a magazine. I had no idea then who the artist was, or why Marion liked it, but I knew that flung profusion of color, those tangled skeins of paint, would keep my brother baffled. At first I couldn't convey such complexity, layer after layer of loose, amorphous form. I had to use both hands; I had to relinquish some control and allow my hands a life of their own. I started at the nape of my brother's neck and let my fingers move where they willed. I worked quickly, impulsively, refusing to render anything familiar, determined to keep my brother in the dark. I felt the planes of Bob's back, the tensing flesh, intrusion of bone, the secret heat from either armpit.

"I don't know what you're doing," said Bob. "Is it something I'm supposed to recognize?"

"Guess," I said.

"You're bluffing. It's nothing."

"It's not nothing." I applied greater pressure. I sensed my brother's concentration shift from the jazz that inhabited the air and settle into the surface of his skin. He was silent for a while, head bent, reverent. I was bringing my brother into himself, taunting him deeply into his body, stealing him from the music, the room, relieving him of regret.

"A rainstorm."

"No."

"Confetti."

I didn't answer.

"This is stupid. No matter what I say, you're going to say no."

"It's so obvious," I said. "So obvious you'll never guess in a million years."

My brother bristled. He was about to stand up, when I shouted, "No. Come on. Concentrate. It's right in front of your nose." He stayed where he was while a frantic abstraction covered his back. Bob lifted his head and scanned the room. He searched everywhere for a clue to what I was doing. Every time he took a breath and ventured a guess, I could feel his ribs expand.

He looked up. "That bumpy stuff on the ceiling?"

"No."

"Is it molecules?" he asked sarcastically.

His frustration was palpable. I gave him a clue. "It's something in this room."

"Molecules are in this room."

"It's not molecules."

"If you're fooling, I'll kill you."

"It's no joke."

Bob looked toward the wall where the painting was taped. I knew it was only a matter of moments, knew the end was imminent. "Aha." He rose to his feet. My hands slid off his back like water. "Pretty clever. You almost had me stumped. It's this thing," he said, ripping the picture off the wall. He turned around and faced the couch. "I'm tired of it. Here. You can have it. It's just a bunch of drips to me." He thrust it toward me.

"Keep it," I said. "It's yours."

"It's not mine." He squinted at the small print beneath the picture. "It says, 'Collection of Mr. and Mrs. Randolph Tremaine.' What suckers to pay good money for that mess." Bob crumpled the picture into a ball. An odd song issued through the speakers, the musicians taking license with the chords. "I'm getting sick of this music too." He plucked the needle out of the grooves. "How about silence for a while?"

"Sure," I said.

My brother remained at the hi-fi. He watched the record spin in circles until it slowed to a stop. "There's nothing wrong with silence, is there?" I didn't realize it was a question until I sensed him waiting for an answer.

"No," I said. "Nothing."

"Good," he blurted, and walked into the kitchen. I stayed on the sofa and let the light sink into my skin. I heard the smack of crumpled paper against the wastebasket, and seconds later a slight suction as the refrigerator door opened. "I hope you're hungry," he called, " 'cause I'm making us snacks."

"I'm hungry," I assured him. A sensation of emptiness chafed my stomach. Something was wrong with silence after all; the room seemed vacant without the music, unpleasantly vacant, despite the flood of sunlight. Raucous shouts from the park had subsided. The tape that had held the picture on the wall had taken with it bits of paint, a sight that filled me with apprehension.

I diverted my gaze to the stack of books atop the end table. Among them was Bob's book from college, *Ways to a Better Memory*. I cracked open the book—the brittle pages smelled faintly stale—and skimmed the index: The Art of Association. Remember with Rhyme. Substitute Words. And under a list of specific topics—Difficult Dates, Names and Faces, Long-Digit Numbers—was a section entitled "Listening to Music." While the sky reddened above the city, while jars and silverware clanked in the kitchen, I learned a way to remember music:

> In music appreciation, the memory method is basically the same as in art appreciation. Study the following examples of ways to associate composer and composition.

Wagner's *Tannhäuser:* Someone crashes a **wagon** into a **townhouse**. Wagner also composed *Lohengrin*. Associate your substitute thought for Wagner to **lone grin**.

Picture a **rose** growing out of your **knee** and putting a **large O** on a **totem** pole, and you'll remember that Rossini wrote "Largo al Factotum." Picture that rose getting its hair cut by a **barber** who is **civil** to remind you that Rossini also wrote *The Barber of Seville*.

For Schönberg's *Violin Concerto,* think of a **con** who's stolen a **violin** and bangs it against a **chair** on top of a **shiny** ice**berg**.

"I'm writing my own version of that book," said Bob. He was standing before me, holding out a peanut butter sandwich wrapped in a paper napkin. "I'm going to call it 'Ways to Forget.' It'll tell you how to make memories vanish, just like that." He snapped his fingers. "Instant amnesia." I took the sandwich and asked Bob why he hadn't made one for himself. "It's funny," he said. "I look at food. I think I'm hungry. . . ." My brother shrugged. "And then I'm not." Bob was framed by the picture window, a thin, sorry silhouette standing in the midst of clouds, clouds with orange underbellies that shuttled through the autumn sky, marbling the lake and land with shadows.

I put down the book and ate my sandwich. While Bob slid records back into their jackets, I invented a sentence to help me recollect "Pick Up Sticks": A man **picks up sticks**. But the method proved ridiculously simple, required too little imagination, and the tune seemed destined to disappear. Besides, if there were associations that would bring back that day at Bob's apartment—an afternoon of erratic light and eventual silence—I found them in the book's ready-made phrases: a crashed wagon, a lone grin, a rose growing from one's own knee, a chair on top of an iceberg.

Without the slightest warning, Mrs. Beswick would drill us on long division or make us stand up one by one and spell tricky words: *cumulus, wharf, tomorrow, vaccine.* "Sit," she'd snap if you made a mistake, and your own blood would scald your face and you'd plummet into your seat. When we groaned and bristled at the mention of a quiz, Mrs. Beswick's posture would improve; our noisy discontent inflamed her sense of duty. Desert Vegetation, Mammal Families, Early Aviation. At least twice a week she handed out mimeographs of multiple-choice questions and fill-in-the-blanks, and while we worked—pencils gnawed, clock watched, erasers ground to rubbery dust— Mrs. Beswick patrolled the aisles in search of the "sluffers" and "dawdlers" and "copycats," whom she considered the scourge of education. "Mark my words," she said, arms folded across her chest. "Someday you'll be grateful you were tested. Sooner or later it will all sink in."

Even though she looked funny in front of the class—her chin wiggled when she turned her head, her arm sagged when she wrote on the blackboard—most of us appreciated Mrs.

Beswick's goal: she wanted facts to stay stored within our minds, mothproofed and neat like clothes in a bureau. She believed that class participation was an especially effective way to make a lasting impression. And so, for the social studies unit on Mexican Culture, we made tortillas from cornmeal and water, slapping the starchy dough between our palms and frying it on a hot plate. In the middle of our discussion on Michelangelo, Mrs. Beswick cleared off a desk and had Carl Bauer lie on his back while Leena Farganis held a sheet of construction paper above his head. Carl lay there, paintbrush poised, blue tempera dripping down his arm, and finally admitted he couldn't paint a cherub because he didn't know what one was. After we learned how electrons generate electricity by leaping from atom to atom, Mrs. Beswick said that if we really cared to understand this boon to humankind, this miracle often taken for granted, we should live without power for a day. The prospect of deprivation was exciting —no toast, no TV; how long would we last?—and we nodded our heads, determined to try. But resolve was forgotten the instant school let out; it was Halloween.

Brad and I made our way home along Ambrose Avenue, bombarded by falling carob pods. Branches whipped back and forth in the wind. Sudden gusts tore leaves from the trees. Nervous light speckled the pavement. The weather was hot at the end of October, as restless and dry as it had been that summer. A mounting electrical charge held sway over the city; the air gathered friction as it raced down the slopes of the Hollywood hills, shaking the streetlights and road signs in its path. With the Santa Anas came pollen and dust, abrasive debris that were heaved through the streets. If Brad and I opened our mouths to speak at the wrong moment, we'd swallow hunks of dusty wind.

"Carl Bauer is such a queer," said Brad. He plucked a carob pod from the sidewalk and lobbed it into the air.

"Why?"

"How should I know why? He just is. Don't you know how to tell one?"

My heart started churning. "How?"

"Do I have to explain everything?" asked Brad. "My brother says that homos speak in code, like spies, and some of them wear trench coats, naked underneath. There are tests you can give to tell if someone is one."

"Like multiple choice?"

"You're hopeless," he said. "What you do is ask a guy to look at his fingernails, and if he looks at them like this"— Brad closed his fingers into a fist, held his fist close to his chest, and examined the nails with cool detachment—"then he's OK. But if he does this"—he held out his hand at arm's length, splayed his fingers, and coyly cocked his head—"then you'd better hold on to your balls. Also, my brother says queers can't whistle or walk backward or see their own reflection in a mirror."

"The mirror thing is vampires," I reminded him.

"Well, the other stuff is true. I swear." Brad broke into a menacing grin, like the grin he had before we tested the effects of g-force on his hamsters, and he dared me to walk backward for the whole block without looking over my shoulder.

It was harder than it sounded. Again and again I felt certain I was about to stumble into a mailbox or fall off a curb or trip over a fire hydrant. Still, I resisted the temptation to glance behind me, holding my gaze fast on Brad, a few feet of hot autumn air between us. I navigated with the aid of a map, a map made up of memory; this was the street on which I'd grown up. Guided by echoes and odors, I gave myself over to intuition. Wind pummeled the nape of my neck. Dry leaves scraped along the sidewalk. I could sense patches of sunlight and shade advancing at my back. Soon I grew used to blind travel and, step by backward step, watched tossing trees and familiar houses recede into the distance. I felt as though I were fleeing home instead of hurrying toward it.

"Goodbye," I sang to Brad, although I continued to face him, our direction and pace the same.

It bothered my friend to see his challenge met with such ease. "Burt," he yelped. "Watch out!" When this didn't cause me to turn around, he began to point at all sorts of imaginary hazards—a stray roller skate, an open manhole—and cover his eyes in anticipation of the awful accident about to happen. After Brad got bored and gave up, I continued to walk backward, never once looking over my shoulder, enjoying his annoyance. "OK," he said, shifting his books to the other arm. "Knock it off. You proved your point." What bothered Brad wasn't only my persistence but the fact that I stared at him, unabashed. I was flooded with fondness for that blunt and husky boy. And because I walked backward, exempt from suspicion, Brad must have interpreted my stare as a kind of teasing and not the romantic trance it was.

Brad's arms dangled from plaid sleeves, his round face ruddy from the long walk home. He blinked against the surges of wind, wind that parted his collar and revealed a luminous inch of undershirt. Hibiscus and ivy and mock orange—the foliage we passed was thrashing back and forth, as if trying to uproot itself. The wind left quick impressions on a lawn, flattening blades of grass. I wanted the air to pick us up and carry us off like specks of pollen.

Those backward, windblown moments seemed to demonstrate the essence of electrics: how all things contain electricity, how an object that touches an electrified body will itself become electrified. I knew these theories to be true because when I touched Brad's hand—what foolishness or bravery impelled me?—a shock fired between us the instant our skin made contact. Brad's eyes grew wide and his mouth fell open and he stopped in his tracks. "Jesus," he breathed. A slight wheeze rode the crest of his breath. We stood there and stared at each other, unable to speak. My show of desire, I thought, had terrified him. The wind absconded with a garbage can lid; it clattered by us and rolled down the street. Brad stepped toward me, lifted his hand, and time wound down. I appraised his slow, deliberate motion; he was reaching for my cheek.

The next thing I knew was a jolt near my molar, the burst of static audible and strong. Brad ran off, shrieking with laughter. I spun around and found him on the brick walkway that led to his house. He was frantically rubbing his hands on his shirt. "I'm recharging," he shouted. "Better not come near me. Unless you wanna fry." His schoolbooks lay in a heap at his feet. Brad shifted his weight from foot to foot, flailed his plump, electric arms, prepared to wield his touch like a weapon. He reminded me of the men in movies who protect their castles and forts from attack, a small sentry guarding the treasure hoarded within his suburban house— board games and hamsters and bags of candy: the loot of a normal life.

As I left Brad flailing in front of his house and made my way toward our kitchen door, a vision overcame me like hiccups, and I couldn't make it go away; I saw myself walking backward forever, whistling to ward off the scorn of the world.

My mother was in the utility room, ironing clothes while she watched "Queen for a Day." A woman talked almost inaudibly about the medical and financial complications of her husband's diabetes. "Darlin'," interrupted Jack Bailey, "just a little louder, please. We want the folks at home to hear." When my mother saw me, she looked out the window and clicked her tongue. "Have you ever seen anything like it?" she asked. "They say an oil derrick tipped over on La Cienega. The Cajon Pass is closed to trucks. And watch this." She dragged the iron over one of my father's shirts and peeled it off the ironing board. The shirt crackled with static and, held aloft by the collar, assumed a life of its own, its sleeves clinging to my mother's dress. "Sorry," Mother said to the shirt. She pulled it off her, patted it flat, and went back to work. "Honey," she asked me, "have you spoken to your brother?" I heard a quaver of fear in her voice.

"No," I said. "Is he OK?"

Mother set the iron on its side and looked directly at me. "It's just that he left a note for your father and me, saying he had to go out of town to take care of some business. That was two days ago, and he hasn't shown up at the office since. We've been racking our brains trying to think what business it could be, and we can't come up with a thing. It's not like Bob to disappear." She let out a feeble laugh. "Well, maybe it *is*. But we'd feel a lot better if we knew what he was up to." She paused a moment and assessed my expression. "Listen. I'm not suggesting that something bad has happened. If something bad had happened he wouldn't have left a nice note: *Dearest* Mom and Dad. Why, I bet he'll be home in no time and our mystery will be solved."

"Right," I said, unsure I believed her.

"Right," she repeated, as uncertain as I.

I left my mother to her ironing and wandered down the hall. The farthest door led into the room that had once been Bob's, a room I hadn't stepped foot in for months. Drapes admitted a faint light, the room as still as a diorama. The bed, the desk, the gooseneck lamp—every piece of furniture was gone, moved to Bob's apartment. Lining a bookshelf were the only possessions left behind, the Hardy Boys mysteries my brother had collected during his adolescence, Frank and Joe Hardy portrayed cheek-to-cheek on the bright-blue spines. *The Disappearing Floor*, *While the Clock Ticked*, *The Mystery of the Criss-Cross Shadow*. After I read the row of titles, I made up some of my own: *The Brother Who Vanished into Thin Air*, *The Strange Girlfriend Who Left Her Records*, *The Mystery of the Backward Boy*.

That evening, Brad and I took Barbara to nearly every house in the neighborhood. Dressed in a flimsy skeleton suit, she thrust a shopping bag before her and yelled, "Trick or treat!" with giddy aggression. Pumpkins leered from dim windows. Soapsuds clogged the fountain in front of the Sunset Royale. Trees were festooned with toilet paper, strips of it hanging from branches in limp and ghostly loops. All night long I thought about Bob. I reconstructed that day at his apartment but couldn't uncover a clue to his whereabouts. My brother was cunning and self-reliant, but I found myself afraid for his safety; the world was a place of shelter or harm, tricks or treats, I wasn't sure which. The harder I tried to picture my brother, to fix his image in memory, the less distinct his face became. Door after door, block after block, I searched for Bob beneath the ocher moon, hoping I'd discover my brother walking calmly up the street or stepping out from behind a tree.

Halloween ended in a vigil. While wind scoured the walls of our house and distant sirens whined through the night, my parents sat at the dining room table and discussed what course of action to take. Aunt Ida and I kept quiet and listened. A vein pulsed in my father's forehead. My mother patted strands of hair made recalcitrant by static. "Irving," she asked, "should we call the police?"

"Only as a last resort." My father's mouth sounded dry. "What can the police do, anyway? After all, he left a note. It's not as if the boy's been kidnapped."

Ida clasped her hands together and whispered, "*Nisht duh gedacht.*"

Mother suddenly straightened her back. "What about breaking into his apartment?"

"And what," asked Father, "would that accomplish?"

Every time my parents faltered, at a loss for what to say or do, they stared into the distance, as if toward a sign that wouldn't come clear. The more mired in helplessness and indecision my parents became, the more necessary Ida found it to divert my attention. She told me she'd heard rumors about people who poison candy and give it to kids on Halloween. She said she only hoped Mrs. King had sense enough to throw out anything Barbara brought back that wasn't in a wrapper. When Ida realized that this topic was just as disturbing to me as the matter at hand, she tried to reassure me that *meshuggena* people were, thank God, a minority, and this poison-candy business was really nothing to get upset about. Finally she changed the subject altogether and asked me about *A Year of Rhymes.* "So. Burt. Have you kept up with October?"

"Mostly," I told her. "Maybe I missed a couple of days."

"Doll," she said, "don't get behind. Time, as they say, waits for no man." She patted my hand for emphasis, tugged at her turban, and the dining room went black.

It seemed to me that the instant before the lights went out, I'd heard in the bulbs of the chandelier a dying hiss of filaments. The blast of wind that drowned out the power sounded like my family gasping. Darkness smothered everything in sight. In the seconds before my eyes adjusted, phosphorescent dots, like a school of minnows, swam across my open eyes. Someone repeated, *Oh, oh,* the pitch of the voice constricted by fear, and I couldn't tell whose voice it was; it could have been my own. Highlights began to burrow through the gloom: the moist, unblinking eyes of my mother, my father's high and shining forehead, the sheen of Ida's satin turban. Through the gray panes of the dining room window there emerged a murky view of our yard. My parents stood up and crossed the room. Two tall and wavering shapes, they felt in the bureau drawer for candles. After some fumbling, a match was struck. Its moving flame left a trail in the dark, like a comet speeding through space. When the flame touched the wick of the candle and caught, the faces of my parents, lit from beneath, looked eerie and unfamiliar.

"Is it just us?" asked my mother. "Or is it everyone?"

"Beats me," said my father. "We'll have to look out front."

Ida and I got up from the table and huddled next to my parents. "Give me some air, for chrissakes," said my father. When Ida sighed, "Oy," the flame shimmied and almost went out. Mother scolded her sister for breathing too close to the candle. "All right," said Ida. "I just won't breathe." My father shushed us. He lifted the candle high above our heads, and clustered together in a circle of light, we blundered into the kitchen, toward the window that faced the street. Sure enough, our neighbors up and down the block had been plunged into darkness with us. In the dormer of the Kings' house, the beam of a flashlight careened around the walls, and then the room turned a muted shade of pink; I was sure that Brad had the flashlight in his mouth, cheeks puffed out like a blowfish, glowing. Other than the light from the dormer window and a few stray headlights winding through the hills, as far as we could see in every direction, the city had disappeared. Even the lights of the Griffith Observatory, ordinarily ablaze like a wedding cake, had been snuffed by the enormous night.

My mother was trying to remember where she'd put the transistor radio, when the back door flew open and in walked Bob. The four of us turned in unison, and my brother was bathed in candlelight. "Hey," said Bob, hands in his pockets, snapping gum. "I guess there's been a power outage." Currents of wind swept through the kitchen, picked up a stack of paper napkins, and scattered them across the floor. Mother broke away from us, rushed over to hug her son.

"Where the hell have you been?" asked my father, relief and consternation in his voice. The candle still flickered high above his head.

"Don't ever do this again," warned Ida. "You made your parents sick with worry." Ida shoved me in front of my brother. "And what about him?"

"What about him?" asked Bob.

"Hi," I said.

"People," said my brother, "let's keep calm. There's someone here I think you should meet."

Bob stepped aside, and a silhouette, framed in the portal, waved hello and glided toward us. A short blond woman in a navy-blue dress entered the circle of light. She stammered, "This must . . . I know I . . . ," but she couldn't surrender the words. When Bob touched her shoulder, the woman grew quiet and lowered her eyes.

"This," said Bob, "is Janet. My wife."

Ida smacked her forehead, but her turban muffled the noise. "Let me guess," she said to Bob. "Your urgent business was in Las Vegas." Ida shot mother her what-next look.

My mother flared her eyes, a signal for Ida to please keep quiet. "I wish we had known," was all she could say.

"I'll be," said my father. He gave the candle to Ida, walked up to Janet, and took her hand. "Mrs. Zerkin," he said, "welcome to the family. *Mi casa is . . .* how does it go?"

"*Su casa,*" said Janet. "That's awfully sweet."

Ida nudged my father out of the way and held the candle inches from Janet. Everyone was embarrassed by Ida's brazen examination of Janet's delicate and—I could almost hear Aunt Ida think it—discernibly gentile features, yet we all leaned in to get a better look, squinting to see in the dark. The wind hadn't mussed her rotund hairdo. Her eyes were a chilly, liquid blue, like one of Arnold's rare liqueurs. "You're nice," I blurted. Janet covered her mouth with her hand and guarded a laugh. Janet was Marion's opposite; the dark hair and eyes of Marion Hirsch were as overwhelming as a power outage, whereas Janet was scentless and plain and pale; she made a pleasant but meager impression. Marion shared her odd thoughts, heedless of the world's reactions; Janet seemed modest, afraid to offend.

And then the low electrical hum. The refrigerator and clock revived, their hidden motors clicking on. The fixture above us sputtered back to life. We had to blink against the glare.

Under the fluorescent light, clutching a purse that matched her outfit, Janet looked even more prim than before. "I know this news is sudden," she said, taking us in with her pale gaze. "There's a lot we'll have to learn about each other."

I was fascinated by this stranger in our midst. I said the word *wife* again and again, under my breath, till it didn't make sense. When I finally turned my attention to Bob, I was shocked by his appearance. His handsome face was different, diminished. Something vital was gone from his body. At first I believed that the change I saw was a lie told by the harsh light. But it soon became clear that an undertone of ash had stained the deepest layers of his skin and sullied the light in his eyes.

In an instant I knew what was wrong with Bob. I kept it to myself in the days to come, afraid to speculate aloud. There was no solace for knowledge like mine. No verses in *A Year of Rhymes* nor any of Mrs. Beswick's lessons could alter what I understood. My brother was changing second by second. My brother was leaving us cell by cell.

WINTER

A dense cloud cover rolled overhead and blotted the sun, the threat of rain sustained for weeks. The stucco walls of our Spanish house, walls padded with lathe and plaster, did little to keep the winter out; I could feel its dank intimation in my blanket, in the cold soles of my shoes.

Something in the dim light, in the moist and imminent air, caused me to long for Marion. Vestiges of My Sin arose like puffs of dust from the pillows, or so it seemed when I sat on our couch. Every red dress, deceptive and distant, was filled for a moment with Marion Hirsch. I refused to resign myself to her absence. She would return, I told myself, though my daydreamed reasons for her return struck even me as desperate inventions. "I just had to see that hula dancer one more time," I imagined her telling my stunned family as she sauntered toward the bamboo bar. Or she'd rap the glass of my bedroom window and ask to borrow *A Year of Rhymes*.

But there was another, involuntary way in which Marion was restored to me: memory. Cryptic remarks were coming back. Asked when she planned to open her own Hallmark cardshop, Marion had smiled and said to my father, "When cows have wings." Listening to my mother complain about the mysterious excess of wire hangers in our closets, Marion had suggested that, late at night, the hangers mated and bred. Mother laughed in disbelief. "Sylvia," teased Marion, "stranger things have happened. Put it in your thinking cap." Morsels of screwy humor, opinions I once dismissed as eccentric, made sense in hindsight, like a joke you understand too late to laugh, and I realized with fresh empathy what had drawn my brother to her.

I never asked Bob what became of Marion. "Ways to Forget," after all, was his primer. If he thought about her, he hid it well. And of course there was Janet.

"What is it that you do again, dear?" It was the second time that night Ida asked her, which in itself wouldn't have seemed peculiar, except that Janet, having arrived from an afternoon shift at Hollywood Presbyterian, was still dressed in her starched nurse's uniform, its fabric crackling every time she moved. Pinned to her chest was an oblong name tag: Janet Cotter. She wore flesh-colored stockings—some other woman's flesh, I thought; her legs were a different shade than her arms—and shoes as white as scoops of ice cream.

"She's a nursing assistant," Bob answered. Janet didn't elaborate.

"Do you get to see a lot of blood?" I asked.

"A little," she said solemnly. "But you get used to it after a while." Janet sensed my disappointment. "Most of my duties aren't all that exciting. I sterilize thermometers, make beds, plan daily menus, that sort of stuff. Really," she said, turning to Ida, "I'm more like a maid than an 'angel of mercy.'"

"You're an angel of mercy in my book," said Bob, patting Janet's thigh. Shifting her weight to pat him back, Janet crackled on the rumpus room couch, an immaculate blank in the midst of hibiscus.

"Looks like you're due for a new name tag," said Ida.

Janet lifted her name tag and read it upside down. "That's right," she conceded. "This'll have to go." She looked at Bob. "Janet Zerkin. I still can't believe it."

Bob winked at her and looked away. The shyness and diffidence between them was a reminder that their relationship was new. It had been less than a month since they met at the Standard station on Rampart Avenue, drawn to each other from different sides of a concrete island. The cap to Janet's gas tank slid off her trunk and rolled away. Bob dove after it. Handing it back, he couldn't, he said, read Janet's expression: "Did she like me or not? It was anybody's guess. What got me was her uniform." The reticence of their first meeting was evident even now. No touch or gaze was allowed to linger. Blond and calm and eager to please, Janet brought out in Bob a kind of decorum; he opened doors for her, draped a sweater over her shoulders, lavished her with those small attentions Marion would have considered absurd. Eyes lowered, sighing deeply, Janet expected concessions to her womanhood. In turn, she'd brush the lint from Bob's lapel or pat the cushion before he sat down, the tidy, inviting gestures of a wife.

All this politeness softened Aunt Ida. Politeness was the antidote to the misery she witnessed at the Nite Light Motel. "So maybe you could plan a menu to fatten him up." Her yellow turban tipped toward Bob.

"We can start right now," said Mother, walking into the room with a tray. On it was a plate of gefilte fish and a package of Manischewitz matzo. She held the tray under Janet's nose. My mother was wearing a green dress, her hair recently tinted with henna, bobby pins holding the high parts in place.

Janet examined the gefilte fish, lumps in a puddle of jellied broth. "That's fish? It looks scrumptious," she added, to conceal her amazement.

"Right from the jar," said mother. "It's ready when you are. And one of Robert's favorites."

"Fish from a jar. My goodness." Janet continued to stare but made no attempt to taste it.

Mother hovered. "Try some, honey."

As Janet lifted a forkful of fish, Ida parted her crimson lips and swallowed exactly when Janet did. Mother stood upright, rested the edge of the tray against her stomach, held her breath, and waited for a verdict. Janet dabbed her chin with a napkin. "Yum," she said. "I can see why Robert likes it."

"It's official," said Mother. "She's one of us." But Mother spoke too soon.

"May I try the matzo?"

"It's not matz-*oh*. It's matz-*ah*. You pronounce the *o* like an *a*," corrected Ida.

Janet squinted at the spelling on the package and confessed she couldn't read Jewish. "I was raised Baptist," she said. "Most of our writing is in English, although some congregations talk in tongues."

"Do you?" asked Ida, braced for disaster.

"Oh, goodness, no."

"What's tongues?" I asked.

"When the holy spirit comes right into you, and you talk in a language only God understands."

"What does it sound like?" asked Bob.

"Yeah," I echoed, "what does it sound like?"

Mother sat next to Janet and balanced the tray on her lap. Her eyes were shining, expectant. My brother and I leaned forward and waited. Even Ida seemed mesmerized, anxious to hear directly from heaven.

"Hello. Hello in there," came a muted voice. "It's me." Eve stood behind the glass doors that led to the patio, waving her arms. When she saw us turn in her direction, her arms fell to her sides. Behind her, the sky and rooftops were equally dark, except for one hazy, lavender patch where clouds intercepted the moonlight. Even in the gloom of evening, I could see that Eve was excited. "It's me," she said again. She looked vaguely foolish, like a child caught making mischief. "We're ready," she mouthed to my mother. Then she cinched her coat and walked away. "We're ready," Mother repeated aloud. My brother looked at Janet and shrugged.

"Ready for what?" whined Ida. But Mother had put down the tray and was headed toward the doors. Ida asked me, "Ready for what?" Then she asked Bob. Then Janet. Then no one at all.

Cold poured into the rumpus room when mother swung open the doors, and with cold came the scent of precipitation, a muddle of smog and sea. The dull shuffle of feet on flagstone. The voice of my father, urging, "Easy does it." I raced to the doors in time to see Arnold and my father rounding the corner, directed by Eve. Dodging the barbecue and chaise longue, they balanced between them an enormous cardboard box, a Heinz logo printed on the side. Mother nudged me aside when they neared the door. Janet and Ida had risen to their feet, uncertain what to do. Janet's hands were folded before her; Ida's hands were clamped to her hips. My brother sank back into the couch, allowing himself to feel fatigue when he thought no one was looking.

Judging from the way Arnold and my father grunted and struggled to negotiate the portal, the box was heavy. After they waltzed this way and that, my father stepped backward into the room, lifting his feet over the threshold and letting them settle gently, gently on the parquet floor. Arnold was next, panting dramatically, bemoaning his sacroiliac, his face a mask of comical anguish. They paused and pivoted their heads, trying to decide where best to set it down. "Over here," said my father, indicating the center of the room with a flick of his eyes. Eve warned them to watch out for their fingers as the box touched down with a muffled thud.

My father and Arnold straightened their backs and caught

their breath, congratulating each other with a handshake so vigorous the earthbound weight of it made them lurch. Eve removed her coat, revealing a tailored business suit, and circled the box, inspecting for damage. When she decided the gift was intact, she faced Bob and Janet, reached out her arm, and made a graceful, sweeping gesture toward the box.

"For us?" asked Janet.

"Ketchup to last a lifetime," muttered Ida. She was mad because no one had let her in on the surprise.

"It's a mystery," said my father. "From an auction at the temple. It was Rabbi Kaplan's idea. You bid on a box without knowing what's in it. Eve and Arnie helped us pick it out."

"We had a hunch," said Eve, "and the rabbi told us to listen to instinct." In the soft, confiding voice of an ally, Eve explained to Janet that she and Arnold had never been inside a temple before. She described the flame ablaze above the Torah, her husband donning a black "beanie."

"There's brand-new toasters and radios in some of the boxes," said Mother. "Or who knows what. That's the fun."

"In any case," my father continued, "our money will go to plant trees in Israel."

"You pays your money and you takes your chances," Arnold chimed in from behind the bar. "Voilà," he said, holding up a paring knife. "Who does the honors?"

"Mazel . . . ," said Eve, unable to finish.

"Tov," Mother prompted.

Invigorated by the mystery, Bob wrenched himself from the sofa, took the knife from Arnold, and dropped to his knees, poised to cut open the box. Janet stood behind him, baffled, her hem grazing his hair. "Don't they have any trees in Israel?"

"It's a desert," said Ida. "They can always use more."

Mother yelled, "Wait," and ran to get the camera. When she returned, she made Bob and Janet kneel side by side and hold the knife with their hands intertwined, like a couple slicing a wedding cake. It took Mother a minute to find the right vantage point. She peered through the viewfinder, swayed back and forth. Light glanced off her bobby pins. My brother and his wife were sheepish, obedient, smiling widely, their bodies bleached by the sudden flash. The bulb in the camera sizzled and shrank, left a trace of burning plastic in the air and blooms of phantom color.

A smattering of applause accompanied the quick, ceremonious slicing of tape. Bob yanked on the cardboard flaps and bent them back, staples popping onto the floor. Brimming in the box were wads of crumpled newspaper, which Janet plucked out one by one, our anticipation deliciously prolonged. "Let me get another shot," said Mother, snapping a new bulb into the camera. While she stalked the scene for a flattering angle, I bolted over to Bob and Janet and parted the place where their shoulders touched. With Marion in mind, I claimed the space between them. Ida clucked her tongue at the brazen way I insinuated myself into the picture. "Burt," my mother scolded, "you'll get your turn." Her head rose from behind the camera, one eye screwed shut. "Take it," I said, refusing to move. In the periphery of my vision, Janet tried to smile. "It's OK," she told my mother. "No," countered Ida. "It's not OK." Adult composure was toppling like blocks. I had wrested their attention. The thrill of it steeled me. I strained my face toward the lens, let loose a wild, defiant grin. When Bob commanded me to scram, I gave my grin more teeth and cheek, and he broke into the helpless laugh with which he sometimes greeted my antics. Bob stoppered his amusement long enough to count backward from five. His eyes were wet with suppressed laughter. A mortar of brief, impromptu threats held the numbers together: "Four—You're going to get it. Three—You'll be sorry. Two—I'm getting angry." I tried to drown him out by saying *Cheese,* the vowel so purposeful, loud and long, it ceased to sound like a word. He reached One, imbuing that digit with all the menace in him, but no amount of menace would make me budge. Mother gawked. She had no intention of taking the picture; the camera twirled from her wrist by its strap. Had Mother possessed the presence of mind, had the shutter been clicked at that instant, the photograph might have captured the blur of my brother thrusting the knife toward my stomach.

Eve shrieked. Ida cursed in Yiddish. An animal moan escaped from my mother. Arnold and my father, at the bamboo bar, glared in my direction, frozen mid-sip. Janet, who saw Bob turn the knife at the last second and jab me in the ribs with the wooden handle, patted her chest in search of her heart, slack mouth in the shape of amazement. Only I was undaunted; we'd played Murder when my brother lived at home; he always won in a tussle to the ground, the intractable weight of a man on my pelvis a private source of such excitement that I'd pretend again and again to die.

I mustered my strength and gave Bob a shove, shocked by the fleshless impact of his chest. That single shove made him teeter on his knees. The ease with which he was thrown off balance, straddled and pinned to the parquet floor, the way he lay there, strangely resigned—his thinness, his weakness, his surrender—enraged me. I held on to his belt with one hand and with the other stabbed him, turning the blade as late as I could. "Stop!" he shouted. "You're killing me!" He said it as though I were telling a joke and he couldn't bear more hilarity. I thrust again, put an end to his mockery. "Stop," he sputtered, this time plaintive, on the brink of labored breath.

And then Bob fell away from me, coughing and wheezing, legs sprawled out at rag-doll angles, clutching his stomach as if it had been pierced; my father had hooked me under the armpits, dragged me off my brother's body, and gruffly set me on my feet. His rapid breath was hot and liquored. He bent over me, held out his hand. Isolation within his shadow was punishment enough. "Give me the goddamn knife," he demanded, and I obeyed.

Not until I relinquished the knife did I feel the floor through the soles of my shoes. Mother hadn't closed the doors, and I smelled the tang of the distant Pacific. Ida and Eve stood side by side, hugging themselves, chilled by the damp November night, by the sight of my brother gasping for air. He tried to rise from the shining parquet, where all our dim reflections were submerged. Janet cupped Bob behind his head and helped him sit upright.

The vision of his son in a nurse's arms—her reflexive mercy, her white assistance—caused my father to bark at Bob, "What's wrong with you?"

"It's a game," Bob answered. "We've played it before." He rested his back against Janet's shoulder, and though he never looked at her directly, her closeness seemed to quell his heaving. Janet dutifully propped him up.

Mother took one step toward Bob. "What your father means," she said, "is what's the matter?"

My brother pulled away from Janet, bowed his head, locks of hair sagging from gravity. His hesitation sank like dampness into every corner of the silent room. We waited, impatient, and I thought of God's impending voice, a message mumbled in an unknown tongue. Bob finally lifted his head to speak, a smirk pulling at the edges of his lips, as if that might negate what he said, make it as light and soothing as music: "I guess I'm sick."

Mother said, "Sick?"

"Sick how?" asked Ida.

My brother raked a hand through his hair. He looked up at Ida. "I get tired," he said, "of eating and breathing."

"What?" cried Ida.

"The boy is overworked," said Eve. "That's all there is to it. I'd be tired, too, if I had to spend my days hunting people down and dragging them off to court."

"You're going to see a doctor," said my father. And after my brother meekly agreed, my father said it again. "Find out," he asked Janet, "who's the best." Janet nodded, stared at her husband as though she didn't know him.

"Drink this," said Arnold. He handed Bob a tumbler of tonic. The hiss of effervescence. Audible swallows. My brother was thirsty, encircled, ill; on one side his wife, grave and estranged, on his other the box, open at last. For a moment no one moved or spoke. Time spun like a wheel in a rut. If it hadn't been for Eve, all that I've remembered could have ended there, in a house beneath a sodden sky.

"Look at me," Eve said to anyone willing to listen. "Do I look worried? Well, do I? Some vitamins and rest, and we'll have a new man." She closed the doors, rolled up her sleeves. "I don't know about anybody else, but I'm about to bust from suspense." She dug into the mystery box and tossed wads of paper to Bob. He caught them deftly, and that seemed to cheer him. "Yoo-hoo," crooned Eve, waving a hand to end Janet's trance. "If you continue to sit there like a bump on a log, we'll never get anywhere."

A ceramic butter dish. A travel clock in a leatherette case. A hardbound cookbook. One by one the treasures were exhumed. Eve oohed her approval at each, held them aloft for all to see. My dazed parents sat on the couch and examined the gifts without surprise or interest. Janet thumbed through the cookbook, now and then pointing out to Bob the picture of a plump soufflé or a boat of brown gravy, watching his face for traces of appetite. When Eve lifted a Hobby-Kraft Microscope Set from the nest of paper, my brother said, "Burt, that's for you." There followed a package of sixty-watt light bulbs, a transistor radio, a pair of earrings. "Zircon," said Ida, peering down at the earrings through her cat-eye glasses.

Once the box was empty, Eve arranged the objects on top of the coffee table, next to the tray of gefilte fish and matzo.

"There you have it," said Arnold, raising his glass in a feeble toast. "Not a bad haul, if I do say so myself." Bob and Janet surveyed the table, their expressions weary, as if looking at refuse from a life they'd lived, not at presents for a life to come.

Bob and I had the job of balling up the paper and stuffing it back into the box. We could barely look at each other, and when we did, the glances were guilty and quick and timid. Instead we saw crumpled drawings of underwear, double ovens, automobiles, photos of President Kennedy, outdated columns of want ads, movies, rooms for rent, all the smeared and useless news blackening our hands.

very day after school, I'd sit at the dining room table and gaze through my microscope, refining the focus, adjusting the mirror. The set included dozens of slides: fish scale, fowl feather, hemp fiber, sea salt. However strange and intricate and bright, those specimens couldn't distract me for long; I'd wonder whether Bob had seen a doctor, what tests he would take, and what the tests would tell. In precise detail that rivaled any lens, I pictured my brother naked to the waist, curling hair in the cleft of his chest, the cold kiss of a stethoscope. Breathe, said the doctor, and Bob and I breathed. And then I'd wake to the dining room, the walls bathed in pale light, fragments of plant and animal life—globules of pollen, ribbons of spore, the tapered leg of a honeybee— pressed in my heavy, forgetful hand.

Sometimes I'd hear a cupboard slam or silverware clank in the kitchen, and I'd fight the impulse to run to my mother and ask about Bob. His health was a matter to be dealt with by adults. My role was to wait, to stay out of the way. Besides, I figured that ignorance was better than bad news.

Mother rewarded my silence with her own; she didn't protest when, restless for new specimens, I plucked threads from our olive-green carpet, snipped off bits of a kitchen sponge, peeled slivers of meat from a frozen roast. She'd watch me plunder bits of the house, impassive in her bathrobe, the henna gone from her hair. Whenever I caught her watching me, I expected anger to change her face, but the moment she sensed my expectation she'd cinch her robe and walk away. Even when I spilled a drop of methylene blue on the tablecloth while trying to dye the veins of a leaf, she regarded the stain as though from a great height, dimly saying that sooner or later she'd find a way to scrub it out.

One day, as I was sprinkling cornstarch onto a slide, my mother drifted through the kitchen and forgot where she was going. She patted her pockets, checked her empty hands. A bill to mail? A list to make? My mother shrugged, and I shrugged back. She began to walk away, when she turned to me again. "What?" Mother asked, though I hadn't said a word. She had heard the rain announce itself, a vast, erratic murmur that drew us to the window. Standing side by side, we watched the pavement of our dead end darken. Leaves wagged on the carob trees, then drooped with the glistening burden of water. The hills and the Griffith Observatory vanished behind the encroaching clouds. I'm not sure how long we stood there, but we listened to the winter rain as though its patter contained some message. We would have listened longer if I hadn't seen Ida dashing up the street. My aunt appeared to crouch and run at the same time, ducking the drops that plummeted from black, overhanging branches, a magazine held over her head. In the hazy setting of rain, her yellow poncho glowed, the only color on earth.

Mother swung open the kitchen door just as Ida, broad as a sail, blew into the room. She was breathing heavily, a few tendrils of damp hair twisting down from the rim of her turban. "I oughta have gills," she said, struggling to extract herself from the poncho. Rivulets of water sloughed off the oilcloth, fell to the floor. "Any word?" she asked my mother.

"Next week he sees Dr. Wexler. The best internist in town, according to Janet."

"*Gutten nachas*," whispered Ida. She set the sopping magazine on the kitchen counter and tamped it with a paper towel. It was the November issue of the *Dell Horoscope,* a configuration of stars on its cover. "Not that," said Mother. She leaned against the stove and crossed her arms. The two of them had read the horoscope together in the past, arguing over their interpretation of various predictions, so my mother's resistance bewildered Ida. "Come on, Sylvia. What's the harm?"

"I'll tell you what the harm is. I walk around this house crazy with worry, and everything that happens seems like a sign. The milk is sour: my son will be sick. The mail's on time: my son will be well. I'm tired, Ida. Tired of second-guessing God."

My aunt grew timid, touched her sister's hand, but Ida was a woman who depended on portents, and she couldn't leave the future to chance. "What if I . . . ?" she asked, holding up the horoscope.

"Go ahead," said Mother. "But I don't want to know."

My aunt had to squint through her glasses and wedge an opal fingernail just so in order to separate the wet pages. Whether or not she meant to entice us, Ida's concentration was compelling. Mother prepared tea, making a show of her indifference. Tap water rang in the hollow kettle. The gas jet hissed and sputtered into flame. I busied myself as well, but after I returned the cornstarch to the cupboard, I turned around and saw my mother peering reluctantly over Ida's shoulder. She laid her hands on Ida's back, bracing herself for a troubled forecast. Huddled together, they could have been children, one sister about to lead the other down a dark hall. The rain had let up, and the lull was riddled with birdcalls. "The appointment is when?" asked Ida.

"Thursday," said mother. "The seventeenth."

"Oh, no," cried Ida.

Mother craned her neck to get a better look. "Oh, no, what?"

"The seventeenth is ruined."

I sidled up to my aunt. The magazine was open to the Daily Guide for Taurus, but beneath the heading, ink bled from the edges of letters, and the newsprint page had become translucent. Text from the other side showed through, and the fuzzy drawing of a crescent moon. I could make out a couple of murky words—*trine, decision*—but that was all. "*Vey iss meer,*" groaned Ida. "Maybe we can save it, put it in the oven or something."

"No," blurted Mother. "I've had enough." She snatched the horoscope from Ida's hands and tossed it into the trash can. "We are going to sit down. We are going to drink tea."

"I thought if—"

"Tea," repeated Mother, and Ida grew quiet.

Hot water was poured. Steam weaved from porcelain cups. Ida and my mother followed me back to the dining room, where we sat at opposite ends of the table. Framed by the panes of the double doors, our yard was enveloped by a passing shadow, and rain began to strike the roof. They dunked their tea bags up and down, sullen and contemplative. I stared into my microscope.

"He's got a wife to take care of him," Ida said at last. "A nurse, no less."

"Let's hope he won't need taking care of."

Ida lifted the tablecloth and knocked on wood.

"Thursday," said Mother.

Ida sighed.

Through the eyepiece of the microscope, grains of cornstarch were scattered like stones.

"Irving's holding up?" asked Ida.

"He works," said Mother. "The more he worries, the more he works."

"It's income," said Ida. "That way you get the best for Bob. My opinion is you should keep busy too."

"The laundry. The dishes. Everything needs doing, and I can't keep up. It never seemed this way before." The chime of a cup set in its saucer. " 'You marry a house when you marry a man.' That's what they say."

"Who's they?" asked Ida.

My mother laughed. "Marion."

Bored with cornstarch, I tore a hangnail from my finger—the stinging made me feel brave—and placed it on a slide. Lit from beneath was the surface of skin, a geography of ridges and gullies as foreign as another planet. I looked long and intently, thinking how skin held us in, bound us to our muscles and blood, divided us from air. It could have been my brother's skin. My mother's. My aunt's. Even today I remember that desolate, magnified landscape, the sound of rain skimming the roof, my queer and inconsolable wonder.

I looked up from the microscope. "Want to see skin?"

"I've seen it," said Ida. She turned back to my mother, expecting to resume their conversation, but Mother put down her cup and gazed at me across the table.

"It's amazing," I said to urge her on. "It's . . ." I couldn't convey what that shred of flesh had made me feel—the thrill, the horror, of being in a body.

Lured by my squeamish excitement, Mother rose slowly to her feet, padded over to the microscope, took my seat, and looked through the lens. When she bent her head, I noticed the nape of her neck shining like an eggshell. She let out a little gasp of surprise, blinking again and again. "Ida," she said, head still bent, mesmerized, "it's really something. Come see for yourself."

My aunt grumbled and pushed herself out of the chair, knees cracking as she walked across the room. She waited her turn beside my mother, picking lint from her pantsuit.

Finally Mother looked up at me. Amazement lingered in her hazel eyes. "Where did you get it?"

I held out my hand. A small drop of blood had congealed on my finger. Mother took my hand in hers. I assured her that it didn't hurt, but she wouldn't let go. Her grip was warm and moist, and I felt as fragile as my brother, as susceptible to harm. I pulled my hand away.

"Let *me* get a crack at it already," said Ida. She nudged my mother up and plunged into the chair. Bowing her head toward the lens, she smacked the eyepiece with her glasses, and the microscope was jarred. Ida removed her glasses, put them aside, and tried again. "I don't see a thing," she said. "Take a look."

I fiddled with the knobs, tilted the mirror. Nothing was there but a circle of light, so empty and harsh it made me squint. "You must have knocked it off," I said. This was my favorite specimen so far, and I cautiously searched the tablecloth, parting the folds that had gathered when the microscope was struck. Ida and my mother leaned over the table and eyed its white expanse, laving me from either side with tea-scented breath. I rooted through the Hobby-Kraft box, lifted the bottle of methylene blue.

"Maybe it fell on the floor," said Mother.

The rumble of rain and a sudden draft; my father walked through the front door, with his briefcase in one hand and a thick manila file in the other. His fedora was mottled by water, and the shoulders of his trench coat bore stains like epaulets. When he shut the door with his foot, the sound of the rain grew dim again. He asked us what we were looking for. Ida said, "Skin," and returned to her tea.

"Burt," he said, "look for it later. There's something I need you to help me with." Without greeting my mother and Ida, he spun on his heel and hurried down the hall; I followed the wake of his gray coat, surprised to see him enter my room. He tossed the briefcase and file on my bed. With one swift tug, he dragged his tie through his collar and draped it over the back of a chair. Removing his voluminous coat, my father disturbed the still air and caused the bomber to twirl on its string. "Where's that book?" he asked. "The one Ida gave you. What's it called?" He snapped his fingers, scanned the room. " 'Time for Rhymes'?" Before I could correct him, he grabbed it off the nightstand, sat on my bed, and thumbed through the pages.

Never looking up to see if I was listening, my father launched into an explanation of his latest case. *Abjure, injunction, domicile*—he used words I didn't understand, words he would use were he talking to Bob. Still, I gleaned what I could from his account of the brief marriage between Hector Ramos and Isobel Nuñez, a young couple who'd eloped, like my brother. The "hitch," as my father put it, was that Isobel had lied about her age—she was only sixteen—and upon her return to Los Angeles from Yuma, Pete and Rafaela Nuñez, my father's clients, took their daughter away from Hector, threatening to have the marriage annulled on the grounds that Isobel hadn't asked for their consent. My father told me to look in his file, where I found some snapshots Bob had taken of the Nuñez house; behind its blurry clapboard facade, the despondent Isobel was confined to her room, kept under lock and key by her parents until the court could make its ruling. The photograph also showed Hector loitering on the sidewalk in front of Isobel's bedroom window. What it couldn't show, said my father, was the frequency of his visits, the unrelenting echo of his voice as he bellowed the love poems he wrote, poems that he hoped would change her parents' minds but only caused the neighborhood dogs to bark and howl late into the night. In order to get Isobel out of the house, Hector's attorney had presented the Nuñezes with a writ of habeas corpus entirely in verse—Hector had insisted, had even written parts himself—and my father planned to respond to their petition with a poem of his own. Seeking inspiration, he flipped through the pages of *A Year of Rhymes,* his brown eyes darting back and forth as he glossed the narrow stanzas.

"I wrote a poem once," he said. "To your mother, a million

years ago." I sat beside him. His wrists jutted from starched cuffs, his index finger riding the lines as though he were reading braille. "It wasn't very good," he admitted. "But I guess it did the trick."

"The trick?"

For the first time that day, he looked at me directly. His eyes were tired, rimmed with red. "She married me, didn't she?" He waited to see what I would say and, when I said nothing, went back to the book.

"How did it go?"

"Go?" said my father.

"The poem," I said.

He closed his eyes, tried to recall. I could see a stirring behind his lids as he struggled to retrieve the words. "Something something time. Something something . . ."

"Mine?"

"Yeah," he said. "Probably. Mine."

"Bob says rhymes can help you remember. He read it in a book. *Ways to a Better Memory*."

"It's funny," said my father, "the things you remember. The things you forget. We met at Aaron Lipsky's party, and I painted your mother's shadow on the wall. But when I look back, I can't see her face. Just the brush and the bucket of paint."

Then and there, I vowed never to let my memory lapse, to bolster my recollections against the effects of time. I'd study my brother's book if I had to. My recall would be effortless, my past, no matter how remote, would flash on command, distinct and stolid, every bit as rich as the present.

"Listen," said my father, sensing I'd been upset by his confession, "sometimes I can't even remember what I had for lunch, let alone what happened that far back. That's what happens when you get up in years. Things become scrambled. Names and places and people are lost."

I was about to argue, to insist there were methods, when

I heard Aunt Ida's distant voice. "Sylvie," she called. "Sylvie, come back."

My mother floated into the room as slowly as a somnambulist, her right hand held out before her. "Look at this. Look at this, will you. It won't come off."

"What the hell?" said my father.

"Methylene blue. It spilled when I tried to tighten the cap." Her hand had turned an eerie blue. Every crease was accentuated. Every pore and whorl was outlined. Cuticles, moons, the striations in her nails. "Washing only made it worse."

Ida peered into the room. "Sylvia?"

Mother wouldn't, or couldn't, answer.

"Irving," said Ida.

Father closed the book, rose from the bed. He moved his wife toward the window to take advantage of the dying light. My father took my mother's hand, turned it over as gingerly as one would turn a frail page.

"What should we do?" my mother whispered.

My father said, "I wish I knew." He let go of her hand, said it again. The drone of the rain. The clicks and groans of our Spanish house contracting in the cold. He gathered up his coat and tie, took my book, and walked out the door. Ida swiveled her head and watched him walk down the hall.

What had attracted my father to my mother—her hands, her breasts, her slender neck? Was my mother drawn to my father's high forehead, the set of his jaw, the slope of his shoulders? I knew it had to be more than their shadows painted on apartment walls condemned long ago in Chicago. Something deep in their skin had compelled them, the other's coloring, scent, and heat, in which they wanted to steep themselves—the very matter of flesh itself and not the shadow matter cast.

Standing before the bedroom window, my mother examined her hand. The light of dusk dimmed behind her, filtered through a scrim of rain. The bed, the walls, the room went blue.

"Sylvie," said Ida, plaintive and soft.

And still my mother didn't answer. Incredulous, forehead furrowed, she seemed to be reading the lines of her palm, darkly etched and otherworldly.

Hector Ramos paced back and forth on the sidewalk in front of the Nuñez house, hands thrust into the pockets of his peacoat. Now and then he'd glance toward Isobel's window and, finding the shade drawn, turn away, his sigh condensing in the chilly air. A black pompadour and smooth cheeks made him look younger in person than in the photographs my father had shown me, but even from across the street I could see he possessed an adult's determination: his shoulders were squared, eyes alert. Every few minutes he'd whip a pencil and a notepad from his pocket and jot a couple of verses for Isobel. His lips moved when he reread the lines, satisfaction bold on his face. Then he'd stuff the notepad back into his pocket and resume his pacing, resolute. Nothing, it seemed, could discourage Hector's vigil—not drawn shades, impending rain, or the threat of a restraining order.

"Lord," whispered Janet, peering through the windshield. "He's wearing a tie."

"Wants to get on her parents' good side." Bob leaned against the steering wheel and watched Hector circle a mailbox, trace cracks in the pavement with the toe of his shoe, run his hand along the back of a bus bench—a lovesick boy inventing small distractions.

"Poor lamb," said Janet. "I wonder if he's hungry."

"Hey," I said, "let's buy him a doughnut."

My brother laughed. "This is surveillance, Burt. Not feeding time at the zoo." He reached into the back seat and yanked the camera out of my lap. He checked the number of exposures left, breathed on the lens, and cleaned it with his shirt cuff.

"I thought Dad already had pictures. How many do you need?"

"I need," said my brother, feigning patience, "as many as I need." Bob took his ledger out of the glove compartment and handed it to me. "OK, Sherlock, in the left-hand column write"—he glanced at his watch—"nine A.M., Sunday, December fifth, corner Grove and Mission. That's Mission with a double *s*. Got it? Good. You two sit tight. I'll be back in a flash."

Janet and I sat in silence and watched Bob pose as a pedestrian. He enjoyed, I thought, having us as an audience, though he couldn't wink or wave and jeopardize his cover. Appearing inconspicuous was difficult; there were hardly any other people on the street. We'd parked in front of a liquor store, and my brother stared into its window, mesmerized, or so it seemed, by a couple kissing on a sign for whiskey, but soon I realized that Hector Ramos, loitering across the street, was reflected in the glass. The instant Hector's head was bent to compose a poem, Bob spun around, snapped a picture, then quickly hid the camera in his jacket and acted as if nothing had happened. My brother walked to the corner, read headlines in a row of news racks, fished in his pocket for loose change, eyeing Hector all the while. Bob continued down the street with a Sunday *Herald* tucked under his arm. From the back he could have been any man—a man taking the long way home, a man with time to kill. High above his diminishing figure, wind drove sluggish clouds across the sky.

"I guess it looks fishy if he sticks around too long," said Janet. "He's probably taking a walk around the block." A bus roared past and rocked the car. Our breath began to mist the windows. Janet crossed and uncrossed her legs, the scrape of her nylons a distant whisper. "So"—she sighed—"how 'bout some heat?" The hum of the heater emphasized our silence. My brother acted as a link between us; when Bob was near, it was nice to talk to Janet; the instant he left, she changed into a stranger. I suspected Janet felt the same about me. Restless for something to say, she shifted in her seat. Janet held her hands to the vent. Her wedding band flashed when she rubbed her hands together, a meager spark in the cabin of the car. "I left Minnesota because of the cold. Every winter we were buried by a blizzard. Have you ever seen snow?"

"On TV," I said. "And Christmas cards."

"Back home, snowdrifts can reach the windows, and the roads turn to ice overnight. People lose their fingers to frostbite."

"Do they just fall off?" My interest was piqued. Janet was happy.

"Not right away. But circulation gets worse and worse, and the only recourse is amputation." The interior of the car grew warm. Janet told me, in technical detail, everything she knew about frostbite. She talked about the body with solemnity and patience, so different from the way my brother had talked about Marion's body, helpless in his exhilaration. Instead of "legs" and "arms" she said *extremities. Hypothermia, internal organs, arteries.* I wondered if she was trying to impress me with her vocabulary. She sipped air at the end of each sentence and studied me for signs of interest, uncertain whether or not to keep talking. Janet had turned to face the back seat. Behind her, framed by the oblong windshield, gray light glowed above the roofs of the city. The silhouette of Janet's hairdo eclipsed the drifting clouds.

She told me about the importance of oxygen in the bloodstream. Did I know, she asked, that the heart is a muscle? She spelled *aorta* and *ventricle*. I nodded often, said *Wow* or *Yuch* to urge her on. I smiled until my cheeks began to burn, afraid to stop and hurt her feelings.

"Suppose," said Janet, "we took a drop of your brother's blood and put it under your microscope. What would we see?" Janet cocked her head and waited for an answer. I looked into my lap, as though the open ledger might contain a clue. Dates written in my brother's hand. Streets noted in slender columns. The name *Ramos* repeated like a chant.

"White cells," she said. "But not enough. Do you know what that means, more white cells than red? It's what we call leukemia."

It sounded awful, unfamiliar, like something Janet made up.

"Your mother asked me to explain it to you. I hope that's all right . . . ?"

"Fine," I lied. And Janet relaxed.

"There's not a lot we know about it. Every day a cure gets closer. Bob might get worse, or he might get well. From here on in, it's up to God. He's awfully brave, don't you think? A real mensch—did I say it right? He still works hard, still wants to make his mark. Determination," Janet added, "is the most effective medicine on earth."

Even if I had wanted to, I wouldn't have known how to explain to Janet that her diagnosis was wrong. If my brother was sick—it seemed irrefutable once I thought it—if my brother was sick, he was sick with love. Why else would he take so many photographs of Hector, a boy with hair as black as his own, a boy whose longing overflowed into poems? Why else would the tassel Marion gave him still twist and shudder from the rearview mirror? If Marion was never mentioned, it was only because my brother was saving her name for himself.

" 'In sickness and health': a vow's a vow. I'm here to help.' " Janet tried to buffer the words with a soft and cautious tone of voice. She reached between the bucket seats to touch me, then thought it better to restrain herself, to let me absorb what she had to say without the intrusion of solace or pity, though pity, clearly, was what she felt, and solace what she meant to offer.

Janet's hand hovered between us. I passed her the ledger. She had trouble fitting it back among wrinkled maps and rolls of film. While she was busy rearranging the contents of the glove compartment, I scanned the street for my brother, eager to see him round a corner and saunter toward us, impersonating a passerby. Except for Hector, the street was unpeopled.

Beneath a relentless procession of clouds, the clapboard walls of the Nuñez house turned a muted blue. The front door swung open. Pete and Rafaela Nuñez, with Isobel sandwiched between them, crept to the precipice of their porch. The parents surveyed the view, checking for Hector's whereabouts and planning a dash to the street. Mr. Nuñez wanted to run straight ahead, Mrs. Nuñez to the left, and Isobel, gripped by either arm, swayed with their indecision. Following Mr. Nuñez's lead, the three of them bumped and lurched across the lawn. Hector, who had been scribbling in his notepad several yards away, turned his back to the Nuñez house, spun on his heel and barreled toward Isobel. I grabbed the armrest. Janet looked up. Commotion broke over the quiet street. Doing his best to run and recite at the same time, Hector held the notepad at arm's length, as though he were chasing the poem itself. Janet gasped when he almost tripped on a crack in the pavement. As Hector tried to right himself, Isobel wobbled in empathy. The closer Hector came, the more forcefully Isobel craned her weight toward him, but her will was tempered by the presence of her parents; she didn't have the strength to disobey, to break their makeshift rank. The more obvious it became that Isobel was her parents' ward, a child who couldn't escape their jurisdiction, the faster Hector ran and the louder he recited.

"Just what does he think he's going to accomplish with all that ruckus?" asked Janet. We rolled down our windows, poked our heads out of the car, the morning cold as metal.

"Ramos," yelled Mr. Nuñez. "Take one more step, and I'm calling the cops. You're harassing a minor. You're trespassing on private property."

"The sidewalk isn't private," cried Isobel.

"You," said Mr. Nuñez, turning sharply to his daughter, "you have nothing to say about it."

Mrs. Nuñez tugged at her husband's sleeve. "Let's go already. Just ignore him. I don't hear him anymore. I don't hear a thing." She took Isobel by the hand and ushered her toward a two-tone Plymouth. Mrs. Nuñez fumbled with a key ring. Isobel fingered the cross around her neck and smiled dimly, pleased by Hector's audacity. Mr. Nuñez remained on the sidewalk, arms folded, legs in a wide, intimidating stance.

It looked as though Hector couldn't have stopped even if he had wanted to. His peacoat bloated with wind; the red tie blew over his shoulder and flapped behind him like the tail of a kite; he and his former father-in-law were seconds away from impact. Above Mr. Nuñez's protestations rose Hector's cracking, adolescent voice:

> We were wed, as God is my witness.
> I hope that you will never forget this.
>
> Come with me, darling, away to the Casbah.
> You are my wife, and I am your—

Hector tried to dodge the man in his path, but Mr. Nuñez stuck out his arm to hold the boy back. Mr. Nuñez's fall was cushioned by crabgrass. He landed in a sitting position. He clutched his elbow—"*Hijo de chingada!*"—and rocked back and forth. Hector careened a harrowing five feet on his stomach and skidded to a stop. The notepad flew from his grip and, completing its course with ghostly precision, sailed along the sidewalk toward Isobel. As she raced to retrieve it, the clatter of her high heels echoed in the air. She plucked the notepad off the ground, reading even as she straightened her back, so intent on her lover's couplets she didn't notice her mother, all haste and indignation, approaching from behind. Rafaela intercepted the poem with one sudden lunge. She backed away from Isobel, waving the notepad above her head, its wire spiral flashing. "I got evidence," she yelped.

"Evidence of love," insisted Isobel.

Hector sat up, puffed apologies to Mr. Nuñez, the tie and peacoat streaked with dirt, a gash across his chin. He touched it and looked at the blood on his hand, but he didn't register pain or surprise.

Janet rummaged through her handbag, extracting a packet of Kleenex and a bottle of Mercurochrome. "I'd better go over."

"I don't think so," I said.

"That cut's going to get infected—"

"Mother," implored Isobel, "read what Hector wrote."

"—and Mr. Nuñez might have sprained his arm."

"Read what he wrote?" Rafaela was incredulous. "I've heard him shrieking poems for a week. I can hear him with my ears closed. *June, spoon. Dove, love.* Is that any reason to promise him your life?"

Janet flung open the door of the car.

"I don't think so," I said again. "I really don't think you should."

Duty made her deaf to my entreaties. She dashed across Grove Avenue, her shoulders squared, Mercurochrome in one hand, Kleenex in the other. She hadn't said not to follow, so I did.

By the time I'd crossed the street, Janet was bent over Mr.

Nuñez, pressing his elbow through his sweater and asking if he was able to lift his arm, lower it, rotate it right, now left. No serious swelling, she announced, but an ice pack wasn't a bad idea, just as a precaution. Janet's attentions, her competent touch, made Mr. Nuñez childlike, compliant. As Janet took his pulse, he stared at her face, her hands, his eyes moist and disbelieving. "Where did you come from, miss?" he asked. Janet pointed to the Pontiac. "Oh," he said, uncomprehending.

"I'm Robert Zerkin's wife. Your pulse is awfully rapid. Better stay put for a minute."

Isobel grabbed one end of the notepad. "Mama," she said, "this belongs to me."

Rafaela tugged in the opposite direction. "We need to have it, *mi hijita*. We need it to help you undo your mistake."

Isobel stamped on the pavement. "There is no mistake. I know what I'm doing. I've known all along."

"Let go, Isobel. *Trata de entender*. Your father's been hurt. I have to see to him."

Isobel refused to loosen her grip. "It's mine, Mama. I inspired it."

Rafaela threw up her hands. "I give up. We'll discuss this later." She prodded her daughter into the back seat of their car, slammed the door, and rushed toward Pete. Isobel brandished the notepad, and Hector, still sprawled on the sidewalk, saw that the poem was in her possession. His smile incensed Mrs. Nuñez. "Happy?" she snapped at Hector as she passed. "Can you walk?" she asked her husband. Mr. Nuñez continued to stare at Janet.

"He'll be fine," said Janet. "The mister's just winded." She moved to Hector and knelt beside him. As she dabbed at his cut with Mercurochrome, I heard a camera clicking behind me.

"I told her not to," I said.

"Dad'll love it. Think how it sounds: A nurse was needed."

Bob shoved me aside to get another shot. "I took a whole roll from across the street."

"You a cop?" demanded Hector.

"Private investigator."

Hector winced.

"Does it sting?" asked Janet.

"Come on, man," Hector said to the lens. "Give me a break."

"Sorry, buddy," said my brother. "Nothing personal. I get paid to take pictures. Why don't you ease up? Why don't you just leave these people alone for a while?"

"Ha!" barked Rafaela. "That'll be the day."

"My wife's been kidnapped, man." We all turned toward Isobel, a prisoner in the Plymouth. She blinked at the havoc in front of her house and held the poem to her chest like an amulet. "What would you do," Hector asked my brother, "if you was me?"

"The same," said Bob. But he kept snapping pictures.

Mr. Nuñez clutched his arm and mugged pain for the camera. "Yes, sir," he grumbled, his vehemence revived. "Wait till the judge sees these."

My brother captured every angle. He must have taken half a dozen shots before Janet had finished her ministrations. "There," she said, her finger propped beneath Hector's chin. "That ought to do you. The bleeding's stopped." Then, in a whisper, "You'd better go home."

"Is this some kind of conspiracy?" asked Hector. "No one will listen to us. What do we have to do?" He greeted our silence with a brief and bitter shake of his head. Hector stood up, brushed himself off, shot Isobel a look of fierce longing. He limped slightly as he walked away, perhaps to prove to Mr. Nuñez that he, too, sustained injuries grave enough to flaunt in court.

When Hector was finally out of sight, Mrs. Nuñez hoisted her husband to his feet. They thanked my brother and Janet for their help. Bob rested his hand on my shoulder and introduced me as his "trusted assistant." I was about to tell Mr. Nuñez that he had grass stains on the back of his pants, when rain began to dot the sidewalk. We blurted goodbyes and ran to our cars. "Don't forget the ice pack," shouted Janet. Mr. Nuñez saluted and smiled. He slammed his door and revved his engine. A plume of exhaust issued from the Plymouth. The intersection of Grove and Mission grew slick and wet and empty once again. Isobel gazed through the rear window, watched my brother and Janet and me fade into the liquid distance.

On the way home, Janet and Bob agreed that there was nothing, absolutely nothing, Hector could do to make his marriage legal. "Not yet, anyway," said Bob. "Maybe in a couple of years, if they can wait that long, but not right away. The court, after all, is bent on her protection. The fact of the matter is: Love can't change the law."

"You're right," said Janet. "One hundred percent."

"The more he tries to persuade her parents, the worse things get. If you ask me," my brother said, "the kid's digging his own grave."

Janet turned and looked out the window. Rattle of rain on the metal roof. Mechanical clack of the windshield wipers. "Isobel certainly looks older than sixteen."

"The hair," said my brother. "The hips."

"Maybe someday they'll end up together," I said.

"What happens later isn't my business. For the time being, I work for her parents. It would be a mistake if I got involved." My brother's voice was strange and plaintive. Janet assured him she understood. She compared Bob to the doctor who can't let his feelings interfere. And still my brother wanted to explain. "I can't take sides. That's all there is to it. When push comes to shove, who can say who's right? Maybe they're better off apart."

Outside, the world was doubled by water. People and cars

were twice as plentiful, trees and buildings twice as tall. I remembered Hector's poem, his swift and desperate trajectory. "Come with me, darling, away to the Casbah. / You are my wife, and I am your . . ." Outlaw? Soda? I pressed my forehead against the glass—cold comfort—and drew a deep breath. Each rhyme sounded ridiculous, the couplet incomplete. Rivulets of water plunged into gutters. Wraiths of steam rose from manholes. When Marion comes back, I thought, my brother will recover.

One morning in mid-December, Mrs. Beswick stood before her sixth-grade class and waited for the noise to die down. Coughs and whispers dissipated, our attention settling as slowly as a feather. "The atmosphere," she said at last, "is everywhere. We live in a restless ocean of air." All of us turned and looked out the window. Palm trees loomed in a placid sky. Light glazed the asphalt playground. The temperature was eighty degrees. Just last week, rain had sent houses sliding down the hillsides and washed away sections of canyon road. Now every trace of rain was gone. Every trace, that is, except for my recollection of Aunt Ida watching the six o'clock news on TV, footage of a buckling house reflected in her cat-eye glasses. "The weather," continued Mrs. Beswick, "is one of the most common topics of conversation because it has a bearing on so many of our agricultural, industrial, and civic endeavors." She whirled her arm in circles and compared heat to a huge spoon that mixes up the atmosphere and makes changes in the climate happen. Some kids took notes. Others just watched, mouths slack, heads propped on their hands. "What I adore about meteorology," said Mrs. Beswick, "is that it tries to find patterns in something as dramatic and unpredictable as the weather."

For the next hour, we heard about colliding air masses, polar and equatorial fronts, the destructive power of floods and tornadoes. Mrs. Beswick drew maps and diagrams and arrows, the brittle chalk breaking into bits when she jabbed at the blackboard to punctuate a point. By the time she was through, the blackboard had become so smeared with erasures, it looked like a blurred and turbulent storm.

When it came to Cloud Classification, Mrs. Beswick expected us to commit the entire sky to memory. One by one, she held up illustrations of different kinds of clouds and chanted a litany rich in syllables: Cirrocumulus. Altostratus. Stratocumulus. Cumulonimbus. Brad, one row over, could barely suppress his laughter; Mrs. Beswick held the pictures in front of her face, and it looked as if she had clouds for a head, as if giant blossoms of condensation spoke in our teacher's nasal voice.

While Mrs. Beswick was eclipsed by clouds, light poured through the schoolroom windows and burned against my back. It was unseasonably hot for the middle of winter; sun bleached the cardboard Christmas trees, the red and green garlands festooning the room. The world seemed wrong, the planets out of kilter. I found myself thinking about my brother; when Bob and Janet came to visit, I'd swing open the front door and search his face for signs of illness in the fraction of a second before I said hello. Sometimes my brother's eyes were moist and his skin looked warm and familiar. Sometimes my brother's eyes were dim and his skin looked cool and mineral. Bob's health changed from day to day, erratic as the weather.

Though he'd struggled with fatigue in mid-December, a vague malaise he blamed on the rain, by the first night of Chanukah, Bob was strong; the set of his jaw and the shine in his eyes reassured me the moment I opened the door. He was squeezing Janet and snapping gum. Stars blinked in the sky behind them. Hills wavered in the evening heat. "Gangway," he said, poking my ribs as he surged inside. "I'm hungry enough to eat a horse." He sniffed the odor of brisket—it permeated the far reaches of the house—then disappeared into the kitchen.

"I'll never get used to California," said Janet, using her hand as a fan. "A person could get heat stroke in December." Janet wore a sleeveless dress—I'd never seen her bare arms—the scar from a vaccination shining on her shoulder. Under her other arm was a gift, wrapped in a print of menorahs. "This is for later," she said. "I picked it out especially for you." Since the day she explained leukemia, Janet had tried to win me over in a dozen persuasive ways. She'd bring me souvenirs from work—a glass syringe with the needle removed, a patient-identification bracelet. She'd turn the beam of her concern on me when I least expected it, asking my opinion of a dress she'd bought, a movie she'd seen. Every so often she'd graze my forehead with a skittish kiss. Each small kindness eroded my resistance, encouraged me to care for her. Eventually I grew to appreciate the alien paleness of her eyes, the whiteness of her legs in regulation hose. If I didn't actually have fun with Janet, if Janet couldn't, like Marion Hirsch, turn logic inside out like a glove, her attentions were pleasant and at least she meant well. I took the box and shook it.

Janet and I joined Bob in the kitchen, where he was trying to bribe Aunt Ida for a bite of her noodle kugel by promising to investigate anybody she wanted, for free. "There must be plenty of attractive gentlemen registered at the Night Lite. Someone you'd like to know more about?"

Ida smiled. "When it comes to men, Mr. Big Deal Detective, I can make my own decisions." She covered the kugel with wax paper and, sentry in a satin turban, stationed herself beside it.

My mother and Eve, peeling vegetables at the sink, glanced at each other; they were startled, I thought, by my brother's hunger. Bob hugged my mother, called Eve "the picture of prosperity," and urged her to model her new suit. Brandishing a stalk of celery, Eve turned in a circle, stirred her hips, primped her wiry, graying hair. When Arnold and my father came into the kitchen for ice, they were heartened by our clapping and laughter. "*A pretty girl,*" sang my brother, chewing the lyrics along with his gum, "*is like a mel-o-dy.*"

And so the evening proceeded, each in his place around the table, my brother defying our fears of his decline. He laughed at Arnold's corny jokes. ("I could shingle my roof with these," Arnold said of the matzo.) He plied Janet with Manischewitz. ("Sweet," she decided. "Kind of like Kool-Aid.") Finally sinking his teeth into the kugel, Bob moaned and grunted and rolled back his eyes, mugging a seizure of pungent joy. Mother flashed in and out of the kitchen, bearing dish after heaping dish, stopping only for a quick check to make sure everyone was happy. Steam rose from oval platters, the dining room humid, fragrant with gravy. It was almost possible to believe that things would get better, that my brother's illness was a headache or a cold, an inconvenience from which he would revive any day now, any day.

Everyone ate and talked at once. Layers of conversation. A clatter of forks and knives. Eve asked Janet about the Salk vaccine. "Why a cube of sugar? Why not, say, a piece of cake?" I described to Bob the wavy path of jet streams, using my wrists, but not too much. My father, his empathy ignited by a second glass of wine, filled Arnold in on the Nuñez case. "They slave to get here from Guadalajara, earn themselves a house and a car, send their daughter to beauty school, and along comes this kid who thinks he can steal her right out from under their noses with a few paltry poems. I'm telling you, it's tragic."

"Me with the liquor business, you with the law. We must have seen it all," said Arnold, shaking his head.

"I think Hector loves Isobel," volunteered my brother. "I mean, *really* loves her. It's like . . ." Bob stopped chewing his food and, stumped as in a game of charades, strained to think what Hector's love was like.

"You can't do it," said Ida. "No one can say what love is like. It would be like trying to describe the taste of kugel. You could get close—a little chewy, with salt and sweet— but you'd never get it exactly right."

"Oh, I don't know," Janet piped up, cheeks flushed from Manischewitz. "Maybe love is yellow like the sun."

"Doll," said Ida, "judging from my clientele, love's a little brown around the edges."

"That's sad," said Janet. She put down her fork.

My father said Hector was too romantic for his or anyone else's good. "The kid's in for a big surprise; I'm prepared to fight poems with poems."

"Huh?" said Arnold.

"You heard him," said Mother, setting down a bowl of radishes petaled like roses. "Irving's composed a poem of his own."

"Hey," said Arnold. "Poem of his own."

"Irving wrote a poem?" asked Eve. "Who's it to? Sylvia, I hope."

"I should be so lucky," said Mother, sitting at last and surveying the table before she served herself.

"I figured if Hector and his attorney could impress the court with a writ in rhyme, so could I."

"Say some of it," Arnold prompted my father.

"Yes," said Eve. "A recitation."

"Recite," said Arnold. "That's the word I wanted."

"Oh, come on," said my father. "You don't want to hear some *meshuggena* poem."

Arnold banged his glass with a spoon.

Janet leaned forward, folded her arms atop the table.

Mother speared a piece of meat. "Irving," she said, "the crowd is getting restless."

"Can you remember it?" I asked. "Can you say it by heart?"

Ida said, "Pass the radishes."

My father stood up, solid as a tree. His shadow fell across the table, all that bounty in my father's shade. He squared his shoulders, cleared his throat. The ridge of his receding hairline glowed in the light of the chandelier.

> "The court lacks jurisdiction
>   To make an order stern.
>   The paper filed by Hector
>   Requires no return.
>   And all the allegations,
>   Including sigh and cry,
>   Each of them now Pete
>   And Rafaela do deny.
>   And for the further answer to
>   This impassioned plea
>   We would remind rash Hector
>   That he should clearly see
>   A child of sixteen is too young
>   To claim a mate for life
>   Without consent of parents, thus
>   Can only lead to strife."

The instant he was finished, my father searched our up-turned faces. Eve said the poem was darling, absolutely darling, and felt that a judge would have to be deaf not to be impressed. Arnold called my father a "regular Bard of Avalon." Avon, said Mother, and agreed the poem was pretty good. "You really like it?" asked my father. "I mean, you think it gets the point across?"

"Clear as a bell," offered Ida. "Now sit and finish your dinner."

My father continued to tower above us.

"You're saying youth is impetuous," Eve suggested. "The poem is a plea for common sense."

My brother clasped his hands behind his head. He tipped back in his chair and rocked on the two rear legs. "Once we show that poem," he said, "the Nuñez case is as good as closed."

A gust of sound from my father's chest. He lunged through the air, thrust one hand toward Bob. The flat of the other hand smacked the table, upset the bowl of radishes. The whole bouquet scattered and bounced, the table creaking beneath his weight. His head must have struck the chandelier. Prisms collided, wagged back and forth. Stripes of light swooned around the room.

Mother yelled, "What's the matter?"

Arnold stood up and murmured, "Irv?" Static held the napkin to his lap. In his hand was a glass of wine, raised as though for an urgent toast.

Janet caught a radish as it wobbled over the edge of the table.

"I thought you were going to fall," said my father, staring at Bob. His voice was deflated and far away, not the voice that had recited the poem. He lowered himself into his chair.

"Thought what?" said Arnold, sitting too.

"I thought Bob was going to fall," said my father, a little louder. "Fall back in his chair. I was trying to catch him."

My brother eased himself forward till the chair's mahogany legs were firmly on the earth. "I wasn't going to fall." Light from the chandelier still swept around the walls. "I wasn't," my brother said again.

"OK," snapped my father. "I heard you the first time." He touched his head where the prisms had struck. "I thought I saw it start to happen."

"The Manischewitz," concluded Eve.

"You think you're drinking grape juice," said Arnold, "but the stuff packs a wallop. Rocket fuel."

A vein darkened on my father's forehead. "Maybe," he said. "Maybe that's it." Mother mouthed, "Loosen your collar," and my father did. I gripped the seat of my chair, felt rough wood underneath.

"Time for coffee," said Eve. "Armenian coffee. Strong and thick. You sit," she ordered my mother, who started to rise to her feet.

My father was perspiring, dabbing the back of his neck with a napkin. His undershirt, a whiter white, shone like a ghost beneath his dress shirt. Mother screwed the cap on the wine. Ida plucked up as many radishes as she could reach from her seat and dropped them back into the bowl. My brother didn't move a muscle; he sat up straight in his straight-backed chair, obedient to gravity, knowing that only his stillness could calm us. The happiness of a moment before seemed soft and insubstantial now, prone suddenly to change its shape, tenuous as any cloud.

"How about that present?" blurted Janet. "You open the presents after dinner, don't you?" My mother nodded absently, and Janet retrieved the box from the kitchen.

"Only one gift a night," sighed Arnold. "How can you Jews stand the suspense?"

Everyone leaned a little closer, braced by the sound of ripping paper. Beneath the swath of torn menorahs, an illustration of braided muscle, a bony hand.

"What on earth?" said Ida.

A labyrinth of red intestine. A long translucent leg.

"It's the Visible Man," said Janet.

"The who?" asked Ida.

"No," joked Arnold. "The *Visible* Who."

" 'A one-sixth-human-size anatomically accurate three-dimensional model kit,' " I read from the box. " 'With see-through body, vital organs, and skeleton. Adult guidance suggested. Glue not included.' " A thrilling tug of suction as the lid slid off the box. Before I could stop him, my brother reached over and pulled out a plastic pole; from it jutted miniature organs, red and plump as fruit. "Cool," said Bob. "Can I take one off?" He gave the heart a twist, and it popped into his palm.

"Right ventricle, left ventricle," said Janet, gingerly tapping either side. She stood behind Bob. Her arm seemed to descend from thin air; her tone was knowing, otherworldly. "About three tablespoons of blood move through the heart with every contraction."

"Oy," said Ida. She pushed the remains of her brisket aside.

The first acrid hints of coffee wafted into the room. "Wait for me," Eve called from the kitchen.

"What's this?" I asked. "It looks like wings."

"Your diaphragm. The muscle that pushes air in and out of the lungs. It flattens and inflates, flattens and inflates." Janet pumped her arms up and down. I watched her and thought about breathing, and the more I thought about breathing, the more difficult breathing became.

"Here's what I feel like every morning," said Arnold, holding up bones in a plastic bag. A small skull sank to the bottom.

"I'm not surprised," said Eve, toting a tray of cups and saucers, "because that's what you look like every morning."

My father let out a sharp and helpless laugh. "You kids are really something," he told them.

"Yup," said Eve. "We're something else. Who wants coffee?"

Mother and Father raised their hands like kids in my class.

Organs were passed around the table, relayed from hand to hand. Each of us deferred to Janet: where in our bodies would such and such be, what does it do, could we get along without it? Pancreas, windpipe, gallbladder, spleen: Janet explained their wondrous functions. Between sips of coffee, Father proclaimed, "The girl knows her business." Mother chanted, "You live and learn." We wanted to believe that Janet had answers, that nothing about the body could elude her, could present her with an unsolvable problem. Janet thrived when asked for explanations. If blue could burn, her eyes were burning. "There's a reason," she insisted, "for everything the body feels and does." Janet hovered above my brother, animated, talkative, made prettier by her convictions. She'd supervise the building of a model man; she'd make sure all the pieces fit. Bob listened quietly. Sometimes when Janet gestured, inadvertently stroking his shoulder or touching the crown of his head from behind, my brother caught her hand and held it. On that clear, hot December night, in a basin of hills and houses and stars, standing at our dining room table, Janet was the medium, and medicine spoke through her.

After all the coffee was gone, after Janet had glossed the human body inside and out, Mother cleared a place on the table and set down our brass menorah. Into the menorah she secured two candles, powder blue and waxy white. She struck a match, cradled the flame.

While Mother prayed, I exhumed the body from the bottom of the box, snapped the empty halves together, and stood him on the table. Highlights shone on the window of his skin, emphasizing biceps and thighs, the arteries etched on his wrists and groin. No nipples or penis or testicles. Only a detailed navel. He faced straight ahead, one foot forward, cold and noble as a swan carved in ice.

"*Baruch atah adonoy, elohanu melach haolum, shehecki anu, vahigianu, lazmahn hahzey.*" A whiff of charcoal when the match was blown out. "Blessed art thou, God of the universe, who has sustained us to this day."

My brother clung to Janet's hand, as entranced as I by the Visible Man. We stared at his vacant anatomy. A physique defined by air and light. A body purged of troublesome blood.

On the last day of the year, I sat on our front steps and waited for my brother. We were going to visit our father's office, though I secretly hoped we'd throw a subpoena to some unsuspecting spouse along the way. In the sky above the observatory, wind changed the shape of clouds as it prodded them toward the east. From open windows across the street there came a commotion of children. Brad's voice carried from the dormer, swearing to a furious Barbara that he hadn't shaved the hair off her Barbie doll's head. "Did so," whined Barbara. "Prove it," said Brad. Deep within the reaches of the house, Stephen yelled at Stephanie to play another song besides "It's my party and I'll cry if I want to"; Lesley Gore had been weeping since I'd walked outside. The more Stephen objected, the louder the music became.

The shouts resounding from the Kings' house made my house seem even more somber by contrast. Following our Chanukah dinner, Bob's health took a turn for the worse. His appetite faded. He lost more weight. A bruise on his ankle refused to heal. Dr. Lock, a specialist in blood disorders at Hollywood Presbyterian, administered a battery of tests and decided to start Bob on a regimen of chlorambucil, a drug that made his mouth so dry, even the briefest exclamations—"That's cool"; "You're kidding"—seemed to crackle with static, like words broadcast from far away.

After Bob began his medication, my mother could always be found on the phone, her movement through the kitchen restricted by a cord that curled from the wall. She sought consolation from Janet, Eve, and Ida; hours were consumed with my mother's questions and the silence that meant they were trying to answer. The telephone cord would go slack and taut, slack and taut, as she went about her routine with the dreamy deliberation of a sleepwalker, scratching grit from the kitchen sink or brushing crumbs from the top of the toaster. Once I saw her frozen in the pose of a woman pouring a cup of coffee, the receiver wedged between her shoulder and her ear, black brew poised at the lip of the pot. "Suppose it doesn't?" she asked at last.

The kitchen remained immaculate, but my mother gave up on her own appearance; the coiffed hair and emerald dress were only for impressing Janet. Her slippers sluffed on linoleum, bathrobe damp from washing the dishes. She still watched "Queen for a Day" while she ironed, but now she watched with a faint indignation, as though no grief dare compete with her own.

Several of my father's cases were pending by the end of December. A land surveyor from Alhambra included the term "malicious snoring" among a long list of annoyances that warranted an end to his ten-year marriage. A Burbank divorcée fought for possession of a beehive in the backyard of her former home. "Stan can have the house," she said. "I want the hive." The Nuñez case was garnering attention from the *Herald-Examiner,* which printed almost every rhymed exchange between my father and Hector's attorney. Even memoranda were immortalized in print: "Let's set a date /

To settle this matter. / The fate of these kids / Couldn't get any sadder." My father composed these poems under the pressure of public scrutiny. One week the *Examiner* would refer to his efforts as "poetic doggerel" and the next as "judicial inspiration." During it all, he must have worried about Bob—the rigors of neither poetry nor law could entirely account for his edginess and preoccupation—but he refused to speculate about the future, except when it came to the outcome of a case.

In those last tropical weeks of winter, Aunt Ida courted Morris Ornstein, a contractor who had installed new sinks in the bathrooms at the Nite Light. "Not just your run-of-the-mill white affairs," Ida told us. "We're talking marble basins with gold veins." Ida expressed her attraction obliquely: "Faucets shaped like swans, I swear! The man can order anything." At the mention of Morris, my aunt became all agitation; she fussed with her turban and collar and cuffs. But when Mother said it sounded like love, Ida swatted the air and let loose with a "Pish."

On the topic of Bob, Aunt Ida was unusually reassuring. One night while she and my mother were clipping coupons from the *Herald,* she insisted there was a perfectly good chance that things would get better once the chlorambucil had a chance to work. What could it hurt to look on the good side? Morrie had a friend who had licked Hodgkin's, she said, and another who was in remission from stomach cancer at this very instant, to the astonishment of those know-nothing doctors.

Before she went home that night, Ida poked her head into my room and caught me scrutinizing my reflection in the darkened window to see if I resembled Bob. "And they say *girls* are vain." She pursed her lips and shook her head. "I cut out some coupons for TV dinners. Did I tell you Morris likes them too? Help your mother out, OK?" Still blushing with embarrassment, I gave a dull nod. She turned to go, then changed her mind. "I'm not saying something strange is going to happen, but if anything does, call me, doll."

As Bob's car rounded the cul-de-sac, Leslie Gore began to wail again, and so did Stephen and Stephanie. I stood up from the steps, brushed off the seat of my pants, opened the door, and leapt inside, afraid to look at my brother directly. The engine revved, and we sped down the street. I fell back into the bucket seat and made the g-force face. "Am I going too fast for you?" my brother asked, stepping on the gas. Bumps in the asphalt caused the car to shimmy. Carob trees flicked past the window. A mailman in shorts sailed by. "No," I said, turning toward Bob. "You're going too slow." The corners of his mouth were chapped. The ashen undertone I'd first noticed the night of the power outage had reappeared beneath his eyes. His skin looked different, thinner, and when he answered back, I could see the apparatus of speech—muscle, tendon, Adam's apple—working within his neck. "Then I guess we'll have to go faster," he said, and floored it toward an intersection, just as the light turned red. I grabbed the dash, pressed a phantom brake, my fear metallic, exhilarating, a knife turned at the last second. The tassel hanging from the rearview mirror rocked back and forth when we lurched to a stop. The Pontiac nosed into the crosswalk, the engine thrumming its low note. A shapely woman wearing orange pedal pushers glided in front of the car. Steady heft of her buttocks and thighs. A taut seam where her pants were halved, like the seam of a peach. Bob ran a pale hand through his hair. "What is it about a shape," he asked, tracking her progress across the street, "that can change the way you breathe?"

It took us longer than usual to get to my father's office. The downtown streets were clogged with cars. Traffic cops blew their whistles, flailed their arms, but no one would be hindered by petty rules. People cascaded over curbs, dodged honking cars, were expelled one by one like gum balls from the revolving doors of banks and department stores.

At the Biscott Building, Sally sat on her stool inside the elevator. An expressionless old woman, her head of white hair was more mist than substance. Sally, it seemed, was a prisoner of the paneled cell, with no idea what year it was, let alone the fact that the year was almost over. My brother asked, "How long have you worked here, Sal?"

"Forever," she said, letting us out on the fifth floor. "Push the button when you want me."

While Bob unlocked the office door, I watched envelopes, mailed from the floors above, drop through a glass shaft that ran down the length of the wall. Message after message fell to earth—a blur of stamps, illegible addresses. "Well?" said Bob, and I followed him inside.

My father was in Westwood on a deposition, and he'd left the office a mess. In the waiting room, pleated paper cups were strewn across the coffee table, along with issues of *Time* and *Life*. Every ashtray overflowed. A camera and a pair of binoculars hung by their straps from the coatrack.

The venetian blinds in the main office had been raised all the way. Shafts of sunlight slanted to the floor, illuminating flurries of dust, precise squares of plush carpet. On my father's desk sat a yellow legal tablet, scrawled with the draft of a poem. And next to that, *A Year of Rhymes*, places saved with scraps of paper. I'd forgotten my father had borrowed the book, and this lapse of memory made me uneasy. I sat in my father's swivel chair—the cushion exhaled under my weight—and studied the glossy cover, an image of a maple tree changing with the seasons. "You can take back your book," said Bob. "Dad wanted me to tell you he's through with it for now." I swiveled around to face my brother. He was leafing through the top drawer of a filing cabinet, lit from behind by a bank of windows, his face in silhouette. "Gotta find the Nuñez file. Then we'll split." Light burned through the sleeve of Bob's shirt, revealing like an X-ray the dark and sorry substance of his uplifted arm. No sound except for manila files scraping against the sides of the drawer, and all

I could think of was my brother's body, the coming to an end of my brother's body, this one thought hushing the world.

All of a sudden dozens of birds, or what I thought were birds, ruffled past the windows. And then there came a second migration, uncanny and fast. Distracted by the flickering light, Bob looked up from the row of files. "What the hell was that?" he asked. We wrenched open a window and stuck our heads outside. The streets beneath us were keening; traffic had come to a standstill, and drivers jabbed at their horns. Pedestrians stopped, heads tilted back, shielding their eyes. The clock on top of the Imperial Savings Bank struck five. "Look out," came a cry from the floor above us. Peering up, we could see beneath the breasts and chins of two women who were laughing wildly and hurling sheets of paper out the window. *"May old acquaintance be forgot,"* one of them sang as paper rained down. She waved to my brother, one finger at a time. "Room 610, if you're interested. We got schnapps and beer. The kid can come too."

"You're with Satacoy?" asked Bob.

"Not *with* him," said the woman. "I *work* for him."

My brother laughed. "That's what I meant."

The sky was dimming, streaked with shades of pink and gray, swirling with fat confetti. I held out my hand, uncertainly, like someone feeling for rain, and plucked a piece of paper from the air. On it was a date in bold red letters, APRIL 10, and a list in pencil: *Call Rich Farley re council budget. Lunch with Dell, 12:30. Folding chairs.* Another landed on the windowsill. JUNE 26: *Who has key to Rusty's apartment? Make dupe.* High above the city, thrust from windows all around us, countless dates went flying by, innumerable things to do. Spent weeks. Spent months. A year sifting down like dust. Men and women leaned from windows, raised paper cups and improvised toasts, eager for a chance to fling handfuls of scrap into the ringing aisles of air between tall buildings.

Bob grabbed the calendar from my father's desk; he yanked off pages and cast them away. They tumbled unpredictably, merged with a hundred other memos. "You gotta try it," he said. He held out the calendar in both hands, like Aunt Ida offering hard candies from a crystal dish—Have a taste. Live a little. I grabbed a clump of December and lobbed it into the air. Written in my father's script, errands and names and telephone numbers rose on a sudden updraft, then scattered toward the pavement below. We passed the calendar back and forth, taking turns. It felt good to stand so close to the edge, to jettison bits of history in the company of my brother.

"Watch this," said Bob. He tore off the few remaining days and crumpled them into balls. After lining them up on the windowsill, he crouched down, cried, "Bombs away," and flicked them into the street. When I asked Bob if we could get arrested for what we were doing, he said, "Arrested? Arrested for what? Reckless paper dropping? Take a look out the window. Everyone's gone nuts. For the next few minutes, nothing matters."

Horns and voices swelled in the street. Makeshift confetti fell from windows all around us, a blizzard of unburdening. "What now?" asked Bob. His eyes glistened like wet ink. I looked around the room, swept *A Year of Rhymes* off the desk, and began to rip out its pages. Summer, fall, winter, spring—the pages were thick and loud. The guilt I felt at ruining Ida's gift only fed my sense of abandon. "Brilliant," said Bob, and he held out his hand.

We fashioned a fleet of paper planes in no time flat. The maple leaf plane. The plane of green grass. The plane of rain and lightning. Along with illustrations, each had a poem emblazoned on its body, stanzas folded at odd angles, rhymes by Blake and Frost and Yeats. "Ready?" said Bob. He stood up, held on to the cord that controlled the blinds. When he leaned out the window to launch his first plane, the blinds clacked, rising higher. "Be careful," I said, and I barred his chest with my arm, just as my brother did with me when the Pontiac came to a sudden stop. Contact with my brother's bones, our perilous height, made me dizzy. Gusts of wind drummed in my ears. The brick wall of the Biscott Building plunged toward the street in red perspective. Bob hovered over the window ledge, yelped as his airplane dipped and zigzagged and disappeared. I watched it and thought about Aunt Ida wanting to rhyme the world into sense, how she emphasized the ends of the lines, hard as bars on a cage. "Summer is ending, Fall arrives. / We lose a season out of our lives . . ." "Oh, lonely trees as white as wool / That midnight makes so beautiful. . . ." We released those poems and a dozen others.

When we lost interest in paper planes, I slid from beneath my father's desk an oval wastebasket, brimming with trash. "You wouldn't," said Bob.

I stared at him, walked back to the window.

"No kidding. You could hurt somebody."

I held the wastebasket out the window at arms' length. "Nothing matters. You said so yourself."

"Listen, Burt, a penny tossed off the Empire State Building can kill someone on the street. Imagine what a wastebasket dropped from the fifth floor could do." If Bob meant this to be a warning, he should have tried to hide his excitement.

I pretended to almost lose my grip.

"Put it back. Now."

Little by little, I tilted the basket. Light glinted off the rim. Shreds of carbon paper blew off the top. Both Bob and I were amazed at my knack for inventing menace.

"Mr. Satacoy, come here, quick. Get a load of this."

When I looked up to find the source of the voice, Bob pulled me inside by the back of my shirt and tried to wrestle the wastebasket out of my hands. We tugged with all our strength in opposite directions, the bright debris of foil gum wrappers and paper clips spilling to the floor. We bantered lame and breathless threats: "You'll be sorry." "No, *you'll* be sorry." We stirred up sunlit motes of dust. And then a streak of my brother's blood seeped from his gums and coated his teeth. Bob must have felt it, must have sensed the fibers of flesh giving way. The salty warmth, the rich, unreasonable taste of blood must have dawned on him slowly. We froze, each mirroring the other's alarm. The oval wastebasket fell to the floor. My brother probed his mouth with a finger and drew it out, smeared with blood. He barred his teeth, asked where the blood was coming from. I moved closer, could hear his heart kicking with each exhalation. Thin ribbons of blood coated my brother's tongue, pooled on the rim of his lips, obscured the gold in his molars. "It's stopping," I said, though I couldn't be sure. My legs were shaking. I closed my eyes.

When I opened them, Bob was in the swivel chair. "If I sit," he whispered. He kept his mouth open, letting in air, hoping, it seemed, to dry the blood like paint. He swallowed carefully, self-consciously, as if he were just learning how. Arms on the armrests. Legs on the floor. A terrified man with perfect posture. Now and then he'd feel for blood, the traces growing more and more faint. Evening light dimmed in the windows. The clamor of horns began to subside. The shadows of straggling memos fluttered across the walls.

We must have stayed in my father's office longer than I thought. Sally shook the white nimbus of her head and remarked that we were the last to leave and it was lucky we hadn't slipped her mind entirely. She didn't seem to notice that my brother, still afraid to move too fast, stood rigid and silent during our descent, staring at the numbered floors rising through the wire mesh. Landing with a bounce in the lobby, Sally yanked open the elevator door with a surprising show of strength and said, "See you next year."

The pavement was a mosaic of numbered calendar pages, torn typewriter paper, handbills, and mimeographs, some of them smudged with footprints. Refuse covered awnings, lay in gutters, blew through alleys. Despite the evidence of mayhem, Alvarado was practically deserted; all the pedestrians had hurried home, emptied the parking lots, boarded buses. One man in a jeweler's apron swept up the sidewalk in front of a watch repair shop.

Wan and dazed, my brother walked slowly, arms at his sides. I was about to mention that he'd forgotten the Nuñez file but sensed it might hurt him to be reminded. On the way back to the car, I gathered up dozens of dates from the pavement in case Brad didn't believe the story of my trip downtown, a story I was already busy embellishing; in the revised version, it was my brother's nose that bled from sheer altitude after we'd flung reams of paper from the roof of a skyscraper, and all it took was the momentary pressure of a handkerchief to make him better.

"Don't tell anyone what happened," said Bob, revving the engine. "I don't want anyone to find out. Except Janet. Janet will know what to do." He checked his mouth in the rearview mirror. "Besides, it's stopped. There's nothing to tell."

Immense clouds drifted above the Hollywood hills. Driving west on Third, we watched the sky's unstable architecture— arches and bridges and broad domes—glowing with the last of daylight, dwarfing the houses and canyons below, as if mocking our dark and solid city.

Half a block from home, I could see my mother pacing back and forth inside a square of light. She appeared more animated than usual and was opening and closing kitchen cabinets with pleasure and purpose. While Bob idled the car in the driveway, I gathered up the memos I'd carried in my lap. And then, as if waiting to be dismissed, I continued to sit. "Do you worry?" he asked. "About me, I mean."

If I said I didn't, I was afraid he might think me unconcerned or, worse, too young to understand the gravity of his disease. And if I said I did, it might imply that I expected the worst. The Pontiac shuddered. I weighed the prospects of yes and no.

"Well," said Bob, "if you do, don't. Let me do the worrying."

I shuffled dates like a deck of cards.

"I didn't mean to do this. This isn't something I meant to do." Bob wouldn't let me leave until I said I understood. And so I said I did. "Janet's at home." He told me this, it seemed, for his own reassurance more than mine. He pulled out of the driveway, searching for a station, and the air echoed with broken bits of song.

At the back door, I was greeted by my mother, who rushed in front of me, blocking my view of the kitchen, anticipating my move to the right, to the left. Holding me back by the shoulders, she looked over my head and into the night. "Shoot," she said when she saw that Bob had gone. "Guess what," Mother asked me. "Or should I say 'who'?" Without waiting for an answer, she cinched her robe and moved to one side.

In the middle of the kitchen, blue teardrops as big as dinner plates turned in aimless circles, along with play money in two-dollar denominations. Suspended within this lazy maelstrom were pictures of household appliances—stove, vacuum cleaner, toaster—spinning in different directions. Among them hovered a photograph of a tiara, actual rhinestones pasted to the peaks. And peering out from the vortex of all these floating objects was the face of Jack Bailey, happy, rotund, with rhinestones for eyes.

"I call it 'Long Live the Queen,' " said Marion. She threw back her head and laughed, disrupting the delicate balance of wire coat hangers and fishing line. Tears wobbled. The tiara sparkled. Money spun out of control. She hung the mobile from the knob of a kitchen cabinet, being careful not to let it get tangled. "I made it for your mother. And for women like her."

"So where's the queen?" asked my mother.

"There *is* no queen. That's the whole point."

"It's a statement," said Mother, a little uncertain. She gazed at the mobile, leaned against the sink.

Marion had gained weight. More voluptuous than ever, she molded a pair of denim jeans; her breasts stretched the front of a man's dress shirt, which was stained with paint. She wore less makeup than I remembered, the subtleties of her face only emphasizing her body's dimensions and presence. What is it about a shape, I thought, that can change the way you breathe? Drawn by my obvious admiration, Marion walked over and stroked my cheek. The scent of My Sin had been replaced by a vague aura of turpentine. "I have to clip them every week," she said when I noticed her fingernails. "Or else I can't work."

"At Hallmark?" asked Mother, rummaging for something to serve, head in the Frigidaire.

"That's just a job. This," said Marion, pointing to the mobile, "this is work. I've been obsessed with these things. Try to finish at least one a week. I want each one to be different than the one before. Repetition is rot. That's my motto. Or it was last week." Marion looked quizzically at the memos I'd been clutching, and when I handed them to her, she read every one, checking both sides. "These are incredible," she said when she finished. "The more you get done, the more there is to do. It's fruitless. And beautiful. Mind if I use them?"

SPRING

Marion had stayed in our dining room for over an hour on New Year's Eve, dunking her tea bag in a cup of hot water and telling my mother and me about an exhibit of abstract expressionism at the Los Angeles County Museum of Art. "The Jackson Pollocks are not to be believed. I'd only seen them in reproduction. Face-to-face is another story. Those paintings talk back. They're big and rude. They keep complaining even after you leave them." My mother had set a plate of *mandel brot* on the table, and Marion, to my surprise, ate the cookies greedily, crumbs dusting the corners of her lips. "Franz Kline, Helen Frankenthaler, Clyfford Still—seeing all that stuff made me more determined than ever. It takes years of work and concentration to find a style and make your mark." Marion held up her cup of tea—"You've got to steep in the chaos of your thoughts"—then set it, satisfied, back in the saucer.

"Why invite chaos, of all things?" said Mother. She stared at her hands, rubbed her knuckles.

"You know what I think, Sylvia? I think you're too timid. You ought to get out of the house more often." In the same haunted voice that Aunt Ida used to recite poems, Marion chanted, "Walls to the left of me. Walls to the right of me." Then her voice returned to normal. "Why don't we make a resolution to see a movie sometime soon. Whichever one you want; you call the shots. Burt can come too. Our official escort."

"Can we?" I asked.

"It's been ages," said Mother.

Marion said, "Movies talk now, you know."

I sensed my mother had just about given up on finding the right moment to tell Marion that Bob was sick. "Can I get you anything else to eat?"

Marion puffed out her cheeks to make herself look stuffed. When Mother didn't react, Marion said, "Get out the muzzle; I'm talking too much. Is something the matter?"

My mother's face grew tight as a fist. "Maybe you've heard. Robert got married."

A quick intake of breath. "Marriage," said Marion. "I'm so sorry."

"That's not . . . it's not that he's married. The problem is—this is hard for me, honey—Robert isn't well. It seems he's come down with leukemia."

Seems. The word lingered. Provisional. A trapdoor.

"Shit," whispered Marion. She wiped her mouth with the back of her hand. My mother went on to explain the details. Inexplicable bruises. Thinning limbs. She spoke slowly, with little emotion, unwilling to slant her story with either hope or despair. The news diminished Marion. Her posture wilted. She listened without comment to the litany of symptoms, absently twisting her teacup as if screwing it into the saucer. For a moment I was Marion, remembering the heat of my brother's breath.

The longer my mother talked, the smaller the room became. Our dark yard pressed against the glass. The chandelier cast a net of shadows. I stared at a spot on the tablecloth, a pale trace of methylene blue.

When Mother was finished, the three of us sat in silence for a while. A party had started somewhere down the block; waves of chatter lapped at our house. Marion was shaken, but preferred to say nothing rather than resort to some cliché. Clichés, however, were what my mother wanted, and she was visibly disappointed when Marion didn't offer up the kind of phrase that came easily from Eve and Ida: *Let's hope for the best. It's in the hands of God. It doesn't do any good to worry.* Marion said, "I'd like to see him." And that was all.

On New Year's Day, my mother, still in her bathrobe, came into my room, holding Marion's mobile at arm's length. "I can't find a place to hang it," she said. "My arm's getting tired." She held the back of the swivel chair as I took down my model bomber and hoisted the mobile toward a hook on the ceiling. From a distance of inches, I could see tiny bubbles of air trapped beneath the surface of the photographs, white beads of dried glue oozing from their edges. Once I jumped down, the imperfections vanished. My mother folded her arms, gazed up at *Long Live the Queen.* Creases formed at the back of her neck. Her bathrobe gave off a musty smell, dank and human, like sadness itself. The cutout of a vacuum cleaner, spinning like a small tornado, was eclipsed for an instant by the passing stove. "It's like trying to clean house in a bad dream. Nothing goes the way you want. She's right," Mother added under her breath. "I ought to get out."

On a Saturday in mid-January, my mother decided to take Marion up on her offer. The house was spotless, and so she'd spent that morning inventing useless chores. I walked into the kitchen, found her plucking cans from the cupboard and wiping the tops with a damp cloth. When she held a bunch of ripe bananas under the tap, I asked her why she had to wash them. "Insecticide. They spray the skin with insecticide. You don't want to eat insecticide, do you?"

"But you peel them," I protested.

"With what?" she asked, water splattering over her arms. "You peel them with your fingers, right? You want to walk around with poison fingers? I know *I* don't. I'm doing it for his protection," she pleaded as though to a third party who saw her indisputable virtue, "and all I get is questions." My mother roughly blotted the bananas, threw the damp towel into the hamper, opened a drawer and removed a new one, watching me watch her all the while. "You're getting a little cranky," she said, "cooped up in this beautiful weather." That's when she dialed Marion and suggested a matinee for the sake of her restless son.

I could hear Marion's faint plans filtering through the telephone. She thought this was a perfect excuse to visit with Bob. She'd surprise him with a call, invite him along. She was eager for us to see her new apartment. We'd decide which movie to go to when we got there.

By eleven-thirty, Bob and I and my mother were scanning the streets of Glendale for Marion's address. Trees lined the tidy residential streets, the apartment buildings and bungalow courts painted in hues of sherbet. Mother couldn't read while the car was in motion; Bob had to stop the Pontiac while she huddled in the back seat and squinted at a scrap of paper on which she'd written slapdash directions. Idling at the curb made my brother impatient; he traced the shape of the steering wheel, checked his hair in the rearview mirror. He must have been stunned when he'd picked up the phone and heard Marion Hirsch saying his name. I'd imagined their reunion a dozen times. My brother enticed by the shadows on her shirt, by the sight of her skin. In Marion's presence, his desire is revived. She takes a step closer, says he looks the same, and countless small mistakes are erased in the blind tunnels of my brother's veins.

"So?" said Bob.

"I'm sure it's left on Arden," said Mother. "Or maybe it's Marvin. Let's look for them both."

"Marvin is a street in Monopoly," I said.

"Where's Monopoly?" my mother asked.

Bob said, "He means the game," and merged with passing traffic.

"I know what he means," my mother lied. "Watch where you're going."

I stuck my arm out the window and let the wind inflate my shirt, a boy cupped in a bucket seat, big and airy with expectation.

Marion lived in a modern building. Part of the stuccoed second floor was cantilevered over a carport, empty except for puddles of oil and a bald tire propped against a post. We climbed the stairs to the balcony—Bob had to stop and rest at the top—walked past rows of sky-blue doors and oblong aluminum windows. An intermittent hiss came from inside Marion's apartment. "What's she up to?" muttered my brother. He knocked on the door and I held my breath, just as I sometimes did at night when, motionless, buried under blankets, I tried to feel what death was like. Three seconds. Four. The door swung open, and Marion was there, gripping a can of silver spray paint, her index finger still on the nozzle. I inhaled the pungent haze that shrouded the room behind her. "Bobby," she squealed. When she threw her arms around my brother's neck, the can of spray paint rattled. She pulled away, held him by the shoulders, embarrassed him with her frank, appraising glance. "You look," she whispered into his ear, "almost like a different person."

Bob wrenched himself from Marion's grip. "You always know the right thing to say. Just like old times. Leave it to you."

"What's wrong?" said my mother. "What are you two saying?"

My brother glowered at Marion. "You think I don't know how much I've changed? Here," he said, lifting his arms. "I barely know my own hands. My bones are showing. My clothes are too big. You don't need to point it out. No kidding, Marion. You don't need to remind me."

"You know me; I say what I see. Don't be angry."

"I'm sick of being sick," Bob continued, enunciating every word with bitter precision. "I want myself back. That's all I want. But I can't have that, can I?" He struck the metal railing with his fist, and the balcony hummed beneath our feet. "Tell me what I'm supposed to do."

Marion mumbled, "I wish I knew."

"You're supposed to . . . ," I said—heard myself saying—and I almost knew what words came next. Bob and my mother and Marion were startled. They turned to face me. I said it again, on the verge of advice. I felt as if I were talking in my sleep, fitful and hot and cinched in my skin. The sunlight stung but couldn't wake me. What could I say that would save my brother? The glaring world seemed to wait for an answer: the pitched roofs, the brown mountains.

Marion said, "You're supposed to come inside. That's what you're all supposed to do." She rested her hand on my back and began to guide me through the portal, when she suddenly changed her mind. "Hold it," she said. "I almost forgot." Marion closed the door behind her, left us bewildered on the balcony.

"What now?" grumbled Bob. "Do I knock again?"

"Give me a minute," called Marion. "Where's your sense of adventure?" The drone of a fan nearly drowned out her voice.

Mother turned to Bob and whispered, "Are you all right?"

"Of course I'm not. Why won't anyone say it? I'm going to die."

My mother gasped.

I told my brother he shouldn't say that.

"Sorry, pal. It's already said."

"I'm ready," Marion sang from inside the apartment. "Enter at your own risk. Well?" she asked, to hurry us along.

Up until that moment, I thought I'd been in a lot of strange places: the dim labyrinth of the Kings' house, with its aluminum foil curtains and scattered toys; the waiting room of my father's office, with its chilly Naugahyde chairs and out-dated issues of *Life;* our rumpus room, with its bamboo stools and a hula dancer whose wooden breasts were tipped with luminous nipples. But no place I'd ever been to had prepared me for Marion's notion of home.

Scraps of photographs and snippets of thread were embed-ded in the shag carpet. A butterfly chair, bright red, begged for attention. It was the only piece of furniture besides a drafting table piled with sketchbooks, templates, and trian-gles. In the center of the living room, a bulging cardboard box contained household objects—a dented colander, a linen bed sheet bunched in a ball, an emerald can of Comet cleanser—artifacts of conventional living, should Marion de-cide on the spur of the moment to lead a conventional life. Every wall was pocked with holes. Pushpins held up handbills for lost cats and dogs, an assortment of matchbooks from exotic restaurants, and the remnants of what appeared to be a ripped-up Dixie cup. Marion had scavenged the city for this collection of refuse, tacking it to her living room walls instead of the usual decoration: seascapes and mirrors and needlepoints of aphorisms. Minor, discarded, forgotten things were destined to find an orbit in one of Marion's mobiles.

Next to the door, an electric fan pivoted back and forth. Every few seconds, blasted by wind, the contents of the walls fluttered wildly, as though in a desperate effort to escape. Even the canvas butterfly chair writhed and rippled like some-thing alive. Marion's black hair flapped above her shoulders, and she had to holler in order to be heard. "Does it look familiar?" she asked me, nodding toward the far end of the room, where one of her mobiles whirled in a circle. "The fan gives it the full effect." The insistent force of the fan at my back impelled me a few steps closer. It took me a minute to recognize, among wire hangers and dancing scraps, the

memos I'd given Marion. *Call Rich Farley. Folding Chairs.*
Dates darted by like timid fish. My mother and brother moved
closer too. Bob reached out and caught between his thumb
and index finger one of several dangling leaves that seemed
to glow with their own light. "Have you ever seen a more
incredible green?" shouted Marion. "I got them from a
ginkgo down the street. Ginkgo trees can pollinate them-
selves. They don't need another tree to reproduce. Isn't that
something? Don't you just love that? They're out of this
world, and completely self-sufficient." Mother asked if Mar-
ion had to water the mobile. "Absolutely not. I want the
leaves to die." My brother asked why. Marion stroked her
throat, paused to find the right words. "Days fly by. Fading
leaves. Those are the facts, and art should reflect them. It's
pretty ambitious, if I do say so myself."

My brother let go of the ginkgo leaf, and the mobile re-
sumed its revolutions. He remarked on the skill with which
Marion had calibrated the balance. It was, he agreed, in-
credible, ambitious.

With every pass of the fan, Bob's clothes trembled against
him and betrayed the brittle figure beneath. Marion was right;
I could see it myself: he almost looked like a different person.
Whatever affinities I had once been able to find between me
and my brother—the shared tint in our eyes and hair, the
rhyme in our laughter or manner or voice—seemed at that
moment to blow away, to scatter out of reach.

Bob watched the funnel of paper and leaves until the wind-
blown motion became too much. Then he gazed into the
center of the mobile as though into the quiet eye of a storm.
He told Marion that he'd missed her. Really. And apologized
for getting so mad.

"So you barked a little. It's good to bark." She switched
off the fan. The walls calmed. The mobile slowed. My brother
surfaced from the blank of his trance, willing to begin our
visit again. Where, he wanted to know, were we going?

It was decided that I would be the one to choose the movie, which wasn't easy since Marion had used that day's *Herald* as a drop cloth on which to spray-paint half a dozen plastic spoons. It didn't seem to upset her that strands of the carpet had been frosted forever with silver paint. She removed the spoons from the newspaper and placed them on the drafting table. "I'm interested in doing something about food," she said, handing me the sticky, metallic pages. "Besides eating it, I mean. I thought of using real spoons, but they'd sort of, you know, bog a mobile down, like anchors on a canary."

I sat cross-legged on the carpet, searching through the paper, silently debating among *The Parent Trap, The Time Machine,* and *Love With the Proper Stranger.* Marion and Bob and my mother hovered above me, sipping cups of instant coffee. "I'd never be able to get out of it," said my mother when Marion asked if she wouldn't be more comfortable in the butterfly chair.

"That would make us roommates, right?" Marion's laughter was breathy, abundant. She talked about how happy she was to be on her own. Her room at home, she said, still contained the canopy bed from her girlhood. "With ruffles," she added sarcastically. Mrs. Hirsch had insisted that the bed be moved to the new apartment, but Marion flatly refused. "The whole idea was to start from scratch. You can't start from scratch with a canopy bed." Marion shook her head and rubbed a fleck of paint off her nail. "Sometimes I wonder if my mom even knows me."

"I'm sure she understands you better than you think," countered my mother, as if in defense of her own powers of empathy rather than those of Mrs. Hirsch.

Marion was still lamenting her strained relationship with her parents as we drove over the hill toward Hollywood. Rocky embankments bordered the road. The sky was white, opaque, immense. " 'Oils or pastels?' That's what my folks ask me every time I tell them I'm making art." She pried off her shoes and scrunched down in the front seat. Bare feet propped on the dash, Marion flexed her toes as she talked. Her hair hung over the back of the seat, and I had to resist the urge to touch it. "It's not that I expect every Tom, Dick, and Harry to love what I'm up to, but parents ought to make an effort, don't you think?" My mother nodded. "Ought to make an effort," she echoed. Bob said, "You've become quite a talker," and wanted to know how that had happened. "Why, sir," protested Marion in a fey Southern accent, "it's not me. It's the coffee talkin'. Besides," she continued, herself again, "who's going to do the talking for me? I want to be heard, that's all there is to it." Our car hurdled the crest of the hill, and I felt my insides lift and give, the bright day like a tossed coin.

Marion interrogated Bob about his marriage the entire length of Hollywood Boulevard. "So you'd describe Janet as practical?"

"Very."

"She's a practical nurse," my mother piped in.

"No ruffles on your bed?"

"Not one ruffle."

"She doesn't have a frilly side?"

"She doesn't require bouquets every day, if that's what you're after."

"I guess what I'm asking is would we get along?"

"Hard to say."

"She does the dishes and laundry, I suppose?"

"Like a dream," offered Mother.

"Marion," my brother warned, "don't get on your high horse. She helps me out. Is that so bad?"

I pictured a horse with soaring legs, Marion stranded on its lofty saddle. "She *wants* to clean," Marion concluded. "She wants to strike a blow for order; that's the distinct impression I'm getting. Listen, you're lucky. And she's lucky too. To have an appreciative guy like you. Sorry she had to work today. I wanted to meet her. She sounds OK. And the main thing is, you love her, right?"

"I do," said my brother.

Marion slapped her hands against her thighs. "I now pronounce you man and wife." And the matter of his union was approved.

It would be years before I understood how carefully Marion, for all her abandon, had asked about Janet—with enough curiosity to demonstrate her concern and enough detachment to assure us that she harbored no jealousy. And my brother may have glossed his marriage for Marion's sake, to prove he could get along without her, to try out the boast of a happy life. That springlike day, however, I was mostly aware of their volleyed conversation, of warm air billowing into the car. Terrazzo stars on the pavement flew past, and shop windows crowded with toys and wigs and mannequins modeling lingerie, hard arms hooked to their hips or twisted into malicious salutes.

We arrived at Grauman's Chinese Theater twenty minutes before the movie was supposed to start. In all the years she and my father had lived in Hollywood, Mother had never been to Grauman's. "I'm here," she said, hugging herself. "I can't believe it." She waved away Marion's offer of money. "I'll treat," she insisted. "Not another word about it." She stood in line and spoke close to the hole in the glass facade of the ticket booth, a small pagoda. "It must be fun to work here," she said to a boy whose pimply face and too-tight blazer should have told her otherwise. He managed a vague and insincere grin, tore off four tickets, and bellowed, "Next." His disposition didn't affect her. That day Mother was determined to have fun, to enjoy her parole from the spotless kitchen. After giving us each our ticket, she purchased a "Footprint Location Guide" from the souvenir shop and proceeded to wander through the crowded courtyard, finally ending up frozen with awe at the sight of Greer Garson's dainty indentations.

Bob explored the slabs of cement without the aid of a printed guide. Neck bent, hands clasped behind him, he stepped into the footprints of Kirk Douglas, Humphrey Bogart, and Alan Ladd. A look of contentment seized him if he fit, as though he had eased through the skin of his own life and stepped into the life of another man.

Marion had discovered near the theater doors a machine that looked like a jukebox, its top a glass dome. From across the courtyard, I watched her jam a coin into the slot, lean forward, and wait to see what happened. I arrived by her side in time to catch the two halves of a metal mold compressing together, then pulling apart. A plastic statuette of Buddha thumped into a trough at the side of the machine. "Still hot," she marveled, scooping it out, "like a bun from the oven." She checked its heft in the palm of her hand. "Nice and light. It must be hollow." She handed it to me and searched in her pockets for spare change. "I have to have more. These'll be perfect. For what, I don't know. But someday I will."

An usher swung open the double doors—a salty wafting of popcorn, a glimpse of the lacquered lobby. The people on the patio began to chatter and form a line. I told Marion to hurry, but she had several quarters and meant to use every one. She handed me another Buddha, the plastic warm and slightly pliant. Bob and my mother were carried past me by the stream of people. Meet you inside, my mother mouthed. "Come on," I whined to Marion. "We'll miss the beginning."

"Go ahead. I'll find you later."

The usherette had to pluck the ticket from my shirt pocket; I held a statuette in each hand. Dragons were woven into the carpet, rearing back on their hind legs. Lanterns with wrought-iron decoration hung from the ceiling like stalactites. A mural of a Chinese landscape stretched behind the concession stand, it's hard-edged trees like nothing seen on earth. I searched for the drinking fountain, found it hidden in a vestibule, and gulped an icy arc of water. At the end of a long hallway stood a gigantic glass case in which three life-size Chinese women surrounded the figure of actress Rhonda Fleming. I couldn't stop staring. Inert and alive at the same time, she was seated on a velvet chair, radiating waxy glamour.

The movie had begun by the time I made it inside the theater. I walked up and down the aisles, hoping to spot Bob, wondering if he'd saved me a seat. Darkness made every face look the same, small and round and awash with amazement. Even after my eyes adjusted, I groped through the void and held cooling Buddhas for ballast. Stopping now and then, I'd squint to force a person into focus, taste my mistake, turn and move on. At last I gave up, plunged into an empty seat, and tried to concentrate on the movie. Rod Taylor barreled through time in a machine as ornate as the lanterns in the lobby. During vivid surges of history, a London neighborhood changed around him: the skyline rose, modes of transportation quickened, women's hemlines blinked up and down. Then something went wrong. The machine began to buck and shudder and erupt with sparks. Rod Taylor, glazed with sweat, loosened his collar, gritted his teeth, tried to get a grip on the throttle. Time spun on the odometer. The future became a haze of gray numbers. Years rose like smoke.

At a red light, Bob let go of the steering wheel and drew back his sleeve. He stared without expression at the veins in his wrist, at the wristbone showing like a frail egg. The blare of a horn behind us woke him to the road. Only minutes later, at another red light, he fooled with the angle of the rearview mirror, raised his lip, and studied his gums. My brother was beyond embarrassment; he never looked over to check my reaction. Bathed by clear, uncompromising light, he searched for clues to his own decay. Like serving a subpoena or trailing a lunch truck, dying had become another job that required his patience and concentration.

I settled back in the bucket seat and tried to ignore him, to allow him the illusion of privacy, but the intensity of his self-examination, his obliviousness to everything except the facts of his physical condition, made him all the more compelling. When he ran his tongue across his teeth, I felt slick ridges. Felt tendons stretch when he flexed his fingers. Dark relief when he blinked.

We pulled into the parking lot of the Rexall pharmacy.

Bob cut the engine, then bent over me to rummage through the glove compartment for loose change. I noticed his scalp, shiny and pale as the belly of a fish, through thinning hair. He exuded a strange and sour odor. The heat of him, falling like sunlight in my lap, filled me with excitement, revulsion, and pity. I could only nod *no* when he asked if I wanted to come inside. My brother shrugged. "Suit yourself." Then he vanished through the pharmacy doors, twin panes of smoked glass. His presence lingered after he was gone. Touching his seat to see if it was warm, I wondered if ghosts were traces of heat the dead leave behind.

In a vacant lot across the street, oil derricks bobbed up and down as though in endless assent to a question. An occasional cloud drifted overhead—a capsized hat, a loaf of bread. People pushed through the pharmacy doors, and it seemed inconceivable that they each possessed a history, saw the world from a different angle, led lives that had nothing to do with my brother. How was it possible that his frailty didn't disrupt the world? The scuttling clouds, the tireless derricks, the rush of people, turned somehow insulting.

Bob had taken the car keys, so I couldn't turn on the radio. I batted at the tassel on the rearview mirror. It spun and exploded with motes of dust. No matter how often I shifted in my seat, I couldn't get comfortable. Time began to stretch and sag. I pushed a button, and the glove compartment popped open. A couple of unpaid parking tickets were stuffed inside, along with Bob's ledger. From the bottom of the glove compartment I fished out a small leather folder. It contained a card from the Department of Professional and Vocational Standards, certifying my brother as a private investigator. And tucked behind that, as intricately decorated as a dollar bill, was a license, issued on January 2, 1962, and signed by the chief of police, entitling my brother to carry a concealed firearm. No detective show on television, no volume of the Hardy Boys, had prepared me for the possibility that my own brother might carry a pistol. It never occurred to me that his job involved any danger greater than missing an incriminating snapshot of some adulterer or finding that a wily spouse, delinquent on his alimony and due a summons to appear in court, refused to answer the door.

NAME OF MANUFACTURER: Smith & Wesson; SERIAL NUMBER OF WEAPON: 2149; CALIBER: .38. Reflexively, I tried to memorize the numbers: *You run for time; pretty late.* And then it dawned on me that the gun might be hidden somewhere inside the car. "If I was a gun," I could hear Aunt Ida say, "where would I be?" A further search of the glove compartment yielded nothing but a pack of Wrigley's gum, the sticks gone soft from weeks of heat. Groping beneath the seats, I braced for contact, inventing an account of the gun's discovery that was sure to pique Brad's awe and envy. *Thirty-eight caliber,* I heard myself telling him, octaves lower than usual, *right there under the seat.* But my brother returned, white paper bag in hand, before I had the chance to conduct a thorough search.

As soon as he sat down, Bob dumped the contents of the bag—three amber vials—into his lap. Pills rattled like rain.

"Have you ever been in really bad trouble?" I asked him.

"What do you call this?" he said, lifting his arm to indicate the pills, his lap, the pharmacy. He picked up a vial and read the label.

"Have you ever had to shoot somebody?"

He looked at me blankly.

"Have you?"

"Of course not."

"With your gun."

"Oh," he said. "I see." He scooped his medication back into the bag, shoved it into the glove compartment. "I'm licensed to carry a gun for business."

"But have you ever had to use it?"

"Never."

"Would you?"

He turned the ignition. The Pontiac shuddered, rumbled to life. "Depends on the circumstances. I mean, if someone tried to jump me or something. In the leg, maybe. Say *they* had a gun." My brother grew edgy with justifications. "What would *you* do?"

"Shoot," I said uncertainly, and pictured a single drop of blood congealing under my microscope. "Where is it?"

"Why?"

"I just want to know. Are you wearing it?"

"You *wear* a hat; a gun you carry." We turned onto Beverly Boulevard.

"Do you keep it loaded?"

"With the safety on. That's rule number one."

"Is it in the car?"

"Could be," he said, smiling in spite of himself. "It's dangerous. Believe me, you hold that thing in your hand and . . . There's no fun in it, is what I'm saying."

"I don't have to hold it. I just want to see it." This was not entirely true. I wanted to press its deadly potential into my palm. The more elusive my brother became, the more clearly I forged in my mind the metal handle, the resistance of the trigger, the sight blade rising at the end of the barrel. "Just tell me where you keep it. You don't even have to show it to me."

Bob shook his head.

"Come on."

"Let me spell it for you: *N-O*."

"I swear I won't tell anybody. Please."

"Did you say something? Your lips were moving, but I couldn't hear you."

I cupped my hands around my mouth and yelled, inches away from his ear: "Tell me where you keep it!"

Bob didn't flinch. "What was that sound? There must be a fly trapped in here."

My throat ached. "You stink," I said.

Bob kept quiet for a moment. "It's the medication. It changes the way I smell. My mouth tastes different. Even my tears."

"I was just—"

"And dreams; dreams are the worst. Dozens of people every night. People I haven't thought about in years. Each of them has something to say. They tell me a secret or whisper a warning, and I always think I'll remember what they've said when I wake up, that I have to remember what they've said, because it's so important. But I never do. And that's not counting the bit players, people in windows and people on the streets, people I think I should recognize but don't. They wave and shout and all talk at once. By the time I wake up, I'm so tired from trying to figure it all out, I'm ready to go back to sleep. Dr. Lock says I'll get used to it, that my body will adjust. Bad dreams, he says, are a side effect of busulphan. But my body won't adjust. I know it."

"I just meant—"

"I know what you meant. I'm calling a spade a spade, is all. I'm telling what there is to tell."

We drove through a residential district, the broad and empty boulevard refuting my brother's dreams. A yawning man, perched in the cab of a street sweeper, left wet gutters in his wake. Near Fairfax Avenue, a small group of Orthodox Jews hurried toward temple. Dark suits emphasized their pallor and set them apart from Jews like my parents, Jews whose belief was amateur, infrequent, a lofty excuse for food and drink. The men talked among themselves and seemed to hold some secret, as mysterious as my brother's illness, behind their intent expressions.

"Janet has it," said my brother.

I looked at him, puzzled.

"The gun. She works around hurt all day and said the idea of a gun didn't sit right. She put down her foot. Couldn't stand knowing I had something lethal. So I couldn't tell you where it was if I wanted."

"Oh, sure," I said, surreptitiously patting the space between my seat and the door. A wad of crumpled cellophane. A ballpoint pen.

"No kidding. She wrapped it up in one of her hankies— the one that says 'Monday'—and put it away for safekeeping." Bob let out a hoarse laugh. "Marion would plotz if she knew."

"Knew that Janet took the gun?"

"Had a hankie embroidered with 'Monday.' "

Then I touched what I thought was a muzzle lodged in a trough by the side of my seat. I tightened my grip, tried to lift the gun from the floor. It was heavy, cold, recalcitrant. Next thing I knew, I shot backward without any warning. Blood rushed to my fingers and face. I heard a hiss like bubbles in soda, all thought squeezed from consciousness. I saw my brother—talking still, unaware at the wheel—in a splinter of vision. For one sorry, distended second, gravity no longer obtained. The car, with its load of rubber and chrome, had someplace to go and was leaving me behind.

I'd yanked the seat release just as Bob, trying to pass a sluggish bus, pressed the accelerator. My seat flew back a good two feet and jolted to a stop, but it felt as if time and space and speed had decided I was unnecessary, had conspired to slough me away.

"What the hell?" said Bob, looking back at me over his shoulder. "Are you trying to ruin my car or something?" He grabbed my pant leg, drew me forward, and the seat slid into position with a click.

We didn't talk much the rest of the way home. It took me a while to regain my composure, to trust the car's solidity. Bob continued his reverie of self-inspection, checking the state of his eyes and mouth every few minutes in the rearview mirror. Although I knew better than to pursue it aloud, I weighed the probability of a .38-caliber Smith & Wesson wrapped in Janet's embroidered hankie. Not impossible. And not very likely. The whereabouts of that missing gun still charged the air like the peal of a bell; it amazed me that my brother didn't hear it, didn't ask me what I was thinking.

We parked in front of our house and we followed voices into the kitchen. Janet leaned against the refrigerator, hands sunk in the ample pockets of her uniform. She barely noticed that my brother and I had returned. Bob walked over and handed her the bag of medication. "Wanna see something adorable?" she cooed. "Just look at those two." Bob and I turned in unison. Abashed to be the subject of our attention, Aunt Ida, smack in Morris Ornstein's lap, raised her hand to wave hello, and because they sat in a cantilevered chair, my aunt and Morris, in tenuous suspension, began to bounce. I had never seen my aunt in the arms of a lover. She had lectured me so fervently about the pitfalls and ruses of love, I assumed the only emotion a man could stir in her was suspicion. But Ida yielded to the force that was Morris, literally clung to his weathered neck, lulled by the gentle, rhythmic bouncing, which Morris prolonged by pushing off the floor. "I'm probably crushing you to death," said Ida, the chrome chair softly squeaking. "So crush." Morris laughed. "That's what I'm here for."

With his horseshoe of gray hair, large features, and khaki clothes, Morris looked like a contractor you could trust. Candor shaded his every statement. "I'm thirsty," he'd announce, or "Let's sit down," as if there didn't exist even the slightest gap between what he wanted and what he said. Though they'd met Morris only a few times, my mother deemed him "a prize," my father "a mensch and a half." "What did I do to deserve him?" my aunt once asked, astonished that her wary nature had led her to such a fortunate coupling.

I hadn't formed an opinion of Morris—his presence in the life of my aunt evoked in me nothing more than surprise—

until that morning. Janet poured a glass of water, divvied up my brother's pills, and proffered them in her outstretched palm. It had become common for Janet to tend to my brother with the cool efficiency her profession demanded, and for my brother to accept her ministrations with a dull and wordless obedience. Bob plucked pills, one by one, from Janet's hand. I hated to see him change into a patient in the presence of others. Morris also saw that Bob had succumbed to a small humiliation, and felt the urge to intervene. "Can you take them all at once without choking?"

"Morris," blurted Ida, "what kind of question is that?"

Bob said, "I suppose I could."

"That's not a very good idea," warned Janet. "It might cause a spasm in the esophagus."

"Let's see," insisted Morris. "Let's see you do it."

Egged on by the challenge, my brother grabbed the pills from Janet. He threw back his head and downed them all with a greedy drink. His Adam's apple throbbed up and down. A rivulet of water glistened on his chin. "There," said Bob. He wiped his mouth with the sleeve of his shirt, pride restored, thanks to Morris.

Before Janet could protest, my parents and the Menassians burst into the kitchen through the swinging door, the Saturday-morning edition of the *Herald-Examiner* open before them. "We found it," said Mother.

"Page three," added Arnold.

"Our Irving," boasted Eve, "is in the forefront of the news."

Morris pleaded, "Read it already."

And my father, grown accustomed to such requests, folded the paper with a flourish and read: " 'Judge Rules Love Above Court in Case of Parted Boy, Girl.' "

"Boy girl?" I said.

"That's boy comma girl," said my father with some irritation. He cleared his throat and continued:

"There isn't any law against love—or even a law that would prevent 21-year-old Hector Ramos from standing on a street corner, reciting poetry and hoping to get a glimpse of his 'Captive Bride,' Isobel Nuñez Ramos, 16.

"So ruled Judge Albert Mosk today in refusing to grant the request of attorney Irving Zerkin for the bride's mother, Mrs. Rafaela Nuñez, for the continuance of a restraining order which would prevent Hector from 'molesting or interfering with' his wife. Mrs. Nuñez admitted that all Hector has done so far is to stand on the corner all day near the bride's home and recite poetry.

"David C. Schmidt, attorney for Hector, charged the girl was being held prisoner by her parents after having been taken away from a wedding dinner in Montebello by her father. Isobel said that she still loved Hector and wanted to live with him, but was told she'd go to Juvenile Hall if she tried."

"Juvenile Hall," interrupted Eve. "That's cruel and unusual."

"Declared Judge Mosk, 'The court has neither the power nor the ability to restrain the courtship of these two young people.' In conclusion, the judge added to the verdict some poetry of his own."

Here my father extended his hand and raised his voice dramatically.

" 'I do not desire / that justice go amiss. / And upon counsel's statements / this matter I dismiss.' "

My father explained that Hector's family and Mr. and Mrs. Nuñez had gotten together and reached a compromise: Hector and Isobel would be allowed to see each other so long as Isobel promised she wouldn't live with her husband until she turned eighteen.

"That's two years," said Mother.

Janet said, "Two years isn't so long to wait if you love somebody."

"It's especially long if you love somebody," said Bob. Janet bristled at his contradiction.

"The point is," interjected my father, "they're married for all intents and purposes."

"For all intents and purposes," said Arnold. "That's why Eve and me got married."

Eve rolled her eyes.

"Whoa," said Arnold, alarmed by an afterthought. "Does that mean they can't . . . you know . . . for two years?"

"I'm certain they already have," said my father.

"Shotgun wedding?" Arnold inquired gravely.

My father shrugged. "Ask me in nine months."

"What's a shotgun wedding?" I asked.

"I don't think Irving and I have been apart for more than two days since we were married." Mother sighed. "All things considered, though, we don't spend very much time together."

"We have different interests," my father explained, to his wife as much as to his guests. "That gives us plenty of room to breathe."

"What's a shotgun wedding?"

"I insist on separate vacations," said Eve. "It's either that or basket weaving."

Arnold snorted.

"Nobody loses; that's the beauty of the verdict. Am I right?" asked Morris.

My father nodded. "Even if Mosk did reject our request for a continuance of the restraining order, there's no such thing as bad publicity."

"And the kids benefit," said Mother. "Don't forget the kids."

Giving up on getting an answer to my question, I climbed onto the kitchen stool and watched couples come together, pull apart. Flushed from all the excitement, Ida tugged at her turban, shifted her hips in Morris's lap. Morris groaned, shaking each leg, disparaging his poor circulation. When Ida tried to rise, however, he caught her hand and drew her back, and she shot him a look of gratitude so stark it embarrassed me to see it. No matter where in the kitchen Arnold and Eve were standing, no matter who they were talking to, they sang wisecracks back and forth like birds calling to one another from the tops of distant trees. Seeing to it that everyone had soft drinks and coffee, my mother and father maintained the stalemate of their orbit, never moving too close together, never veering too far away. Bob and Janet had stepped out the back door, but I could hear and see them through the screen.

"Two years isn't such a long time," whispered Janet. "Grant me that."

"What does it matter?" said Bob. "We're not the ones who have to wait."

"But we *are* waiting. Don't you feel it?" Bob remained silent. Across the street, Brad and Barbara began to quarrel. *Did too*s and *Did not*s—a metronome of accusation—echoed over the neighborhood. "I don't know what will help," said Janet. "Not anymore. I thought I'd learned what to do to help." She shivered a little. "I went to nursing school," she said flatly, as though this fact should have protected her from a future on our back steps with a husband whose health was failing.

"Everything is going to be fine," said my brother, his voice remote, mechanical, each word a brick meant to seal them from hurt. Janet glanced at her watch. "I'll be late for my shift if I don't hurry." Bob guided her back into the kitchen, his hand slowly cascading off her shoulder as she walked out of reach to say her goodbyes. How long would my brother feel her on his fingers? Does sensation, I wondered, evaporate like water?

Late that night I lay in bed and pressed my stomach, the inside of my thighs, timing the life of every touch. Sometimes the pressure lingered on my skin, and sometimes it died right away. *A Year of Rhymes* was gone from the end table, and I was thankful that Ida, preoccupied with Morris, hadn't visited my room and noticed it was missing. From my parents' room came vibrations of talk, floorboards creaking with the weight of their bodies. Down the hall, my brother's room sat empty—except for the shelf of mystery books—the impressions of desk legs pocking the carpet, his fingerprints clouding the doorknob, the light switch, the window through which our neighbors' lights were extinguished one by one.

In April, Janet took the train back to Minnesota to visit her father, a salesman of backyard athletic equipment—jungle gyms, teeter-totters, trampolines. "He's got the gout," Mother called from the closet.

"Oy," said Ida. "Swollen toes." She was peering into the mirror above my mother's vanity table, tapping the wrinkles around her eyes. "Don't gawk," she said when she saw me reflected from my parents' bed. "It stimulates the skin, promotes elasticity. I read about it in a magazine." I tried it myself, and it felt pretty good. Ida had just washed her hair, and gray tufts stuck out in all directions. Freed from her turban, my aunt looked older, less oracular.

Mother walked out of the closet with a towel. "Janet bought him a pair of sandals before she left. Can you imagine? His feet won't fit into regular shoes."

Ida mumbled something back, but her mouth was pursed for a coat of lipstick, and the words were unintelligible. She blotted the excess pink on a Kleenex and studied herself in the same somber way my brother had in his rearview mirror. Right profile, left. Ida exhaled, her posture deflating. "If this is what Morris sees when he looks at me . . ."

"Do me a favor and don't start. It upsets me when you insult yourself. You might as well be insulting me." Mother sat beside Ida, addressing her reflection. "You were always the pretty one."

Ida said, "*Were* is right. Just don't tell me I'm well preserved."

My mother draped the towel around her sister's shoulders. They gazed together into the mirror. "Why is it so hard to grow old?" asked Mother. "We knew it was going to happen all along." It was then that Mother noticed me in the background, reclining on the king-size bed and pelting my face with my fingertips. "What's he doing?" She whirled around. "What are you doing?"

"Stimulating my skin."

"It's all right," said Ida. "I taught him how."

"It promotes elasticity," I informed my mother.

"You, my friend, are too young to worry about elasticity."

"I'm not *worried* about it." I continued to tap, playing intricate chords of sensation, mesmerized by the hardness of my skull beneath a negligible padding of flesh.

"Go ahead, then. Pound away. I don't have the energy to argue." Mother opened a jar of setting lotion, the same cloying smell as cherry Jell-O. She slathered strands of Ida's hair and wrapped them onto spongy pink curlers, which fastened with a click. For the sake of self-improvement, Ida kept her head in whatever position it was tilted. Mother explained to her captive audience that there was no one else to take care of Janet's father, and he couldn't afford to hire a nurse. Not only had Janet volunteered; she'd paid for the train fare with her savings.

"The girl's a *mensch*," Ida offered.

"I suppose so. But I wish she hadn't left. Not right now, when Robert needs her."

I asked why Mr. Cotter's toes had grown.

"That's what gout does," my mother said.

"How does it do it?"

"Honey," said Mother, "I'm not Janet. Ask her when she gets back. I'm sure she'll tell you all about it."

"Robert's OK on his own?" asked Ida.

"Burt," said Mother, pointing at the table next to her bed, "look what Ida brought from the Nite Light."

Old issues of the *Saturday Evening Post* and *True Experience* were meant, I knew, to protect me from hearing whatever came next. And so I lay back on the bed and pretended to read while I listened. Mother whispered something about Bob being too sick to go to work. The slightest exertion made him dizzy—without any warning he'd have to sit down or brace himself against a wall—and although he swore he could still run errands and organize files, my parents insisted he stay home and rest. Was he, Mother wondered aloud, dizzy from the illness or the medication? Doctor, pharmacist—who knew for sure? The matter was strictly chicken or egg. Janet had had the foresight to leave a two-week supply of pills, each day's dose in a plastic bag, but Mother had doubts about whether Bob was following instructions. "You know how he is sometimes. He wants to forget. And who can blame him?" At the appropriate moments, Ida grunted and sighed and clicked her tongue, a spectrum of empathetic sound. "What can I do?" continued Mother, desperation invading her voice. "I can't control his eating and sleeping. How many times can I call in a day? I wish I had eyes in the back of my head. I wish I was God. I'd watch him every minute."

This sacrilegious wish made Ida uneasy. "Oh, Sylvia. You wouldn't want to be God."

"I would," countered Mother.

"Well, you can't be, doll. There's one of Him. We're only mortal."

"That's the trouble," said Mother. "Mortal's not enough."

As if to illustrate my mother's point, the back pages of *True Experience* were blanketed by black-and-white ads for

bunion pads, asthma tablets, bust cream, and trusses. END
THE TORTURE OF AGONIZING ITCH. DRINK YOUR UGLY FAT
AWAY. KILL UNWANTED HAIR AT THE ROOT. SHED YOUR OLD
COARSE SKIN. The human body was bound to falter. Coupons
for nursing schools featured photographs of smiling, well-
groomed women who could have passed for Janet. *Doctors
rely on them! Patients appreciate their cheerful, expert care!*
And still farther back, if science failed altogether, small ads
touted the power of prayer. POOR HEALTH? MONEY, LOVE,
OR FAMILY PROBLEMS? SERVE THE LORD AND EARN WITH
WORLD'S ON FIRE MINISTRY. One ad in particular intrigued
me: a drawing of a naked man lying on a cruciform slab. His
pectorals were well defined. The drapery that covered his
groin seemed intended to tantalize. Above him hovered the
word ROSICRUCIANS and the phrase DISCOVER THE SECRETS
OF THE AGES. Who were Rosicrucians, and what had they
done to him? The word conjured an alien life—Martians,
Venutians. Other than an address for a free brochure, the ad
contained no explanation. Was he dead or merely sleeping?
I suddenly felt that I had to know, that hidden within this
vexing image were secrets that might help my brother. I sat
up on the bed, ready to ask about Rosicrucians, when I saw
that my mother's shoulders were shaking. "I'm so tired," she
told Ida, trying to keep her back to me. "Maybe I'm dreaming
this. Tell me I'm dreaming."

Ida cupped my mother's face in both hands and repeated
"Sylvie, Sylvie," as if to rouse her sister from a trance. My
aunt saw me staring and motioned for me to leave by tilting
her head, a chrysanthemum of curlers, toward the bedroom
door. "Did he see me crying?" I heard my mother whisper
as I closed the door behind me. "No," said Ida. "He didn't
see a thing."

I didn't know what to do with myself in my unexpected
exile. I wandered down the hall, but everything seemed un-
familiar; the house no longer belonged to my family; it be-

longed to the inevitable, a force against which we had no effect. As I passed my room, *Long Live the Queen*, stirred by the draft from an open window, turned in aimless circles. Rhinestones winked. A toaster trembled. I picked up the hall phone, dialed Time, and listened to the dirge of minutes. I jumped when something touched my shoulder. Even after I recognized Brad, it took me a minute to understand that he must have found the front door unlocked and decided to let himself in. "You scared me," I snapped. "You can't just walk into people's houses."

"Why not?" he honestly wanted to know.

Still clutching the receiver, I searched for a way to explain. *At the tone the time will be . . .* "What if my mother was naked?" I said.

"What if?" Brad laughed. "Hang up the phone. We're going on a ride." As I followed him outside, Brad told me that his mother was working late at Miracle Match and his father was at a convention of used-car salesmen in San Diego. The King children were temporary orphans once again, given the run of the house. That morning they had eaten vanilla wafers for breakfast and raced rolls of toilet paper down the hallway. Later, working with a bent bobby pin, Brad's older brother jimmied the lock of Mrs. King's jewelry case and pilfered the key to the used Valiant, compliments of her husband, that now idled at the curb.

Stephen sat tall in the driver's seat, trying to appear as if he had more authority than the learner's permit I knew him to have. Opposite him, Stephanie filed her nails and yawned and did everything in her power to act blasé, which made the trip seem even more illicit. Barbara squirmed in the back seat, humming—the national anthem?—off key. "Are you coming or not?" Brad demanded, holding the car door open. When I asked where we were going, he smiled and repeated the question. I looked back at my stucco house—windows open, doors unlocked—Ida and Mother waiting for solace within its walls. As a final enticement, Stephanie said, "There's a mirror that shows you as you really are. If you want to see it, get in already."

"Yeah," grumbled Barbara. "Make up your mind."

Like the inside of the Kings' house, the floor of the back seat was littered with toys: pieces of a jigsaw puzzle, loose Crayolas, scattered jacks. An armless Barbie doll rolled out from under the front seat each time the car accelerated, and rolled back each time we stopped. Ashtrays overflowed with candy wrappers and Popsicle sticks. There wasn't much space between Barbara and Brad; obsessed with the exact perimeters of their personal territory, they argued and drew imaginary lines and reached over me to deliver slaps and pinches, each squealing that the other was taking up too much room. Unperturbed and parental, Stephen and Stephanie looked straight ahead, their hair an identical yellow.

We drove up Los Feliz Boulevard toward the Hollywood hills, the lawns in front of apartment houses freshly mown and blooming with flowers. At the gates to Griffith Park, Stephanie spotted a police car in a vacant lot, half hidden behind a stand of lanky sycamores. She turned to face the back seat, eyes enlarged. "Act normal," she exhorted. Legally, Stephen was supposed to be accompanied by an adult when operating a vehicle. This sent ripples of panic through the car. We sat as rigid as crash-dummies, good kids within the limits of the law. Hands at ten and two o'clock, Stephen navigated the street like an overcautious, myopic old man, constantly checking the rearview mirror. "Heat's off," he said at last. Everyone turned around to make sure. The cops were a black-and-white dot in the distance. Brad and Barbara resumed their slapping. The Valiant picked up speed.

Roads curved dangerously in the higher altitudes of the park, some turns so extreme they almost took us full circle. Stephen veered into the adjacent lane even on blind curves, ignoring our pleas to slow down. On one side of the narrow road, breaks in the foliage allowed fleeting views of the city below, a few clouds casting their shadows on the infinite grid of streets. On the other side, charred patches of hillside were still visible from last summer's fire, the bare earth eroded by rain. Parked at scenic overlooks, people sat on the hoods of their cars or stood on dirt promontories and gazed into the distance; they'd turn and scowl as we screeched past, higher and faster into the hills.

"Rag doll," screamed Stephanie as we made an especially wrenching turn. On cue, everyone went limp, including Stephen, though he hung on to the steering wheel and managed, somehow, to control the car. The force of the right turn sent us tumbling left. I fell onto Barbara, whose head hung out the window, her long hair whipping into the air. The door handle poked her in the ribs, but the rigors of the game—it demanded compliance to gravity, required we abandon our bodies completely—made us numb to pain. Brad slumped across my lap, his elbow digging into my crotch. And just as I began to savor his weight, the Valiant made another sharp turn. All of us flew in the opposite direction. I saw the back of Stephanie's head arc above the front seat before it set like a sun. Barbara slid across the vinyl upholstery and leaned into me like a drunk, cheek flattened against my shoulder, body wobbling with every jolt of the car. Her breasts, or the softness that would one day be her breasts, pressed against my arm. The sensation of her flesh wasn't nearly as strong as the hard rise of Brad's hip prodding me from the other side. His shirt came untucked from the force of his laughter, pale stomach exposed. Practically on top of my friend, breathless and grateful, I clenched my legs, tried to hide my erection. I gave in to a pleasure bigger than my body as the car barreled close to the edge of a cliff.

Stephanie screamed. I snapped to attention. It seemed we might sail right off the road and tumble into the canyon below. Stephen pretended to stir from unconsciousness. He shook his head like a wet dog, applied the brakes, and turned the wheel, sparing our lives at the last second. "Saved!" he exclaimed in his most heroic voice. "Was that ever close!" Stephanie slugged her brother for frightening us and, even worse, for causing her to lose her composure. Arms folded, nostrils flared, she refused to speak for several minutes.

Even after the game was over, my breathing came fast and ragged. Brad stared out the window with the dreamy, slack-jawed look of a kid drained by horseplay. Pine trees flicked past and scented the wind. I wondered if I was in love with him.

The parking lot of the Griffith Park Observatory was almost full. Dozens of people milled on the promenade leading to the front entrance. A banner over the doors announced NEW EXHIBIT: HAMMOND'S MIRROR. As we searched for a parking space, Stephanie, seeing one couple kissing in a car and another admiring the view with their arms around each other, inched closer to her brother in the hope that someone might mistake them for lovers. She tried to be slow and subtle in her movements—feigned a yawn, fiddled with the ashtray—knowing Stephen wouldn't stand for her pretense. Even from the back seat I could tell she was embarrassed by her need to be seen by strangers as someone who was desired. "Don't touch the merchandise," Stephen snapped when they were shoulder-to-shoulder, brushing the sleeve of his T-shirt as though he'd been contaminated with uranium. He had known all along what his sister was up to, had waited to rebuke her until she'd relaxed in the pose of worldly woman. Radiant with satisfaction, Stephen was as proud of his cruelty as he was of his stunt driving. Stephanie took out her emery board and punished the nubs of her nails.

Like an infantry landing on a beachhead, we shot from the Valiant as soon as it stopped, running in a cluster through the parking lot, asphalt soft in the afternoon heat. We passed an obelisk decorated with the figures of famous scientists:

Galileo, Copernicus, Kepler; granite men dreaming the Secrets of the Ages. Each held a globe of the world to his chest and stared into the distance with wide, pupilless eyes.

At the front steps, a guard in a blue uniform informed us that there was no admission fee. "But we do," he said gently, "accept donations." "So do we," said Stephanie, forging past him. All of us followed behind her like ducks. Once we entered the crowded marble rotunda, shouts, voices, exclamations of wonderment echoed. An enormous pendulum, suspended from the center of the ceiling, hung above a circular depression in the floor. Swinging back and forth, it knocked over a small wooden pin on the perimeter every half hour, demonstrating the planet's rotation. The felled pins were a matter of excruciating anticipation for families leaning on the railing and waiting, the babies in their parents' arms growing heavy as sandbags. A pin must have fallen as we made our way to the Hall of Science; a collective groan of relief rose up, like friction released between plates of the earth.

Various marvels were displayed in small, enclosed chambers on either side of the long hall. A scale model of the moon, pocked with gray-green craters, revolved against a backdrop of painted constellations. A three-dimensional cross section of the earth, lavish as layer cake, showed deposits of oil, fossils, and lava. Ultraviolet light revealed not only the flecks of ore in otherwise bland rock samples but the luminosity dormant in our teeth; skin and hair invisible, we assaulted one another with smiles.

A line had formed outside the new exhibit. I waited with apprehension, certain that my longing for Brad would swim to the surface of Hammond's Mirror like a gasping fish. The King children made a ruckus about having to wait in line. They tapped their feet and pulled their hair and consulted imaginary watches—a vaudeville act of pure impatience. This amused the woman standing behind me. She chuckled and sniffed, told me she had allergies and speculated that, what with the line moving so slow, we could all drop dead before we got a peek. Plucking a handkerchief from her bra with the aplomb of a magician, she yelped, "Pollen!" and her nose exploded.

Another blue-uniformed guard was letting people into the exhibit in small groups. They must have exited somewhere out of sight, because once they walked through the black curtains, they never came back. A diagram on the wall showed the complicated geometry of planes and lights that ". . . allow you to see your reflection as though you were standing outside of yourself." I imagined finding a hidden door in the confines of my body.

The guard asked if the five of us were together and, seeing us nod, drew back the curtain. Our reflections entered from the far end of the mirror. We met ourselves in the middle. Our faces contradicted what we'd seen all our lives: noses crooked at a different angle, smaller eye on the opposite side, expressions of awe inverted. Forehead furrowed, Stephen reached out one arm, but the opposite arm lifted in the mirror. It looked as if he were being introduced to someone he mistakenly thought he knew. He laughed as he shook his own hand, but it was one abrupt and helpless sound, strong as a sob. Stephanie slowly turned her head. Made pensive by this revision of her image, she couldn't bring herself to speak. Brad and Barbara danced around the room, flung their bodies crazily, trying to catch the mirror off guard and cause their reflection to miss a step. "Time for someone else," said the guard. I waved hello to my second self—another skinny, mortal boy, unexceptional except for his secret—who appraised me uncertainly, waved goodbye, and burrowed into the dim room as I walked into the light.

"Let's do it again," suggested Barbara. But Stephanie was already making her way up a flight of stairs, following an arrow that read TO TELESCOPES. We raced after her, shouldered open the double doors. The view from the roof was broader than any vantage point along the road. To the east, City Hall overshadowed the smaller office buildings. Foliage growing around the La Brea tar pits stained the heart of the basin green. A metallic band of ocean glittered in the sunlight, marred only by the mound of Catalina Island. The horizon curved perceptibly, ending in hazy, unknowable edges.

I dropped a dime into one of several telescopes bolted along the balustrade. The aperture opened, and I scanned Los Angeles, startled by the clarity of telephone poles and swimming pools. Miniature cars floated along the freeway or lifted mutely up and down the hills. I retraced our route to the observatory until I reached Ambrose Avenue, houses surrounding the cul-de-sac magnified in the lens. I was about to tell the Kings that I'd found our street, when I saw my father's car pull into the driveway, a puff of exhaust as the motor died. The car doors swung open, a beetle's wings. My father walked to the passenger side, bent down, and lifted my brother to his feet, their mutual effort visible even from this great a distance. Arms around each other, they stood for a moment, waiting to trust their tenuous balance, stiff and small as letters on a page. Ida and my mother rushed out the back door, watched Bob and my father amble toward them. Ordinarily too proud to accept assistance, Bob leaned his weight on my father wholly. Hands rising at her sides, Ida seemed to be asking questions, uncertain what had happened, uncertain what to do. Mother held the back door open, a woman assuming an awful duty she'd expected all along. Their figures shook if I so much as breathed—I held the telescope tightly—and so I spared them by holding my breath, a consoling bit of omniscience.

Gears hummed in the telescope. Time ran out. The aperture contracted. I looked out from the observatory, tried to find my family again. Muddled roofs and trees and roads, the world stretched before me, a map of their absence.

M y father told the story over and over. Mother heard it. Arnold heard it. Eve and Ida and Morris heard it. Anyone who would listen heard. Each telling overwhelmed my father, but the details never varied. Veracity became a challenge, an obsession, as if in recounting the incident exactly my father might at last believe what had become of his healthy son.

After serving a subpoena to a Glendale dentist (the job became my father's when Bob stayed home from work), he'd decided to drop by and see how Bob was doing. It was noon on Saturday, the weather warm, clear except for a trace of smog settling on the horizon like silt. "An innocent visit," my father would protest. "Not like I had to go out of my way. Not like I was spying or something. I'm his father; don't I have the right?" Driving into the hills of Echo Park, negotiating the narrow roads, he was shaken by a sense of dread he could neither dismiss nor explain. He parked in front of Bob's apartment, sat in his car, procrastinated. My father paused at this point in the story and slowly lifted his leaden hand to illustrate how he knocked on the door. He wondered what was taking so long, shifted his weight impatiently, heard slippers shuffling on the wooden floor. Bob answered the door in striped pajamas, blinked against the uninvited light. The two of them stared, not sure for a moment who the other was—a man who knocked, a man who answered. My brother's cheeks were shallow depressions, his eyes frozen in dull surprise. Bob tried to speak, to say hello; he moved his mouth, but no sound came out. "What?" cried my father, and the forces in him gathered, rallied at the sight of his speechless son. He swept Bob inside, ordered him to sit, firmly pressed a hand on his forehead. My brother looked up, dazed and grateful, his fever filling my father's palm. Bob was given a glass of water, and when he was told, "I'm taking you home," he nodded once to show his compliance and folded his pale hands in his lap. My father rushed from room to room, collecting a hasty assortment of belongings—hairbrush, car keys, a balled pairs of socks—and tossing them into a paper bag he found on the kitchen counter. What did Bob want him to do, he asked, with the mound of mail, most of it unopened, sitting on top of the kitchen table? "I can't," Bob mumbled by way of a reply, "tell what's important anymore." At first my father didn't understand. And then it hit him: my brother had trouble sorting the mail. Bills and fliers and personal letters had dropped through the slot, had blurred together, news from a world that had grown remote, the life outside his small apartment a vague and unreliable rumor. Each letter was printed with my brother's name, and his name, like any word repeated, had begun to lose its meaning.

This lapse with the mail frightened my father. He mediated the tragedies of others, believed his renown and prosperity might allow him to sidestep grief, but driving home that afternoon, he knew Bob's condition would never improve; he would watch the son beside him die. At my father's insistence, Bob had worn his pajamas for the ride, and a woman in the adjacent lane would not stop staring. "Just ignore her," implored my father, shooting the woman an angry glance. "If people want to look, let people look. A man in pajamas is nothing new."

But the man who entered our house that Saturday *was* new, more forlorn and meek and disoriented than the brother I'd talked to just days before. I raced into Bob's old room the instant I returned from the observatory, and found him standing in the middle of the floor. "I saw you through a telescope," I said, panting hard.

"You did," he answered flatly, as if such sightings happened every day. "I'm supposed to wait," he said, changing the subject. I couldn't bring myself to ask for what. He hugged himself and asked if I was cold. I told him no, which seemed to disappoint him. I remembered cartoons with the screen split in half—rain on one side, sun on the other—and that's how I pictured the rift between us, brothers standing face-to-face but conversing in different climates. Mother was talking in hushed tones on the hall phone, confirming a checklist of ailments—chills, yes; nausea, no—when a daybed, the mattress folded in half, glided through the door. My father lumbered into the room, pushing it from behind. "You're here," he said when he saw me, a trace of amazement in his voice. Ida followed with an armload of linens, her coiffed hair like a cumulus cloud. She patted ethereal curls in place. "Well," she asked me, "what's the verdict?" Ashamed to have let her vanity show in a moment of crisis, Ida didn't wait for an answer; she busied herself with an inspection of the room, righted a row of fallen books—the Hardy Boys peered out from blue bindings—and dredged her finger in the dust along the shelf.

The bed was pried open, with no small effort. A folding chair my father retrieved from the closet squeaked into three dimensions. Bob sat in it without expression and watched as his narrow bed was made. Ida flapped open the starched sheets. She tucked the corners "hospital" tight, to please my mother as much as Bob. Next my father returned with the card table, each of the legs swinging wide on its hinge. Blossoming like a time-lapse flower, the room became a sad facsimile of the room it once had been. The paper bag full of my brother's possessions only emphasized its makeshift decor and made the very notion of home seem pallid and provisional.

By the time the bed was made, my mother had arranged to take Bob to Dr. Lock's office first thing Monday morning. "There's nothing more we can do until then," she announced, full of false cheer. "No aspirin," she added, propping herself against the portal. "It might cause bruising. The fever will have to run its course."

"It's best to get some sleep," concluded Ida.

My brother made his shaky way from the chair to the bed, a boy so frail an aspirin could wound him. It hadn't occurred to me that all of us were staring, the air oppressive with the weight of our pity, until Bob said, "Please don't watch me." My family instantly turned away—we studied the walls, the ceiling, the floor—our attention flung to the edges of the room by the centrifugal force of his shame.

My brother slipped between the sheets like a letter into its envelope. Mother piled blankets on top of him, thinking heat would help break his fever. To intensify this remedy, she decided to make a pot of barley soup; Bob could sip it while he lay beneath the blankets, the fever attacked from within and without. "Like an Indian in a sweat lodge," said my father, hoping to make the discomfort sound fun. He volunteered to return to Bob's apartment for medication and clothes and mail, things he'd forgotten to bring in his haste. Ida offered to cancel her theater date with Morris in case she was needed, but we vetoed her in unison, and my aunt could barely hide her relief. "Well, I wouldn't want this hair to go to waste," she conceded.

"You don't have to sit here," said my brother after the

adults had left the room. Perspiration glistened on his fore-
head. Now and then he shook with chills. "Everybody's mak-
ing too much of this." But neither statement was voiced with
conviction; things were exactly as bad as they seemed, and
he didn't, I knew, want to lie there alone.

To relieve the tedium of my bedside vigil, I squirmed in
the metal chair and imagined it folding closed with me inside.
"Do people really get trapped in Murphy beds?" I asked. My
aunt, who slept in a Murphy bed, had once suggested this
awful possibility during a lull in dinner conversation. "Doz-
ens of innocent people," she said, "are killed each year by
their foldaway beds. Statistics show, if you don't believe me."
She wanted to make us grateful that, having survived another
night, she was free to join us for brisket.

"You bet they do," said Bob, revived by the romance of
tight spaces and narrow escapes. "They get swallowed while
they're sound asleep and suffocate inside the wall." *Suffocate
inside the wall:* unthinkable, thrilling; the phrase unrolled
like a bolt of red silk.

"That's sick," I said with relish. I wasn't sure I believed
him, but the object of this game was to wish for the worst,
to scare each other with tales of entombment. "What about
trunks? Do you think people really stow away to foreign
countries inside trunks?"

"Happens all the time. Air holes. That's the secret."

"But how do they eat or go to the bathroom?"

"Think for a minute. They can get out of the trunk once
they're in the cargo hold. Walk around. Do what they want.
You don't have to be Harry Houdini to figure that out." The
more Bob talked, the less he shivered. "Houdini promised
his wife that he'd come back from the dead. That was going
to be his greatest trick. Bet you didn't know that, did you?"

A tree limb scraped against the house, the rising wind like
a wave about to break. Bob turned his head to look out the
window, and I saw where sweat had seeped into the pillow,

my brother drained of everything essential in the blotter of his makeshift bed. The breeze carried with it the smells of car exhaust and roasting meat and wet grass—all the pungent, invisible evidence of the lives around us being lived. Nostrils flared, eyelids heavy, Bob surrendered to a brief and restless sleep. As I sat there and watched him, a chill from the metal folding chair sank into my back and thighs. Against my better judgment, despite everything I understood about the physical universe (splattered stars, luminous rocks, the strata of the planet layered like cake), I found myself waiting for Houdini to appear, his hair mussed, a little out of breath, but matter-of-fact at his resurrection, asking me where he might find his wife. Every nerve, every grain of my concentration, was funneled into the wish that he'd appear, until I felt I was nothing but longing, nothing but an urgent need to see a man squeeze through a hole in the hereafter and resume his life in my brother's room.

"Did he do it? Is that what you were going to ask?" There was scorn in Bob's voice. He must have wakened to see me pinched in wishfulness, eyes boring into the heart of the room. "You slay me," he said. His ridicule made me feel hot and small. Bob sat up, and the stack of blankets slid off his chest, revealing a V of perspiration. "Jesus Christ," he said. "I'm soaked to the skin." He put his hand on my shoulder for leverage and rose to his feet. I followed him into the bathroom, where he peeled off his pajamas and tossed them toward me. I didn't know which was more shocking, his damp and heavy bedclothes in my hands, or the sight of him naked as he knelt to draw water, the skin too tight around his ribs. Water thundered into the tub and echoed off the tile walls. Steam billowed from the faucet. He stood up, folded his arms, and waited for the tub to fill. His penis hung from a mass of black hair, testicles retracting. Too intrigued for comfort, I fixed my gaze on my brother's face. "What am I supposed to do with these?" I asked, holding out his pajamas.

He pointed to the laundry hamper and asked if anything of mine might fit him in the meantime. Dropping Bob's pajamas in the dark and fetid hamper made me feel I'd made a mistake, thrown away something I should have saved, abandoned hope completely.

I sifted through the shirts and pants in my bureau drawers, choosing an old pair of shorts with a threadbare elastic waistband and an oversize T-shirt from an outing to Marineland, a school of faded tropical fish swimming across it. Back in the bathroom, I presented my selections to Bob; he eyed them without excitement. Beads of steam shimmered on the walls, fogged the mirror above the sink. My brother sank in hot water, his bald knees like desert islands, the hair on his chest and calves matted flat. He soaped himself slowly and didn't object to me sitting on the toilet lid, watching him work up sheaths of lather, which melted off his slick skin and dissolved with a hiss on the surface of the water.

Bob submerged himself up to his neck. Waves lapped at his unshaven chin. He opened his mouth and let water pour in, as if he might swallow the contents of the tub. I heard a click as he closed his throat, mouth remaining wide beneath the water. The law of refraction made him look broken, arms and legs at odd angles. He sputtered and coughed, resurfaced into a sitting position. After he caught his breath he said, "Someday we'll find a way to breathe water, easy as air." This mention of the future turned him morose. He paddled the tepid bath. "I might not make it. You know that, don't you?" I pretended he meant make it out of the tub, make it to his feet without my assistance. "Yes," I said, and my own throat closed.

Bob toweled himself dry and put on my old clothes, both of us surprised that, although they were a little snug, the shorts and T-shirt fit him pretty well; most of his own clothes had grown too big. He combed his hair and brushed his teeth, spitting out toothpaste pink with blood. Feeling for his fever with wrinkled fingers, he said he thought it was almost gone—leached into sheets that would have to be washed. Bob stripped the bed and, wrapped in a blanket, sat atop the bare mattress.

He was sipping dinner, the odor of barley welling in the air, when our father returned. He brought Bob fresh pajamas and a bathrobe. Vials of medicine were set in a neat row on the card table, along with a stack of edited mail, the unimportant pieces removed. "You look better," said my father. "Do me a favor: this time don't skip your medication."

"The fever broke. Maybe I should go—"

"You're staying put." Father raised a finger to finalize his point. He reminded Bob that this was still home, admonished him to finish his dinner, then turned and left the room.

Bob tilted the bowl and gulped the dregs of his soup. "Janet's coming back," he told me, waving a letter he picked from the pile.

"Wasn't she supposed to?"

"You never know. Sometimes people don't." He saw that I was puzzled. "Come back," he repeated. "Like Harry Houdini." He savored the letter, mouthed her words, and hard as he tried to fight it, fell asleep when he finished. The pages slid from his hand, fluttered to the floor. Written on onionskin stationery, Janet's printing had been jarred from the motion of the train, but it appeared as if the words themselves were warped by the force of some inner turmoil. Here and there the ink was smeared and entire lines dipped toward the right-hand margin. "Dear Husband," it began:

> Just out of Union Station and I'm already wondering how you are. This is not easy for me to say except in a letter but when we were first married I had to know that you needed me to worry about you and tend to your wants and generally make a fuss. (Remember when I would serve you breakfast in bed? I hate to think about

bringing you food on a tray because there would be so much of that later, and I just didn't know.) For me to be worried was a kind of happiness, and then you got sick and I had to worry in a real way and things were different.

For better or worse. That vow keeps me on the straight and narrow because I figure if there isn't that promise between us life is petty and mean and nothing good is left. Abiding is a word from the Bible that always filled me to the brim. But I would be lying, Bob, if I said that there weren't times I see you suffer and there is nothing I can do or say and I feel empty and have no ideas for the future. Don't hate me if I say that with my father at least I know what will help: (1) a change of diet (2) anti-inflammatories (3) exercise. Is it bad to admit that his situation is easier for me? I'm going to stay with him as long as it takes to get him back on his feet. After all, he helped me through nursing school and now I can pay him back. Whatever else can be said about me, I try to meet my obligations.

The city is falling away and the landscape is changing. It makes me feel far away from you. I hate to think, what if we never met. I hate to think that I might have pulled into that gas station a minute later and would have missed you forever. You were so handsome and different from anyone I ever knew. I was ready then and there to walk into a new life. And now I have to make that life my own. I don't want to pine because that is more sadness and we've had enough, but I hate to think I could have missed you. Whenever there's a coincidence my dad says, "Everything is attached by a thin thread." Don't you think so?

The whole point of this letter is that I want you to get along without me for the time being. I want you to tend to your own needs while I'm gone. I want you to remember how I am with you and I want you to be that way with yourself. Otherwise, what has my caring been for, what will my coming back mean?

Your Wife

What has my caring been for? Into the evening that phrase played in my head like the refrain of a song, pointed and plaintive, and I wondered whether Janet meant *caring* as in "being fond of," or "taking care of," or some combination of both. While Bob twisted in a fitful sleep, I joined my parents in the rumpus room. My father sprawled on the couch and stared at the blank TV. Jiggling the change in his pocket helped him collect his thoughts. "I've got to, Sylvia. There's no way around it. I've got to hire someone to serve subpoenas."

"It'll kill him if he finds out." Mother amended her prediction when she saw my father wince. "It'll hurt him, Irving. How are you going to tell him? How are you going to put it?" She sat on a barstool, *Art Through the Ages* open before her. Marion had loaned the book to my mother the day we went to Grauman's Chinese Theater, promising that a crash course in aesthetics would give her something to think about besides cooking and cleaning and, though it wasn't added to the list aloud, my brother's illness. For weeks, Mother lugged the volume from room to room, slammed it with an authoritative thud on the kitchen counter or the dining room table, ceremoniously licking her index finger and turning the pages, a woman trying as best she could to pry wide her narrow horizons. But she was always drawn away from the book—the telephone rang, the teapot whistled, the philodendron needed water—back to a set of domestic concerns more compelling and varied than the history of art. She never got further than the paintings in the caves. "You can't just say to him, 'Son, I'm replacing you.' "

"Of course I wouldn't put it like that. Give me some credit, for God's sake. I'm going to tell him it's temporary." And then, as if to reassure us, he added, "It *is* temporary."

I pulled up a stool next to my mother, peered at drawings of spotted horses, a writhing bison shot with crude arrows.

"Who on earth can you hire who knows the ins and outs? No one will do as good a job as Robert. I can tell you that right now."

"It's not a competition. I'm not out to hire someone better than Bob. But business is business, and I can't do everywhere and be everything at once."

"*Be* everywhere and *do* everything."

My father stopped jiggling his change. "That's what I just said. Is there an echo in here?" he asked with consternation. "Anyway, I thought I'd ask Hector Ramos. He could use the money; no question about that. He can't make a career out of waiting around for Isobel. He sure as hell can't make money writing those poems of his. And the kid's persistent, which is just what it takes."

"Hector Ramos?" My mother barely stifled a laugh. "I don't think Hector Ramos wants to do you any favors. Not after you hammered him in court." She barely noticed when I slid the book away from her. Cows grazed on the ceiling of a cave. On the facing page, a painted handprint, fingers splayed, memento of an ancient presence.

"I didn't hammer him in court. They wouldn't be getting legally married if it wasn't for me. Besides, I'd be doing *him* the favor. I'm sure Mr. and Mrs. Nuñez wouldn't mind their future son-in-law getting a head start on what could turn out to be a lucrative future."

Bob said, "I think it's a good idea." He shuffled into the room in his slippers and bathrobe. My parents fell silent, sorry he'd heard, exchanging looks that blamed each other. He sat beside my father and yawned. "I could help him get started. You know, introduce him to Delaney at the bail bonds office and Elevator Sally, or fill him in on some of my tricks." Yielding this easily wasn't like him. "It's only for a while, right?" Either my brother really believed this or he said it to bring the debate to a close. Bob lay down, rested his head in my father's lap. Pinned to the cushion by Bob's groggy weight, my father stiffened, stared into his lap as if something had spilled. He let his arm fall near my brother's face. He warily touched my brother's hair. He inhaled the odor of sickness and cradled the face of his son.

Outside, the night was ubiquitous and black. My brother's breathing wavered like a flame. Mother and I leaned close to each another, studied the pictures in *Art Through the Ages*. Shapes of vanished animals. Imprints of absent hands.

Our household grew somber and absentminded, yet agitated, too mindful to sleep. Could we remember the days before he was dying? Only a murky reminiscence, smothered under the enormity of mourning. A chair leg scraped, a filament hummed inside a light bulb—every object we thought we possessed was wearing thin, burning out. Plates and glasses were set down softly, and our feet on the floor, and our bodies in beds. We resorted in private to superstition, tossing salt behind our backs, folding our hands as we murmured prayers. Hear us. Protect him. Make it not so.

Even our guests grew polite and quiet, as if Bob's disease were a sleeping child, fussy and shrill when awakened. Knowing that my brother was somewhere in the house, Morris Ornstein whispered when he spoke. Ida, too, grew less voluble, stirring a pot or emptying an ashtray, her sense of obligation glorified by silence. The need for quiet gave Morris and Ida another excuse to huddle together, to rehash the miraculous fact that they had met, to sink into the ample cushions of the couch and nuzzle and stroke and implode.

Far from being an annoyance, their inability to stay away from each other reminded me and my parents that emotions apart from fear existed. Falling in love this late in life entitled them to make up for lost time. And they managed to share their surfeit of feeling. Once, hugging in the hallway, they loosened the braid of their tight embrace and snared my brother on his way to the kitchen. Caught unawares, Bob did his best to break away, and when he realized they wouldn't let go, that my aunt was aiming to kiss his forehead and Morris to pat his back, Bob struggled to slick down his dirty hair and straighten the placket of his sour pajamas. They persisted with their mission until he'd been enveloped, broken of timidity, his sleepy, sallow face beginning to glow with blood.

The Menassians came over less often, and usually Eve arrived alone. At first she made excuses for Arnold: "He honestly wanted to come, but it's spring inventory, and the man's no whiz kid when it comes to stock. He'd lose his head if it wasn't screwed on." The bar became crowded with the booze he sent in lieu of a visit, each bottle remaining in its oblong gift box. Arnold had made a business of abandon, thrived in a climate of unimpeded play, but recently my father had become a moody sidekick, less prone to laugh at his pranks and sample his expert highballs. The strain between them was never discussed. What could they say? Arnold sympathized with my father's sorrow and my father with Arnold's need to have fun; their mutual understanding only strengthened the impasse.

Eve, on the other hand, made the most of her visits, even if that meant sitting with my mother and saying nothing, her gold bracelet clinking as she drank a cup of tea. Sometimes I wondered if Eve, for all her kindness, inspired my mother's jealousy; impeccably dressed, adventuresome when choosing from a menu, an ace at bridge and reading maps, Eve believed in her own luck. Unlike my mother, she moved fluidly between her home and the world, and assumed she deserved a place in both. Arnold swore that Eve's intuition had kept the Cap 'n' Cork in the black. "Horse sense," Eve argued, tapping her head. "Not intuition." On those long nights when Bob was at home, I saw my mother lean across the table and yearn for the respite of being Eve.

If Bob ventured out of his room, Eve rose to greet him and pulled out a chair, the two of them shy and deferential as a couple on a date. "You're OK?" she'd ask him. "I'm OK," he'd say. "If there's anything you need . . ." "Nothing, Eve." Courtesy passed between them like music, a duet that made my mother sad, and she'd stare at Bob as though from far away. "Take a picture," he'd tease her. "It might last longer."

Hector Ramos made no attempt to hide his surprise at the change in my brother. The Bob who had stood over him on the lawn of the Nuñez house—agile and handsome, camera in hand—must have born little resemblance to the sickly boy who sat before him the day he came over. Hector had jumped at the chance to "earn good money," to "provide for the wife," to "show his in-laws what he was made of" (phrases my father dangled like carrots), and a meeting had been arranged, with Bob's permission. The four of us sat at the dining room table, Hector jotting important points in the dog-eared notebook he once reserved for poems. His eyes grew wide and bright with alarm whenever Bob struggled to swallow or lost his train of thought.

"So you were saying," prompted my father, "that it's best to strike at dinnertime."

"Oh, yeah," said Bob. "That's when people don't expect a knock on the door; their guard is down, and they'll put up with just about anything to get back to a meal. Ask their name, and if they so much as nod, you shove the papers in their hand and run."

"That's easy," said Hector. He printed, STRIKE AT DINNERTIME.

"But don't forget to tip your hat." My father laughed.

Hector said he didn't have one.

"You can have mine," my brother offered.

"Loan," said my father. "You'll loan him a hat."

"He can have it," said Bob.

My father flung his hands in the air. "This is ridiculous. I was just making a joke. What does he need a hat for? Let's skip to the useful stuff. I don't want to drag this out forever. Hat," he mumbled under his breath. Then his rage ignited again. "You'll keep your goddamn hat, and that's final."

Drawn by the noise, Mother peered through the portal, then fluttered away as softly as a moth.

Hector shifted in his seat and tried to act businesslike. "Supposing no one answers?" he asked. He brushed back a lock of hair, thick and black as my brother's had been.

Bob said, "You've got lots of options. Gun the motor so it sounds like you're driving away, then sneak back in a couple of minutes."

Hector gnawed his pencil and imagined.

"Here's another one," said Bob. "Take a vacuum cleaner with you and pose as a door-to-door salesman. Works pretty good, but it's harder to get away fast if you have to. Or—I used to love this one—catch a guy on his errands; you know, run up to him at the bank or the post office like you're an old friend. 'Joe Schmo! It's been forever. How ya been, buddy?' And he says, 'I'm Joe Schmo, but I don't think I know you.' Then boom, it's over, and there's nothing he can do. That one really pisses people off, but it's practically foolproof."

Hector scribbled frantically, hesitating when it came to spelling *Schmo*.

"And if none of this works, you can always use Burt."

"Use Burt?" said my father.

"Don't," I warned Bob.

"He does this little-lost-kid routine, gets the person to

say their name, then throws the subpoena so they have to catch it."

"You can't get away with that," cried my father. "Burt's a minor, for chrissakes, and that makes the whole thing . . ."

"What?" said Bob.

"Invalid!" shouted Father. "You know that as well as I do."

"Well, it works," said Bob, happy to get a rise out of someone, a break from the steady diet of politeness. He grew lucid and large, remembering mischief. "At least it worked on Mrs. Vixen's husband."

"Just stick to the rules," my father advised Hector, taking a breath, tamping his anger. "There really isn't too much that can go wrong. With subpoenas, I mean." My father turned to Bob. "Worked on Charlie Cantrell, did it?"

"Like a charm," said Bob. "Look, Hector, if worst comes to worst, there's a Declaration of Service on the back of the subpoena, and if for some reason you can't get the person to take it, just fill it out and leave it on their doorstep or tuck it under their windshield wiper. They'll take the thing sooner or later, believe me."

I said, "Curiosity killed the cat," and waited for Hector to write it down.

Hector just sat there. "Fill it out how?"

My brother tried to recall but couldn't, and my father intervened. " 'On such and such a date,' " he recited, " 'I, So-and-so, served So-and-so at such and such an address, and declare under penalty of perjury that—' " Here Bob joined him, their voices harmonizing, almost elegiac: " 'the above and foregoing is true and correct.' "

Wind rattled the patio doors. When my father swung them open, the rim of the tablecloth trembled and the notebook flapped like a startled bird. Trees shimmered at the edge of our yard. Purged of clouds and smog, the sky was blue and flawless and broad above our flagstone patio. My father stood up and stretched, a signal that the meeting was over. Hector picked up his notebook and slipped the pencil into his pocket. "You still writing poems?" my brother asked him.

"Not really," said Hector. He shifted his weight self-consciously, held the notebook to his chest like a schoolboy. "Well, sometimes. I write them when"—he looked at my father and brother and me, apprehensive that we might not understand—"when I get depressed." Our lack of reaction spurred him on. "I write them when I have to say what I feel about Isobel, when I can't hold thoughts inside me anymore. It's too much sometimes, the way I want her." He blushed deeply, cleared his throat. "That's when I write them."

"Does it help?" asked my father, with a minimum of interest, ready to usher our guest to the door.

"Sort of." He sighed. "But there's always more."

"More to write," Bob asked, "or more to want?"

"Both," said Hector. "How did you know?"

My brother shrugged. "That's what love does. Once you've had it you always want it, and how much you want it never gets less." He reached out to seal the meeting with a handshake, but Hector balked at my brother's hand.

Hesitation cracked the air like glass.

"I'm glad you two boys got along," blurted Father. Strain tightened the features of his face. "Don't get too comfortable, though, Ramos; Bob'll be back in a couple of weeks."

"I'm not contagious," said Bob, his voice thinned by indignation. He hunkered in his chair, held out his hand until Hector shook it.

"Hey, man," said Hector, firming his grip in apology.

The meeting with Hector Ramos enervated my brother; he'd recounted every trick for his proxy, made a convincing case for deception, and he took Hector's sudden temerity to heart. But if Bob was skilled at fooling strangers, he was less skilled at fooling himself. In the days that followed, he couldn't forget his sickness for a minute, couldn't tap some vestige of will and tell himself that he might survive. Hector's momentary fear of a handshake, no matter how unwitting or innocent, set my brother's death like cement.

In those first, brilliant days of May, my brother settled into his death as he'd settled into a tub of hot water—a slow, labored, painful submersion—and rather than watch him suffer, I decided to wage a campaign of distraction. I showed up repeatedly at his bedroom door, bearing a succession of colorful boxes: Parcheesi, Monopoly, Chutes and Ladders. But accumulating paper money or hoisting a little plastic marker up and down the rungs of a ladder wasn't enough to rouse him from bed. With every appearance at the bedroom door, I found my brother tending his body. He rubbed my mother's moisturizing lotion into his chapped hands, hypnotized by his own touch. He clipped his toenails, brushed the brittle pieces onto the floor, where they lay like slivers of a broken cup. Each day he sank deeper into himself, until even his vanity seemed like despair.

Almost every night he spoke on the phone to Janet, reporting the slightest nuance of sensation, a tingling in the legs or a stiffness in the joints, as well as pains that were harder to assess, the unfamiliar weight of his blood or a spiteful ache whose location traveled. Bob and his wife had developed, like children, a secret language that excluded the world and fortified their common bond, a code made up of degrees, milligrams, side effects, and contraindications. My brother fondled the mouthpiece and played with the coiling telephone cord, his voice so intense and intimate, his descriptions so vivid and physical, that he and Janet, despite the distance, seemed to be making love. Only after his own complaints had been aired in their entirety did Bob inquire about Mr. Cotter, fishing for news of improvement. He wanted Janet to come back but couldn't find the courage to ask her directly.

Occasionally, when Bob was asleep or reading, my mother

called Janet to confer on his condition. It was during an especially hushed conversation between them that Janet decided to cut her trip short. Not only was her father walking without the aid of a crutch ("Cute as a newborn foal," she told my mother), but he'd seen the folly of a life drenched in oil and butter and cream ("A poor man," he lamented, "with a rich man's disease"), thanks to his daughter's tireless lectures. I pictured Mr. Cotter, fit and reformed, a vigorous and fatherly figure bounding from one of his trampolines into the gray Minnesota sky. Mr. Cotter's quick recovery was the reason for Janet's early return; at least that's what my mother told me.

My father was unusually forgetful the day that he and my mother were to pick up Janet at Union Station. The persistent wind, the mild electrical charge in the air, seemed to unhinge him. He'd gone back into the house, where I could hear him curse as he searched for his car keys. Bob and I were lying in the chaise longues on the patio, wearing our shorts—currents of air washed over our bodies—languid as swimmers drifting in a river. My mother had goaded Bob into going outside, her alarm at his listlessness causing her to harp continuously on the need for sun and exercise; long after I'd given up on my program of distraction, Mother took over, another runner in the relay race of familial concern. "You boys should do something while we're gone," she said, standing over us and shielding her hair, as gray now as Ida's, against the wind. "We are sunbathing," said my brother, enunciating every word as warning for Mother to leave him alone. "I can see that for myself," she said. "Why don't you two take a walk or . . . I know"—she brightened—"pick flowers for Janet. I'm sure she'd just love that." She pointed to a hibiscus bush nestled in a shady corner of the yard, the heavy blooms drooping, carnal and red.

"They die . . . don't last in water," said my father, stepping through the dining room doors with his key ring. "You'd be better off with the irises. Pick them all if you want. It doesn't matter." He slapped his forehead, turned on his heel, and mumbled, "Wallet." From inside the house, more searching and cursing.

I lay back and closed my eyes, the light molten behind my lids. Sparks writhed like living fire. The world, I thought, must have looked like this before it cooled, and would look like this when it came to an end.

"Marion's going to drop by for that book of hers," said Mother. "There's food in the fridge, so offer her something. We should be back in an hour or so."

When I opened my eyes, she was staring down at Bob as if to recall, with immeasurable effort, what he looked like, though he lay before her, shirtless and prone, as tangible now as yesterday, sunlight shining on every pore, every hair and pale-blue vein. "Bob?"

He lifted his head. "What is it now?" he said.

She continued to stare, years of knowing and loving her son running in reverse. "Nothing," said Mother.

My father returned with his wallet. "Are we ready?" he asked. He patted the pockets of his shirt and pants, touched his buttons, the buckle of his belt. Abstracted, afraid, he frisked himself and could not move, and I felt the power of my father's forgetting, airless and swift and strong as a vacuum.

A knock at the door brought him to his senses. My father led Marion out to the patio. She carried with her a small portfolio, black as her sunglasses. Her hair was tied into a ponytail by a scarf—years later I would be able to identify the Mondrian print—that fluttered in the wind, a flag of primary colors. Before Marion could say hello, my mother told her that Bob and I had been sitting around the house all weekend, and wasn't it a shame when the weather was this beautiful and there was so much to do. "I'll take care of it," said Marion. She shooed my parents like chickens. "You guys get going. I'll think up some recreation. From the Latin," she added. "*Wreck:* to ruin; *creation:* to make." Marion threw back her head and laughed. Soothed somewhat by her peculiar assurances, my parents excused themselves and left for the train station. No sooner had my father's car rumbled out of the driveway than Marion announced into the microphone of her closed fist, "Attention, please. This is your cruise director."

Bob looked at me and mumbled, "Mutiny."

"I heard that," said Marion with mock indignation. She sat at the foot of my brother's chaise longue and set the portfolio on her lap. "But first"—she peered at us over her sunglasses—"pictures at an exhibition." Marion unzipped the portfolio, the ragged metallic tug like the sound of anticipation itself. My brother sat up grudgingly. I moved next to Marion. Encased in acetate was a drawing of a toaster floating in an empty room. Gradations of graphite gave the appliance a three-dimensional appearance; set against the adumbration of a ceiling and walls, the toaster seemed to pop out from the page.

"What is it?" asked Bob.

"A toaster." Marion was momentarily alarmed. "Can't you tell?"

"I know it's a toaster, but . . ."

"What you want to know is why." She turned the pages, sunlight glancing off acetate and sweeping over our huddled faces. The same vague room appeared in drawing after drawing, but hovering at the heart of each was an ordinary object—a book, a dress, a potted plant—its shadow a puddle of darkness on the floor. "Levitation. The logical evolution of what I've been doing all along. No strings this time—that's the big difference."

"How do they stay up?" I asked her. "I mean, it's impossible."

"Impossible," she echoed. "But I made it happen."

Bob took the portfolio from Marion and thumbed through the drawings, impressed by refinements in Marion's craft, the folds in fabric, the highlights on chrome. Anything is possible, the drawings seemed to say; substance is something to overcome; ordinary objects have a life of their own, might unmoor themselves from one's expectations and defy the laws of gravity and chance. Staring into imaginary rooms, my brother seemed selfless, lost in thought, sleek perception stripped of a body. His admiration pleased Marion, and she reached out to stroke the nape of his neck, the ridge of his spine defined by sunlight. If there was pity in her gesture, I didn't see it. But my brother looked up, his reverie ended. In a sudden show of modesty, he reached for the T-shirt I'd given him and pulled it on, hasty, self-conscious, wrestling with the sleeves, slammed back into the limits of his skin.

Marion ordinarily trusted her impulses, and she was startled by my brother's reaction to her miscalculated touch. She drew back her hands and settled them heavily into her lap. "Let's do something," she said, more out of obligation than enthusiasm. "I promised your mother."

"How about—"

"No board games," said Bob.

We sat together in silence, leaves rattling all around us, and I believed that Marion had been defeated, her powers of invention finally run dry, nullified in the face of sorrow. What could she do for a dying boy? What amusement could matter? What pleasure was there left for him to have? How could Marion, for even a moment, divide him from the betrayal of his body? Her expression remained inscrutable. Until she reached back and untied her scarf.

Strands of hair at the back of my head were pulled when Marion tightened the knot. She held me by the shoulders and spun me around, darkness churning in all directions. And yet I knew right where my brother was, heard a rustle as he tried to run away. I dove through the swoon of gravity and instantly encircled his torso. With my head against his sun-warmed chest, I heard a heart's code of growing excitement, and didn't know whether it was his heart or mine.

"No fair," he protested, prying me away. "I wasn't ready. I didn't have a chance."

Even before Marion slipped the blindfold from my eyes, Bob insisted that his turn was next. She stretched the fabric across his face and tied it from behind. We turned him gently, and Bob abandoned himself to our hands, revolving in my borrowed clothes. "That's enough," he said. He straightened his back and looked around, a blind man piqued by heightened sounds, content in the refuge of a woman's scarf.

Marion took me by the hand, and together we backed across the patio and onto the lawn. "Bob," she called. He turned toward her voice, felt emptiness before him. He took one uncertain step, and another. His hair blew back, his stance alert. The T-shirt flapped like a sail from the mast of my brother's bones.

I ran in the opposite direction and called out to him too. Marion and I kept moving, circling, dodging Bob if he came too close. He cocked his head and twisted his torso, relying on all the stealth he had in him. He lunged at the hibiscus bush, a swath of pollen staining his face. He stumbled on a sprinkler head and righted himself before he fell. Marion flattened herself against the fence, grimacing when my brother nearly grazed her. I called his name, and he pivoted just in time for Marion to make an escape. "You're getting cold," she yelled, as my brother moved away from us into the shady reaches of the yard. "Really cold. Freezing!" All our tramping on the grass released a musky odor of growth, as complex and pungent as breath or sweat. *Remember this,* I told myself.

My brother forged toward me with his arms extended.

"Bob," I said, to give myself away.

"You're getting warm," shouted Marion. "Warmer. Boiling. You're burning up."